The Weeping Mulberry Bush

By

Rachel Hawadi

 New Generation **Publishing**

For my mum

Southern African Terms

Bass: An Afrikaans word for 'boss'.

Dagga: Marijuana/Hash.

Ek se: An expressive term which is used for emphasis and literally means 'I say' in Dutch.

Fusekhi: An Africanisation of the term Voetsek (see below).

A Gas: A good time.

Kaffir: A derogatory term for a black African person equivalent to 'Nigger'.

Lekker: Afrikaans word which means 'nice', 'good', 'pretty', 'desirable'.

Old Bali: A slang term used largely by coloured (mixed race) people in Southern Africa which means father/dad.

Pikinini: A pejorative term used by white colonialists to describe black African children. It is thought to be derived from Portuguese *pequenino* meaning 'little'.

Robots: Traffic lights.

Sis: An expression to denote disgust.

Stoep: An Afrikaans word for a 'step' or a raised platform in the front of the house. The word is derived from Dutch.

Voetsek: Means 'go away' in Afrikaans.

Bekezela

Luveve Township

January in Rhodesia 1976 was a warm soothing month after the endless December rains had filled the moody, intense Zambezi River. Along the edges of the meandering river the thick horns of black rhinoceros poked through the still waters. Crocodiles bathed alongside grey herons while zebras strolled carefree across the dusty plains. In the north of the country the Zambezi gives birth to the magnificent theatrical Victoria Falls where elephants watched the mysterious spray from a distance swiping away nuisance flies with their ears. At the border between Rhodesia and Zambia the river ages into a black, slow undulating marsh flowing to the Congo before giving up the ghost into the Indian Ocean. In Mana pools and Chimanimani sleepy hippos and pockets of noisy buffalo herds shared their land with awkward giraffes and bouncing kudus.

In the vast fields farmers produced acres of tobacco and farmed juicy beef for export. Mango trees grew big as their fruit hung heavy against their flimsy branches. Thick aloe trees were thriving alongside Mopane and the strange looking inverted Baobab trees.

The beautiful Savannah held a great secret amidst the beauty, a secret of a bush war that had killed and maimed thousands of people for twelve years. Most people continued their lives as if nothing was happening. In the 'white only' suburbs, little white children played in the turquoise blue swimming pools. Their black nannies in starched uniforms, aprons and hats looked after them better than they did their own children in the black townships. The white bosses tried to ignore the threat of landmines and guerrilla attacks and did their best to carry on their work in green or beige khaki shorts and safari hats.

The televisions all over the country had shown pictures of Ian Smith reluctantly giving in to Henry Kissinger's proposals for 'Black Rule'. Televisions were for white people; for most Africans a dusty broken down radio muffled and out of tune would be blaring out the same news in their native languages.

In Bulawayo in a small African township called Luveve, Bekezela woke up at 7am to go to her first day of school. Her mother had called her Bekezela, which meant patience, patience for the end of suffering. Bekezela was oblivious to the importance of skin colour. She didn't even know there were white people except the funny looking albino with yellowy-white hair and the green squinty eyes that made 'looking' seem painful. The people in the township cruelly called him '*inkawu*' which meant monkey. Everyone ignored the inkawu and from how painful the albino's skin looked, Bekezela knew she didn't ever want to be white.

In the small kitchen in the back of the house cups with boiling hot steaming Tanganda tea were served from the brown teapots on the new European stove. Even with the new stove there was always a fire outside next to the chicken pen with a drum for heating up the water for baths. This was Bekezela Hadebe's Grandmother's house where food was eaten in a hurry.

In this house full of children, Bekezela had learnt to always eat in a hurry just in case she didn't get her share. Bekezela knew that if she was too slow then she might miss the hot water to wash and have to wash in the ice-cold water. There were so many children and grandchildren that everything was a competition, even washing to go to school. Being late for tea or the hot water meant she could only wash her face once. This meant not getting all the sleep from her eyes and only washing the front of her legs in one swoop. If she was not too late or too worried about someone stealing her freshly baked half a slice of Lobels bread, then she would spend the time scrubbing her heels with a communal pumice stone. The stone would be an ancient syenite igneous rock found by an unknown somebody somewhere in the fields or on the road. The stone found its home in the lavatory and sat faithfully on one of the two corners of the outside toilet. If it was unlucky it fell into the waste hole but often it sat staunchly until the next person wanted to scrub their cracked heels full of sand and mud.

Bekezela scrubbed her feet very hard to make sure that no new cracks appeared or so hard that she made sure that old cracks disappeared. Nobody liked or respected cracked heels. They showed that you came from a bad background.

After scrubbing and shivering she ran into the bedroom and dried herself with an old dirty dress or something else that was not her brand new school uniform. The school uniform was a bottle-green polyester affair, clever because it did not need to be ironed at all. Clever also because the belt was really attached to the middle of the dress by ten little stitches that traversed in the middle to form an 'X' so that the children never lost the belt or the uniform.

All uniforms had on the left-hand breast a badge with a yellow 'owl' underneath it the word 'Matshayiskova', the name of Bekezela's new school. Underneath were the words 'Knowledge is power'. The girls' uniforms had a yellow collar the same shade as the corn that ripened in December. The boys wore only boring khaki shorts and trousers with the owl on the right-hand side of their shirt pockets.

Shoes at Bekezela's new school were not mandatory but they showed that your family were not too poor. If a child wore white socks all week then they were seen as well-to-do, especially if they were clean. Clean white socks with polished shoes every single day won the respect of the teachers. Bekezela knew from her older uncles and aunts that cleanliness could guarantee a place in the top stream. All the Grade 1 children had to bring 5 cents to school with them if their parents could afford it. For that they would get a warm glass of fresh fragrant milk in thick plastic resin cups. The cups were nearly always a deep translucent turquoise colour with the odd aluminium one which you got if you were last in line.

Gulp, Gulp, Gulp.

Milk was often devoured in fewer than five gulps followed by an exaggerated 'hahhh' to prove that the milk was indeed finished and had indeed been enjoyable as usual.

Some of the children, especially the boys, would run off into the dust to play football. The footballs were made from blue and white maize meal bags stuffed with general house rubbish or old clothing that was skilfully moulded into a sphere. Once the sphere was the right size the boys would twist the top of the sphere with their hands. The children would then cut off the top and secure it with an old bit of elastic from someone's underpants.

The girls played '*ntsoro*' using ten freshly ground holes on the earth with five to seven equal amounts of pebbles in each hole. The girls would sit on the dusty ground and move the pebbles in their tiny hands with steely concentration. They would stop either when they reached an area with no pebbles or an area full of pebbles where you would collect them into the next hole. The game would end when there were no more stones to move and the winner was the person with the most stones. The skill in playing *ntsoro* was about strategy, tactics and mathematics.

When the children were tired of *ntsoro* some played *'uAra'*, which involved two or more people using a stick to draw a series of rectangular blocks on the ground. The blocks were divided into two columns: the first rectangle was *umam* one then *umam* two, three, four and five. The aim was to use a small, smooth, flat flint like stone which you would move from block to block with your foot until you beat your opponent by securing a home that they could not throw their stone onto. Most of the children spent their time laughing and teasing each other in the playground.

The sun always blazed through the gigantic rows of gum trees and penetrated through the fine particles of dust. The trees were so tall they looked like they were on wooden stilts that reached the heavens. Their generous, shiny leaves were the same colour as the girls' uniforms making the playground feel as though it was under a big bottle-green umbrella.

The bell always rang too soon.

'Goooo-oo duh Mooh-ni-ng Miss Sibanda,' the children bellowed out their ritualistic chorus in response to their teacher. Their teacher Miss Sibanda was really Mrs Sibanda but all female teachers were called Miss something or other whether they were married or not. Mrs Sibanda was a beautiful teacher with slight bow legs, dimples and big black eyes like *uMtshwankela*, a sweet black berry that looks like olives. Her smiley black eyes were hidden behind black horn-rimmed *Nana Moskouri* glasses that she pushed up her nose now and again. She had perfect even white teeth that would suddenly appear to light up her coffee coloured face and make her dimples deepen into her high cheekbones. Her skin was smooth, matt and velvety. Beke had overheard her telling another teacher that her family were *Chewa* people from Malawi.

Miss Sibanda wore plain, colourful A-line, knee-length skirts and smelt of a fragrance with a mild tone of sandalwood and a top note of Johnson's baby powder. Her fragrance permeated every molecule in the classroom in subtle but powerful ways that created lifetime memories.

Grade 1a was the first class you came to when you turned left from the headmaster's office. This was the class for all the clever new children. There was also Grade 1b for those who were not so clever, were troublesome, too loud or didn't have socks and shoes.

The teacher's table always faced the door and was full of books, pens, chalks, newspapers and other things. The clever children in the class sat in a group of tables of five or six next to the teacher. They were called group 1. Groups 2, 3, 4 and 5 followed according to intelligence. Group 5 were those children who got things wrong often. Beke was proud to be in group 1 of Grade 1a.

Samson and Cornelius

Bekezela was excited about school and was getting used to the cycle of school, home, school, end of term, holidays and school again. Bekezela was now in Grade 3; she was now 'a big girl' at eight nearly nine years old. She was lucky to still be in group 1. It showed that she was still very clever and she was very proud of this.

In Bulawayo young white boys of sixteen had been called up to Llewellyn Barracks to train alongside British mercenaries.

It was the year that Air Rhodesian flight RH825 was brought down by guerrillas. The 'terrorists' based in Zambia had been aided by Russia. The attack had angered the Rhodesian Army and led to a retaliation causing unrest throughout the country.

The new term and New Year had brought many new faces including Samson a tall, dark boy from an arid African reserve near Lupane. Lupane was one of the areas that the white Rhodesians had 'given' to the natives. Samson was older and bigger than the other children. There was Precious, a small quiet girl who had come from Gaborone in Botswana who sat next to Bekezela. Cornelius was a tall, orange-coloured boy whose family lived opposite Matshayiskova School. Clara was also another new girl who had come from The Reserves. Clara had two menacing tribal scars on both sides of her cheeks just below each eye that looked like the number 11. Like Samson, Clara looked much older than the children in the class. She had already started to sprout breasts which protruded through her second-hand faded uniform.

Samson and Cornelius had quickly formed an alliance and were secretly known as 'Fanta' and 'Coca-Cola' by the other children. This was because Samson was as black as midnight; he was a tall, gangly boy with knees that knocked together as he walked. Cornelius was a light-skinned boy who could have easily passed for a 'coloured' in any of the coloured suburbs like Thorngrove, Fambeki, Trenance or Saucertown. While he was in Luveve, talking Ndebele, eating *sadza* and walking barefooted, nobody questioned that Cornelius was a just a light-skinned African.

In Grade 3, Miss Sibanda with her flowery perfume, chalk dusters and her chocolate voice had disappeared to teach her new children, who believed in her paradise for a year or two. Miss Sibanda would no doubt teach the new children all the skipping songs, the alphabet and give them little nicknames. Bekezela's new teacher was Mr Moyo. The first time the children saw Mr Moyo they knew he had not been cut from the same soul cloth as Miss Sibanda.

Moyo was a rotund man; in fact everything about Mr Moyo was round. His face consisted of two layers of roundness: the lower layer was occupied by his cheeks which protruded smugly below his round forehead which always glistened with a round shiny patch. His tummy formed the next level of circular-ness which more than likely had been hurriedly covered by a tight-fitting shirt that permanently had round sweat patches underneath his armpits.

The children soon learnt that Mr Moyo was special, not only was he their teacher but he was also the deputy headmaster. A fact the children felt forced to be proud of. They had certainly graduated from being small children, cute and helpless, drinking milk and singing silly songs.

Mr Moyo wasted no time in letting the children know that he would not be addressing them in Ndebele. If they wanted to grow up and be successful they needed to learn to speak English.

'Waal Good morning Chi-d-ren,' Mr Moyo's deep reverberating sing-songy baritone voice silenced the children and brought them to attention.

'Guuuu-du m oh-ning Sah,' the Grade 3 children replied even more sing-songy with their hands behind their backs.

'Siiiiii,' Mr Moyo silenced the children who immediately became quiet as mice. A little snigger came from the corner when the children realised that Mr Moyo could not pronounce shh and had a speech impediment. Mr Moyo quickly restored order and dispersed the new children to their new tables. Precious sat next to Beke in group 1 and they became friends immediately. Samson and Cornelius sat in group 5 within view of the teacher but closest to the door. Mr Moyo was a busy man who spent most of his time attending important school matters. After the morning greetings Mr Moyo would waste no time in giving the children their readings.

'Ooooh-kaaay Na-wu,' Mr Moyo drew out his sentences for so long that the children thought he might fall asleep.

'I want you to read from page 3 to 10 of *Benny and Betty,*' Mr Moyo would say in a loud whisper to make the children pay attention more.

'Aaay wan-t-i the-e class to be sah-y-len-ti while-est-i ree-di-ng.' Mr Moyo would raise his fat fingers which looked like centipedes with heads much smaller than the rest of their bodies. When Mr Moyo raised his fingers the children knew that he meant business. Before Mr Moyo left the classroom all the children would hurriedly find their reading books and compete to be the most silent in the few minutes that Mr Moyo gathered his official papers. Mr Moyo would stuff his papers into his brown leather briefcase and put on his tan cotton jacket which like the shirt was getting too small. The children remained silent until someone at the back sighed loudly, or yawned loudly or dropped something on the wooden floor loudly.

'Shhhhh,' another child would reply. All the children would remain as silent as possible in spite of the distractions in case Mr Moyo came back suddenly. Mr Moyo had come back suddenly before and had never hesitated to come back and roar like a lion. Mr Moyo never hesitated to punish any children who were found not following his instructions. A whack in the ear with his bare hand or three strikes with his rubbery *shamboc*k was usually dealt out to the boys. Mr Moyo seemed to genuinely enjoy giving out punishments to the boys but never touched any of the girls.

Sometimes Mr Moyo would be gone for an hour or two and at times he had to drive with the clerk in his black Ford Zephyr. When Mr Moyo and the clerk drove to town they could be away all day. One Tuesday afternoon Mr Moyo unexpectedly came back holding with him the hand of a little girl who would be joining Grade 3. Cynthia Ncube was a small girl with sleepy, hooded almond eyes and little black freckles that looked like the little girls in the *Ladybird Fairy Tales*. Bekezela had never seen freckles on little black girls. Bekezela had never seen little white girls or their freckles except in the books. Bekezela was secretly pleased that Mr Moyo had put Cynthia Ncube near her and Precious where they would form a trio of the prettiest girls in the class. Cynthia had recently moved to Luveve with her mother who was a teacher at the school.

Beke immediately liked Cynthia and they became firm friends. Cynthia lived in the new township called Gwabalanda which was at the edge of Luveve. Beke could see Cynthia's house from her Grandmother's house at Luveve.

After school Cynthia had invited Beke to her house where they played with Cynthia's dolls, with their silky long blonde hair and blue eyes with the exception of one doll called 'Lady', who had short brown hair and brown eyes. Beke could not believe how neat and tidy Cynthia's house was. There were no clothes or dirty plates with scraps of food anywhere in the house. There was no trail of dust from the hundreds of feet walking in through the front door. In fact they had a little mat that made people wipe their feet before they walked in. Cynthia's family had a sink inside the house made of metal and there was no smell of urine and blocked toilets that came from outside. Beke envied Cynthia's idyllic existence.

Most of all Beke loved the golden sunrays that poured into Cynthia's living room through the white lace curtains and the silence that comforted the children as they ate slices of bread and jam.

From Cynthia's house Beke could see the old dog Rex from Grandmother's neighbour walking past her Grandmother's house to lie under the midget mango tree on the left and the peach tree that the women used for shade when the sun got too hot. The banana trees in the corner stood next to the old two-tone blue and yellow broken down 1961 Holden Special. The car would have been special once upon a time but as it sat in the corner it had a broken down engine, no wheels, missing doors, torn red luxury interior leather that the children played in—it was far from special.

**

As the term progressed Mr Moyo began to spend less and less time in the classroom. The children got used to the routine and even stopped pretending to be quiet in case Mr Moyo came back. They talked openly to each other about what they did over the weekend, football, and the new dresses they had bought. Precious, Cynthia and Bekezela talked about their families and the pretty dresses they had been given by relatives in South Africa or Botswana. Precious's father had died mysteriously while working in a mine in Selebi-Phikwe before Precious was born. Her father's family had been forced to support Precious, her mother and older sister. This had caused much resentment within the family and caused Precious's mother to move back to Bulawayo where her own family lived.

'*Bafana!*' (Boys!) Cornelius stood at Mr Moyo's podium making the children stop their loud chattering and mischief.

'*Lalelani Bantwana.*' (Children listen.) Cornelius stood in the assumed authority in front of the classroom of 27 children.

'Siii,' Cornelius mocked Mr Moyo and the whole class burst out in uncontrollable fits of laughter.

'*Zwanini,*' (Listen,) Cornelius said in a loud whisper.

'Samson and I are planning a party for the whole class,' Cornelius stated in a fit of sudden grandiosity accompanied by a sweeping gesture when he said 'whole'.

'We want to have 25 dollars by Christmas for a party which we will have in here or there or in the playground or by the football fields.'

The class responded excitedly at the idea of having a party here, there, outside or by the football fields. Most of the children saved 1 cent a week if they could afford it from their milk money or promise to pay it back later. Every week Samson faithfully read out how much was in the party pot.

'I have to tell you that in total we now have 1 dollar

and 75 cents for the party.' Everyone clapped loudly.

'Hey today we want to find the prettiest girls to dance at the party.' All the boys cheered loudly and clapped while the girls looked at each other nervously.

'Safira!' one of the boys in the corner in group 4 shouted.

'Precious.'

'Ye u Precious.' Another child agreed with the second shouter.

'Safira!' The lone voice repeated disguising his voice under his hand.

'*Bekezela mina,*' (Bekezela for me,) another boy shouted.

'Clara,' a boy from The Reserves stood up demonically to demonstrate his loyalty to Clara, the only girl from The Reserves. Clara was generally thought of as ugly so his outburst let out a raucous chorus of jeers and laughter that would have reverberated through the concreted corridors, through the assembly quadrangle to the deputy head's office had he been present in his office.

'Precious, Bekezela and Cynthia let the class vote for you,' Cornelius said with syrupy charm. The class voted that Precious was number 1 and the most beautiful girl in the class. Bekezela was number 2 and Cynthia number 3. Bekezela was pleased that the class had voted the three best friends as the most beautiful girls in the class. This made her feel even closer to the other two girls and sealed their bond.

After the beauty parade Samson and Cornelius brought the money and spread it out on the wooden platform.   Mr Moyo stood up to write on the blackboard when he would be back to teach the class. The class formed a line one by one and circled the kitty. When the parade had completed Samson asked the children to clap and cheer Cornelius's hard work at

21

masterminding and caretaking the party.

**

June came and lowered the sun's heat. Women wore
jerseys to cover their arms while men wore thicker
jackets and sweaters. The gum trees that lined the
streets of Luveve swayed obediently to the wind's
unpredictable sonnet. Babies were wrapped in brightly
coloured towels or traditional *mbelekhos*, their fat
cheeks pressed too hard against their mothers' backs.
At the school gates women wearing headscarves sold
fruit, sticky buns and sweets wrapped in pink, yellow
and green crinkly wrappers.

When Bekezela got home the dusty old radio was
talking about the bad heat and drought which had
caused people to share baths in faraway countries. All
Bekezela could think about was how much she missed
Miss Sibanda. She saw Miss Sibanda frequently
chatting to the other teachers flashing her perfect white
teeth excitedly from ear to ear. Bekezela imagined Miss
Sibanda's soothing perfume creating a warm archway
for her new children. From a distance Miss Sibanda's
new pupils could be seen holding hands, walking two
by two in a line behind Miss Sibanda. How Beke
missed her; she wondered why school did not allow
children to have one teacher for the rest of their lives.
Now she had to put up with Mr Moyo who scared her
not because of his voice or his stomach but because he
looked like the frogs that Beke had seen in the
Ladybird Fairy Tales. Beke did not wonder if Mr Moyo
would turn into a prince if he was kissed by the right
princess; she knew that he wasn't a real frog, he just
looked like one.

'Siii,' Mr Moyo quietened the children and left.
These days the children did not bother to open the

books or pretend to be serious, they simply waited for Mr Moyo to leave so that they could find out what games Samson and Cornelius had up their sleeve.

'Today, Precious the most beautiful girl will be Samson's wife,' announced Cornelius to the rest of the class.

It became clear from that point on that Samson was the boss and Cornelius was No. 2. It was unclear how the hierarchy had come about. Cornelius did most of the talking while Samson didn't say anything except for the odd whisper of orders to Cornelius.

Samson was taller than Cornelius by about 3 inches although Cornelius was by no means short. Although they were in Grade 3, Samson and Cornelius were two of the tallest boys in the school. Both the boys were much older than the other children, in normal circumstances they would be in secondary schools.

Precious sat down shyly, her big brown eyes and gentle face looking at the reading book.

'Beke is my wife,' Cornelius proudly thumped his chest with his right fist. Cynthia Ncube was given to a third boy who had decided to be the second lieutenant because he sat in group 5 with Samson and Cornelius. Beke did not mind the idea of being Cornelius's wife as she found him handsome because of his light skin. '*Bantwana,*' (Children,) Cornelius beamed with his beady, black sparkling eyes half imitating Mr Moyo. 'Some of you have not been paying your party money. How are we going to have the party without money? No money, no party—some of you haven't paid for weeks.'

'Boss, what are we going to do?' Cornelius turned to look at Samson who was chewing gum and tapping his desk with a wooden ruler menacingly.

'They have to be taught that this party is very important,' said Samson. Samson stood up while

23

Cornelius pulled Xholani, a small boy at the back, and whacked him with a ruler for not paying any money for weeks.

The Grade 3a children got used to paying for the party and got used to being hit with a wooden ruler or slapped in the face if they did not bring their 'party money'. They got used to the idea of the main boys having wives and in the playground and tuck shops the girls would frequently be referred to as 'Corny's wife' or 'Mrs Samson'. The children did not tease Cynthia that much because everyone knew she was Miss Ncube's daughter. Cynthia spent all breaks and lunch times in her mother's room. As soon as the bell rang Cynthia would be the first child out of the door.

'Precious and Clara,' said Samson, standing up and taking the reins from Cornelius for a while. Clara dragged her athletic, sinewy body to the front exaggerating her chewing to show that she was not afraid. Precious was a quiet, fragile girl, with big frightened eyes and small hands.

'Fight,' Samson whispered calmly to the two girls who obeyed without questioning. They eyed each other menacingly. The class was surprised to see Precious squaring up first, eagerly cupping her small hands into a fist the size of tiny lemons. Clara and her number 11 tribal scars were taken aback by the gesture; she had expected the small girl to be weak. The two girls stood transfixed, neither prepared to throw the first punch.

'*Limeleleni?*' (What are you waiting for?) Samson shouted a little louder from his desk. The two girls continued to stare at each other. Clara smiled nervously, temporarily pushing up the number 11 scars between the crease of her smile and her flared nostrils. Then Clara let out a fit of uncontrollable laughter so that her number 11 scars were now completely hidden by her hands.

24

'Right Clara by laughing you have volunteered to throw the first punch,' said Cornelius pointing and shouting then sitting down in one swift move.

'Hit her or Corny will come and hit you with his bare hands,' said Samson not wanting to be outdone by Cornelius's threats. Clara hit the smaller girl with her left hand. Precious's tiny frame should have sent her reeling but instead she remained rooted in her spot. Precious responded swiftly by giving Clara a hard lemon smack on the bone of her cheek.

Within seconds the two girls were tousling, tugging and pushing. Precious fell on the floor with Clara on top of her. Precious pulled Clara's short hair tightly between her little fingers and Clara screamed. Precious was soon back on her feet kicking Clara, pushing and biting. By now the whole class was on its feet cheering and shouting.

'Hit her!'

'On the head.'

'Don't bite it's not fair.'

'Ha, ha, ha I can see your panties.'

The two children were out of breath, panting and checking their arms for scratches and bite marks. As the noise became louder and louder Samson instructed Cornelius to stop the girls from fighting. The children slowly stopped shouting and went back to their seats. The excitement of the fight that had erupted so suddenly like a sleeping volcano had left its *samskra* on all the children. Samson and Cornelius were stimulated by the power of the fight, half the girls were pleased that it was not them in the fight while the other half wondered if it would be them next week. Most of the boys were exhilarated by the fight and thought about how much they would ensure they won if they were in a fight.

Shebeen

Beke walked home. Alone. She had waited for Cynthia for twenty minutes outside her mother's door. She was sure Cynthia had said to wait there. What had she said she was picking up? She wasn't sure. Beke waited for Cynthia to return from her mother's room and wondered what Cynthia might be talking to her mother about. She thought about Cynthia's mother's face which was pretty but unfriendly. She had smooth, cocoa coloured skin with an unusual hue of red mixed in. Her hair, which was always pulled back in a tiny bun, made her seem austere. She had the same freckles that Cynthia had but a little bigger.

After twenty minutes Beke sauntered away excited that it was Friday. Friday was her best day and today was better than most Fridays as she was going to see her mother tomorrow. The mood was always lighter and bearable on the days she knew she would see her mother. The dull ache in the middle of her chest would ease by itself. She strolled past the shops and said hello to naAndriya the fat lady who lived on the corner on the way to the railway station. On the way home she went past the women selling things under the trees opposite the butcher and grocery stores. There was MaKhumalo selling ripe red tomatoes, big onions and kale. MaDube was suckling her baby and selling sweets and chewing gum. A young girl who did not go to school was sitting next to the two women selling *umbhunzu* and *umsosobiyane,* beautiful sweet and sour berries in amber and mahogany colours.

The women sat on *amacansi,* mats that had been woven from dried long reeds of grass. They were often busy weaving a new mat, knitting a new garment for the baby on their backs or gossiping away loudly to each other.

Nangu umama, nangu umama (Here comes mummy) was the cry of all the children that lived in 203 when Lucy Nkomo came home from a hard day's work at Security Mills.

Nangu umama. At least ten children would run up to her, some were neighbours that lived three doors down, behind and some didn't live anywhere near 203.

203 was Lucy Nkomo's house. Most people called her 'MaNkomo' or 'uMama'. Lucy Nkomo had lived in 203 New Luveve since 1969, the year that Beke was born. Lucy had nine children with five different fathers; all her children had been born with a two-year gap between them.

Maria was Bekezela's Grandmother's first born child who had the same father with Nancy and James. When it came to the fourth boy, Michael, there had been some debate as to whether he shared the same father as the first three children but most people thought he had his own father because of his lighter skin. They thought his father may have possibly been a coloured man. Except for Nancy all of MaNkomo's children were given biblical names by the Reverend Lewis who she had worked for as a nanny in Essexvale. Nancy was named after Mrs Lewis.

MaNkomo's fifth child was called Hetta because most people could not pronounce Heather. Hetta was born on the same day as Rev. Lewis's mother whose name was Heather. After Hetta came Gabriel who was born on Christmas eve and named after the Angel Gabriel. Hetta and Gabriel were thought to share the same father because of their darker skin and square faces which the other children did not have.

By the time the sixth child, Anna, was born in 1965 MaNkomo had left working for Rev. Lewis who had moved back to Wales. Anna too had her own father who was thought to be a Kalanga man, Mr Nkala, from a village in Tsholotsho near Plumtree. Anna was the source of many jokes as Kalangas were thought to be inferior because of the funny way that they could not pronounce 'r's and used 'l's instead. The Kalangas were originally Shona speaking Rozwi people who had been invaded and integrated into Mzilikazi's Ndebele tribes.

David was the eighth child, was born in May whose father was a teacher. The last child in her mother's family was Alison, whose father was a tall Xhosa policeman from whom Alison had inherited almond shaped eyes, a straight nose and high cheek bones.

**

Ngomvulo yi babalazi (On Monday it's hangovers)
Ngomvulo yi babalazi (On Monday it's hangovers)
Obalesihlanu sidl' imali zethu (On Friday we spend our money)
S*idl' mali zethu Imalizethu!* (We spend our money!)

Every Friday this song would bellow like Jumu'ah to Muslims from the record player that only one of her four uncles was allowed to play and maybe her Aunty Hetta, who was the life and soul of the Shebeen.

One crate of Castle beer would be brought in from the local beer hall, Hetta would carry twelve bottles of beer on her head. The next crate would be bottles of Lion beer, which was a favourite with most of the people that came to the Shebeen. When she got tired or when the boys were home or if she could find people to help her, by the time MaNkomo came home from a hard day's work she would find at least ten crates of beer tucked away in her bedroom waiting for the visitors to the Shebeen. In the fridge would be a few cartons of African beer made with hop. The favourite was *iNdlovu* which had a little red elephant on the front of the carton.

Beke's Grandmother had spent most of the profit from the Shebeen extending her three-bedroom house, adding two extra bedrooms. She now had a free-standing fridge freezer which had square ice blocks, at least one beer, vegetables and eggs. In the kitchen was a white four plate electric cooker which was hardly ever used mostly because they did not like how it cooked. The romance of cooking outside with as much smoke as possible was inherited from their pastoral Nguni ancestors. It was unity with the primal elements of fire to succumb to its wild power when the match was first lit. To harness that power when the mealie pot boiled or the beef fried in harmony with tomatoes, onions and *tshomoliya.*

Those who watched that fire knew that its purpose was to give spiritual sustenance to the children of Lobengula. The electric cooker depleted the passion and the love from the art of cooking so it remained a symbol to tell the world that they too had embraced the white man's gadgets.

Before going into the house Beke played *iBora* as the sun set, painting the sky with maniac brushstrokes of intense metallic oranges and blues which could only be found in Bulawayo.

Kwa Bulawayo.
Lobengula's city.
Bulawayo.
Bullies
Blues.
Skies.

'*Nangu mama, Nangu mama, mama,*' the children would shout in one chorus excitedly. The children

29

would abandon all their balls and smooth stones and run for Grandmother and give her a kiss and pull her handbag to see what she had brought for them.

Usually Grandma brought pieces of fresh bread from the factory where she had worked since 1969. The pieces of bread were usually wrapped in a plastic piece of paper and sat in her handbag along with her knitting, an old broken watch and breadcrumbs from last week or even last year. Grandmother's handbag had old lipsticks with no caps worn all the way down until the winding contraption was visible. Deep inside the vestigial lipstick container would be a wiry hairpin which had been used to dig out as much of the remaining lipstick as possible. The handbag always had a small tin of snuff which was kept in an old, miniature Vicks tin, the size of a 10 pence coin which was a light green colour with tiny blue writing.

Qo, Qo, Qoki. Grandmother Lucy would knock on her own house that she had lived in since 1969. She loved having her grandchildren with her especially Beke, her first grandchild whose mother was now married to a white man and lived in the suburbs. The children made her house a noisy, vibrant abode that reminded her of growing up in the thirties in Essexvale.

'*Alike linginike I Bhiya mani,*' (Please give me a beer,) Grandmother said with an exhausted sigh of relief. She was glad to be away from the heat and salty sweatiness of the claustrophobic factory. The children would clamber over each other fighting to be the first to get her beer. They all wanted to show her how much they loved her the most. The fastest child would run to not only get the beer but then to open it with their teeth. The winner of the challenge would normally have another piece of bread or something special like ice mints or chewing gum that Grandmother had in her other plastic bag that she didn't allow the children to

30

look in. The children who hadn't run fast enough to get Grandmother's beer would nearly always be involved in a fight over who had tripped who or pulled who back while the winner thought of a new place to hide their ice mints or chewing gum.

The sun would finally disappear beyond the horizon as quickly as it had arrived. As the evening settled and distant stars sparkled, the air became warm and still and the crickets started to chant.

After everyone had eaten, the metallic plates would be washed in the heavy duty Belfast sink made of sealed concrete. Clank, clank, clank was the cacophony of sounds made by the aluminium plates as they violently pushed each other out of the way fighting for space in the dirty, grey water. After the washing was finished and the plates stacked together, starchy pieces of hardened *sadza* formed a translucent carapace cruelly orphaned before being thrown away in the communal drain.

The plates were often washed by hands by whoever was on duty. Aunty Hetta usually created a rota but she nearly always ended up doing the dishes herself as she could not trust her younger sister Anna or her lazy good-for-nothing brothers who just ate and left the plates. Most Fridays even Hetta would leave the plates. Friday was for dancing, drinking beer and laughing.

The evening would start off slowly and Hetta and Grandmother would share a bottle of Castle beer between the two of them before the first customers arrived at the Shebeen around 7pm. Shebeen was a Gaelic word that was originally written as *Sibin* hundreds of years ago in Ireland where potatoes were peeled and fermented into spirits. Shebeens were the speakeasies of the prohibition era that had made their way from Galway to the anthracite mines in Pennsylvania.

Most customers came to the Shebeen because of the cosy atmosphere and if you wanted you could get a plate of *sadza* and some meat cooked over the hot coals outside near the chicken pen. Beke and all the young children loved to watch the adults dancing, singing and talking at the top of their voices from 7pm.

They got louder and louder.

'Heeey another Castle. Hey MaDube.'

When the sky matured and turned a deep velvet purple and black with a fairy dust sprinkling of pure silver stars the talk would turn to the war. The conversations at MaNkomo's Shebeen were always about Joshua Nkomo and what 'the boys' were doing in Zambia to defeat Ian Smith.

The guerrilla fighters were discussed in hushed, apocalyptic tones. If one of your relatives in The Reserves went to join ZIPRA he was sure to never return, or go mad or kill his own family. There were stories of ZIPRA guerrillas recruiting young boys as vigilantes-some as young as ten.

'My nephew's school, all of them taken,' Mr Ndlela, a regular at MaNkomo's Shebeen, would say in a low voice, the gramophone lowered and they gathered closer to hear more of his story.

'*Abafana! abantwana babelinde inkomo,*' (Young boys were looking after cows,). he spoke with a weary insouciance which either came from witnessing a war that seemed to have no end or from the warmth of the beer.

'*Sitshele Baba Ndlela,*' (Tell us father Ndlela,) MaNkomo pleaded when it seemed Mr Ndlela would either cry or fall asleep.

'*Baba tshaya, tshaya ngama AK47, igazi yonke ndawo, babathatha, batshiya ikaya zwi!*' (They beat them with AK47s, blood everywhere; they took them and left not a soul in the village!) As the drinks flowed late into the night the conversations became more pugnacious and the children could hear voices, music and laughter in their bedroom as they tried to sleep.

'*Hm, hm, hm hayi wena,*' everyone in the Shebeen expressed their anger and powerlessness. Many of them felt that they did not want to be a part of the war that wiped out villages and took away their able young men to die. Young men who could have been working to provide for their families.

Mr Ndlela's story went on to describe the landmines that were all over Zambia and Mozambique, which killed and maimed numerous young soldiers who would be mercilessly returned to their villages.

Cotton Buns

Bekezela felt that the sun on Saturday mornings shone very differently to the sun during the week. The dishes were still unwashed from last night, bottles of beer in their crates empty now. One or two of the visitors to the Shebeen had fallen asleep on the sofas or the hard cement floor on a reed mat. They were woken up by the brown and black cockerel or by one of the children sweeping the floor.

Beke loved joining in with the chores and picked up the smallest broom, the one that was just the right size for her. Sweeping always started in the living room and on Saturdays was a more thorough job. Once the last visitors had woken up from the floor the dining room or 'e Da' would be swept thoroughly. All the dust was collected at the veranda and put into the grey steel bin in the front. Beke didn't like getting down on her knees to mop the floor because it took so long to find a cloth to mop with. This morning didn't take too long; her Aunty Hetta had found an old baby's cotton napkin. Beke rinsed the holey napkin and got a bar of Sunlight soap and rubbed hard against the palm of her hands.

Scrub, scrub to wash off the dust and sand brought in by the dozens of people walking in and out of the house. One time to change the water, twice and a third time until the end. Aunty Hetta was like quicksilver at putting the red wax of Cobra polish on the floor. In little defined circles under the gramophone, under the sofas with the foam hanging out. In and around the table that everyone bumped into, all the way to the window in longer strokes. She let the polish dry so that the whole house smelt of comforting wax. Aunty Hetta left it for an hour or two and would bark at anyone who dared to walk on her floor before she polished it. The smell alone was usually enough to deter any would-be tresspassers.

On Saturday mornings after the mess from last night's Shebeen was cleared was time for hair. It nearly always happened magically. Before she knew it Aunty Hetta sat facing away from the blazing sun. Beke would sit on the hard cement *stoep*, not caring to keep her already dirty dress clean. Nobody enjoyed hair being done, but it was important for looking pretty as long hair always made little girls look nice.

Aunty Hetta was a ruthless hair terrorist with her metal toothed silver comb which resembled an elongated pitchfork. She would start combing the hair without warning or ceremony. Every brush made Beke feel like she was walking naked through a thorny bush. If her head moved too much in one direction to avoid the pain, Aunty Hetta would shove it back to the centre with the force of a shepherdess pulling a wild ewe.

A small break in the pain would be interspersed with momentary pleasure when Aunty Hetta would disturb the layers of sleeping dandruff by slanting the teeth of the comb at a 30-degree angle and gently scratching the flakes. She would then blow them away rhythmically from her brown skin.

'*Yebo sisi.*' Every five minutes a stranger would walk in to disturb them to ask for directions or to want to chat not realising that hair was a painful and serious business. Aunty Hetta's body language always let them know that she was in no mood for chatting and the hair drill would continue. The first parting to create the first row was done once Aunty Hetta was happy that the whole of Beke's head was free from dandruff then the process of making *Amabhanzi* (buns) would begin.

'Your mother is coming today,' Aunty Hetta said matter of factly creating her first bun. A bun was made from a handful of hair held between the forefinger and thumb and secured tightly with a three-ply length of black cotton.

'You must look pretty; your mother likes you to look pretty.'

Beke knew that the extra cleaning that was being done was to impress Maria, Beke's mother who was the eldest daughter who was coming to visit.

The only solace was the sound of the radio in the dining room, which sounded like the echoes of a hypnotist speaking into an empty tin. The gentle breeze blew the door open to make the sound clearer so that Beke could hear her favourite song.

Let your love flow… Beke danced waving her thin arms and little fists when her aunt talked to someone walking by.

'*Hey wena, akhucume!*' (Sit still!) Aunty Hetta shook Beke to show her irritation at the sudden crazy dancing that made her have to restart the bun she had been working on.

One row, two rows, three rows. Beke's hair had grown. Only two months ago she had started plaiting her hair and needed at least six rows now all she needed was four rows. By the time Aunty Hetta was finished Beke's hair was pulled so tightly that her forehead shone like a mirror. Her neck was so tight that she could not move it spontaneously but rather swivel like an owl.

The pain was unbearable but Beke would not dare tell her Aunty Hetta how much it hurt. How could she tell her aunt who had spent two hours combing, twisting, blowing and threading that she could not bear the pain. Instead she sat in the corner with her little knees until her mother arrived and the tears spontaneously rolled down her eyes.

'Yebo Mama, what's wrong?' her mother said, gently wiping the tears from her daughter's cheeks.

Beke didn't know why she was crying. Was it the pain of the hair? Was it that she missed her beloved mother whom she saw only now and again? Or was it that she couldn't find the words to tell her mother she wanted to be with her every day.

Everything changed when mother walked through the door, even pain. Suddenly the sun would shine with a perfume that made the birds sing sweeter songs. Mother was a beauty with high cheekbones, full lips with red lipstick, flawless skin with soft dustings of powder, eyes with blue eye shadow. Very few women in the townships especially Luveve wore lipstick, powder and eye shadow. That was not all. Mother wore shiny, gold earrings that played duels with the sun's rays. Her eyes were covered with sunglasses with two tones: brown and taupe. She walked rhythmically and provocatively as if she was in the 'Berkshire baby' silky pantyhose advert. Wherever she went men would stop talking and stare at her in an openly lascivious way that was tamed by the respect she automatically commanded.

Most of the women in Luveve didn't envy her. Envying her would have been like envying Queen Elizabeth of England. She was beautiful and untouchable. Out of reach. Most of the men no matter what age treated her like a sister that they secretly wanted and wished they could be good enough to be her lover.

When mother visited Luveve it was always without warning but it meant that all plans would be put aside. There was always a new surprise.

'Come and see my new car,' mother cooed at Aunty Hetta, as Gabriel and Anna ran out to the front of the house to find a shiny Mini Cooper with red leather seats.

'Ah, Ah, Ah.'

'It's so nice, hey wena.'

'When did you learn to drive?'

She answered all their questions with visible pride before commanding them to take out the bags of shopping from OK Stores. There was a big bag of salt & vinegar crisps, Chipstix, chocolate, orangeade, cola, sweets and chewing gum for the children. Another bag, with fresh, thick juicy chunks of beef from the butchers on 3rd Avenue. Mazoe cooking oil, big bags of rice and 25 kg of the fine blue bag of polenta that they could not afford at Grandmother's house. There would be a feast and laughter laced with the smell of European perfumes when mother came on her surprise visits that wiped away Beke's tears.

Mummy and Daddy

By 4pm in the afternoon the dust in Matshayiskova School had risen high up in the air. The afternoon was set aside for commemorating the death and funeral of Mzilikazi who had built the Matebele nation. Some of the older children in the schools in Luveve, Njube and Mzilikazi were carrying spears and shields dancing like warriors within the school playground.

Beke had seen the Grade 6 and 7s re-enacting how Mzilikazi the great warrior son of Matshobana had valiantly fought uTshaka and subjugated what was now Bulawayo: the place of slaughter.

The boys wore the three-legged leopard-skin hoods around their necks and over their khaki shorts to commemorate Matshobana who had fought many battles and was known as 'The Leopard' for his courage. Matshobana's enemies had amputated his hand during battle leaving his blood gushing on the soil to scare any enemies. The three-legged leopard was said to be the spirit that protected Bulawayo's children.

'*Bayethe Dingiswayo,*' shouted the smaller Grade 6 boys waving their spears saluting Dingiswayo the revered Zulu chief. The drummer wearing the Ndebele tribal headgear and footwear made of goatskin sat at the edge of the dance banging his drum rhythmically. The sound of the drum seemed to lift everyone's spirits hypnotically forcing them to clap and sing along.

A cloud of chaos and ululation ensued with all the children pretending to fight with their harmless spears. The children dreaded going back to the classroom— Cornelius's and Samson's classroom. Class 3a were now used to the routine: Mr Moyo would walk in and say something sententiously in English, write a few things on the board then walk out and Samson and

Cornelius would be in charge. 'The party has been delayed until Christmas.' Cornelius would strut down the classroom with a menacing presence. Those who did not have the money would be asked to fight their friends or be beaten by Cornelius. The beauty pageant had progressed to new levels. Cornelius felt that it was important for all the beautiful girls to have a husband to look after them. As the weeks went by the children were asked to lie down on the benches where Samson and Cornelius sat.

As the weeks went by the children became comfortable with viewing whichever eight-year-old mummy and daddy partnership was selected for viewing.

Beke didn't know why she felt so uncomfortable with the tingling sensation she felt when Melusi or Mandla put his hands down her panties. Sometimes she would cry and when she cried they would then make her fight with her friend Precious or her friend Cynthia or even her enemy Clara, who seemed to grow taller and taller.

'Beke you have not paid any money for three weeks.' Beke sat silently looking down at her new shoes that her mother had brought her this weekend from OK Bazaars.

'Beke answer me,' Cornelius roared far louder than necessary making Beke jump.

'*Hayi,*' (No,) she answered in a quiet whisper.

'Where is my money?' Cornelius took the young girl's left ear and pulled it up until she was upright.

'*Angilayo.*' (I haven't got it.) Prickly tears flowed from her face.

'*Uthini? Uyadlala manje.*' (What? You are playing now.) 'Your husband goes to work every week but spends all his money on beer, huh?' Samson said to Beke who sat with her eyes glued to her black shoes and white socks.

'I am talking to you, mummy,' Cornelius shouted again making Beke jump for a second time.

'*Ye,*' (Yes,) she replied with a tear escaping from her brown eyes.

'Well maybe you are not very nice to your husband.' He said standing up to face the rest of the classroom.

'Who didn't you pay party money?' Cornelius said staring menacingly at the children.

'*NguMfazo,*' (It's Mfazo,) said one of the boys whose desk Cornelius was standing next to.

'Mfazo boy, come here.' Mfazo was a small dark boy with a permanent string of green snot that hung a centimetre from the base of his flared nostrils.

Mfazo stood up obediently and looked Cornelius in the eye knowing what was to come.

'It looks like your wife has not been paying the money she owes boy, have you been spending it all *amasese e bhawa* heh?'

'*Ye amasese amnandi njani,*' (Yeah *amasese* are very nice,) Mfazo said dancing in a mocking way.

'Look, he is still drunk,' Cornelius shouted to the rest of the class, which was now roaring with exaggerated laughter.

'*Beke mama lala lapha,*' (Beke mummy sleep here,) Cornelius commanded Beke to lie on the bench where he and Samson normally sat, his voice menacing and gentle at the same time.

As Beke sat down staring at the ceiling with her green uniform tucked in between her thin legs she wondered what would happen. Cornelius and Samson were very unpredictable. Cornelius could find another victim and completely forget about her, he could call another fight between the children or he could invent a new game. Beke's heart beat faster, the fingers of her

41

right hand in her mouth while her left hand wiped away tears.

She wished Mr Moyo would come back unexpectedly but he never did. If he did he would simply shush the children before rushing out to meet the Mayor or the headmaster. If all the children were naked and jumping up and down he probably wouldn't notice.

Beke missed Miss Sibanda and her dimples; she imagined Miss Sibanda was missing her old class and would suddenly wander down the corridor and stop Samson and Cornelius.

'*Bakhithi buyani lizobona,*' (People come here and see,) Cornelius shouted to Samson and the rest of the children.

'*Khuyini?*' (What is it?) Samson looked up reluctantly as he was nearly always only interested in the money that the children brought.

Samson dragged his knobbly knock knees over to where Beke lay on the bench. Cornelius had yanked up Beke's uniform.

'*Maye babo!*' (Oh my God!) Samson laughed clapping his hand. Samson came back for a closer look at Beke who started to cry loudly lifting up her shoulder blades to see three of the boys looking between her legs.

'*Uloboya entweni yakhe,*' (She's got hair in her thingy,) one of the boys laughed and ran back to his desk before Samson and Cornelius asked anything further of him.

'*Uboya!*' (Hair!) They all laughed and screeched as the entire class walked up to Beke to look at her premature pubic hair that had started to emerge. None of the children had ever seen anything like this, pubic hair on a small child of eight years old.

By the end of the week a miracle happened. Mr

Moyo didn't go out of the classroom five minutes after arriving. He even called the register, something he hadn't done since January or February.

'Sabelo Banda, Musa Dhliwayo, Nancy DhloDhlo, Phathani Hadebe …'

'Pre-Ze-nthi.' Each child stood up.

After the register Mr Moyo did not put on his jacket and leave the classroom. Instead he picked up the board duster which spewed all its disused chalk dust into the air.

'Today chil-dren we are going to do some M-A-T-H-S. Then some 'E-N-G-L-I-S-H. Then some reading from *Benny and Betty*.' Mr Moyo said the last activity without writing anything on the blackboard. The children were confused by Mr Moyo's presence; he didn't leave once except to speak to the headmaster through the door. Mr Moyo's jacket sat clung to the chair like a scared child.

During the lunch break he sat down marking and filing his books away. Samson and Cornelius were very quiet like church mice once Mr Moyo was back. The children were still scared that Mr Moyo would disappear and Samson and Cornelius would ask the children to fight or pay them.

Monday the children learnt to subtract and read. Tuesday Mr Moyo taught them some more subtractions with difficult numbers and told them there would be a test on Friday on what they had learnt.

Wednesday Mr Moyo was still there and the children became more comfortable: Precious was smiling, Clara was smiling, Cynthia and Beke were exchanging smiles across their table. All the children did their sums and exchanged looks while Mr Moyo told them what the answers were.

'Well done, I am very pleased with your hard work,' Mr Moyo said putting on his jacket even though the sun was hot and he was already sweating.

'The best in the class today in sums is Miss Bekezela, stand up Beke.' Mr Moyo started to clap with the rest of the class following. Beke did not hear the rest of what Mr Moyo said or who was second as she was so proud that she had been the best at sums.

Once Mr Moyo had finished he said in a low voice, 'Beke please stand up and come with me.'

Beke stood up, proud and tall. She forgot all about the classmates jeering at her last week. She forgot all about the fights with Clara and the money she had to pay Samson and Cornelius. She was sure that Mr Moyo would stay and the nightmare would be over and she would be crowned the queen of sums this week and the queen of English and reading next week. Mr Moyo closed the door behind him, his eyes narrowed and his forehead curled up like a scared centipede.

'What is this I hear about you using that kind of language?' Before Beke could answer or knew what Mr Moyo was talking about, his sausage fingers had formed a flat surface whose velocity and power smacked against Beke's jaw leaving her neck spinning with heat and confusion.

What had just happened? Beke couldn't even cry, what language was he talking about? Who could have told him such a thing? Did Mr Moyo not know the truth about what Samson and Cornelius were doing when he was not there? The pain was too much for Beke to cry. Mr Moyo told her to go back into the classroom and never again to use such language. Beke went back to her desk still confused; she thought she was going to get such praise from the teacher who had returned to save her and her friends.

Trenance

Rhodesia was always racially separated since Beke's mother, Grandmother and great Grandmother could ever remember. The white people lived in their suburbs with lawns, big gates, nannies, garden boys and barking dogs. The Africans who worked in their factories and cleaned their cars lived at the opposite end of Bulawayo in special townships. There were 'the coloureds' who were neither black nor white. They were not quite good enough to be white but good at fixing cars and too good to be black. They lived in little special pockets of Bulawayo. Sometimes they lived in pockets between African townships or in pockets between expensive white suburbs. Trenance was one such pocket where quiet coloured people lived. Bekezela's mother had moved there with her new husband. A white man.

Friday afternoon, school had finished at lunchtime and Beke was excited about the journey to visit Trenance with Uncle Gabriel. Trenance meant 'farm' or settlement in Celtic Cornish and referred to a place on the Southern Cornish coast near St Mawgan. Uncle Gabriel, only six years older than Beke, was asked to take Beke to her mother in Trenance for the first time. Uncle Gabriel and Aunty Hetta had at first fought about who was going to take Beke to Trenance, each one of them giving reasons why they would be better for the job.

Grandmother had decided that Uncle Gabriel was to go. It was Friday, Shebeen night and Aunty Hetta worked faster than Uncle Gabriel, cooked for customers who wanted *isitshwala la mathumbu* when they were drunk. She kicked out the troublemakers and the men loved her lithe body swinging from side to side when they got drunk.

Decision made.

Aunty Hetta helped Beke pack all the lovely clothes that her mother had bought for her in Botswana or South Africa. Little green suits, a blue floral dress, bell-bottoms, platform shoes that all the other little girls didn't have. Beke was very proud of the fact that nearly all the little girls and boys in Luveve envied her nice clothes which she liked to wear on weekends.

Uncle Gabriel decided to look after the suitcase and clutched it with his left arm. His right hand was deep in his pocket, protecting the money for the bus tickets. The two children left at 3pm when the sun was starting to loiter heavily in the deep blue sky and workers were starting to drift back home for the weekend.

The children seemed to wait forever at the terminus opposite the Luveve beer hall listening to the rising voices which grew louder and louder like the sound of distant humming bees. The beer hall always had the same smell of *iNdlovu*, beer hops and the smell of communal sweat. In the distance were pockets of blue smoke rising from where fresh, tender, juicy slabs of beef were being grilled. The man grilling the meat was standing over an open fire with one eye closed to hide from the smoke and one hand fanning away the flies.

Eventually the bus came and the children paid the bus driver who was wearing a bottle-green uniform that looked like Beke's uniform without the yellow stripes. Luckily the bus driver did not waste any time but put the heavy black gear stick into motion and sped out of the terminus. A quarter of a mile from the terminus children piled into Luveve swimming pool in their pairs and trios skipping over the grey pebble pathway. The lawn on either side of the pathway was freshly cut, the smell of chlorophyll permeating the air to mix with the heavy scent of the blue chlorinated water that lay past the six-foot brick walls. From a distance she could hear the relentless sound of people diving, shouting and screaming with the blue and green joy that matched the water and the grass. For a moment Beke wished she was there but she knew she much preferred the mysterious Trenance.

The bus meandered into Fambeki then past Magwegwe, Mzilikazi and finally the bus terminus on Third Avenue and Lobengula Street. The walk to City Hall was confusing but Beke's mother had explained to Uncle Gabriel many times how to get there safely. In the hypnotic late afternoon heat, the uphill walk from Lobegula Street to Main Street was like wading through tar. They came to the imposing statue of Cecil John Rhodes standing at a junction close to the main post office.

At the post office, Beke and Uncle Gabriel turned left onto Fife Street and could see the City Hall without moving a muscle. The City Hall was a beautiful square setting of neo-classical buildings surrounded by gardens and fountains neatly trimmed with conifer hedges reminiscent of Tudor England. On the perimeter of the gardens were pockets of giant mountain Strelitzia trees with their serrated fan-like leaves casting shadows on the walkways that led to and from the city. In-between the walkways were triangles, rectangles and square shapes of neatly manicured lawns bursting with different flavours of lime green. The sprinklers were moved by the African gardeners between the numerous species of colourful, succulent shrubs with their rosettes of yellow, purple, red and orange.

On the edges of Bulawayo City Hall surrounding Selbourne Avenue, Eighth Avenue and Fife St were giant Jacaranda trees which seemed to whisper symphonies as well as producing a breeze that calmed the harsh afternoon sun. Beke and Uncle Gabriel marvelled at the geometrically manicured lawns and hedges and benches that said 'Whites only'. Beke and

Uncle Gabriel could not help themselves from staring at the 'Madams' with their shopping from the Spar or Woolworths all carried by the garden boys wearing khakis or white uniforms with matching hats.

The children got into the bus going to Trenance and gave the bus driver their money for their journey.

'Where you going?' the driver asked nonchalantly, drivers were getting used to more and more Africans catching the buses to white only areas.

'Last stop, Trenance,' Uncle Gabriel said in his best English wondering why the African man would not speak Ndebele to them.

The bus was emptier, cleaner and more luxurious than the buses to Luveve. There were only five people on the bus along with Beke and Uncle Gabriel. An old couple sat behind them.

'Mr Smith says "fifty–fifty",' said the middle-aged man.

'Mr Smith will never give the blacks 50 per cent of anything, I don't believe it do you?'

'It's a trap. Smith said there would never be any black rule, never in a million years,' the woman responded excitedly to the man who must have been her husband.

'He had better give them what they want before they kill us all, damned savages.' The man ruffled his pages. The children looked straight ahead mesmerised by the floating trees and houses that seemed to glide past as the bus drove out of town.

At the back of the bus sat two schoolboys wearing maroon blazers and khaki shorts talking at the top of their voices so that the rest of the bus could hear. Beke sat by the window, her little hands holding onto the bar of the seat ahead. The suitcase was tucked away under the seat. Beke and Uncle Gabriel hardly spoke but were deeply absorbed in their endless journey.

The bus stopped for a while on Third Avenue before floating along Athlone Avenue. The trees lining the road seemed to go on for miles forming a warm, soporific velvet tunnel as the bus moved further away from town. The noise of the town's engines, hawkers and car horns drifted away until they were just waves of undulating silence, black in colour then white.

'Last stop.' The driver had left his seat and was walking through the bus; the children had fallen into an anaesthetic slumber and missed most of the journey. They were frightened of finding themselves somewhere strange. Uncle Gabriel rushed Beke out as he remembered that he had been told to start the next walking part of their journey at 'Garden Cash' store, which he could see from the bus.

'*Asambe, asambe,*' (Let's go, let's go,) Uncle Gabriel pulled Beke away. Once outside the bus they walked up to Garden Cash and saw the little collapsed wire gate that NaBeke had told them to climb under and walk in a straight line.

'*Pangisa, pangisa,*' (Hurry up, hurry up,) said Uncle Gabriel pulling Beke's arms out of her still dozy state.

The children walked through unfamiliar bushes surrounded by thorns, mud and unexpected potholes. In the distance they saw brightly coloured mansions that looked haunted and unlived in. After 20 minutes the children were relieved to find a similar gate to the one that they had seen at the beginning of their bush assault. NaBeke had told them that as soon as they saw a yellow house they had arrived. Uncle Gabriel felt an incredible sense of achievement when he saw NaBeke's house.

The house was situated at the end of a huge plot of land. On the right-hand side was a piece of fertile land that had been ploughed recently. The middle had an overgrown unkempt lawn and reeds as tall as Beke. On the edge was a wild mulberry tree whose curved branches hung down to the gravel driveway.

The left-hand side of the yard was uncultivated and had several trees that provided shade for the neatly lined stones that led to the front door of the house. The front door was made of double doors with window panes that framed the shiny glass.

Beke and Uncle Gabriel went through the side door which led to the kitchen. They had always been taught by Grandmother that it was very impolite for young children to enter through the front door. The side door was directly opposite the 'boys' *Khaya*'. Every white person's house had a boys' *Khaya* or servant's quarters with running cold water and a toilet. To make the boys feel more at home the toilets were a hole in the floor, something that they felt Africans were more comfortable with. One *baas* had been dismayed to find his African servant crouching on top of his European toilet. This had inspired the *bass* to build his servant something that was more to his liking.

The boys' *Khaya* was small and only sufficient to hold a suitcase and a few things. This stopped many of the boys bringing family, friends or girlfriends late in the night making the dogs bark. The windows were normally high up and close to the ceiling making the room stuffy and claustrophobic.

The Bass was not obliged to buy the servants a bed but most did provide a bed of wooden slats and two or three blankets and sometimes a pillow.

'*Qoki*,' (Knock knock,) said Uncle Gabriel in a low voice which had recently broken.

'Come in, come in.' They were ushered in by Baron, NaBeke's houseboy. Baron was a confident, friendly Ndebele boy with a big smile and a gap between his sparkling white teeth. Baron was probably a couple of years older than Uncle Gabriel.

The two children walked into the kitchen and were greeted by the wafting smell of freshly picked *tshomoliya* that Dade the nanny was cooking. The smell of freshly cooked stew and spices permeated the air and made the children hungry.

My mama lives here, wow, Beke thought to herself, her eyes moving from the neat yellow chairs to the big fridge to the white stove.

'Madam is in the bath, she will not be long,' said Dade respectfully to the two children.

There is a bath in the house, Beke wanted to ask her Uncle but the words stuck in her throat.

The two children knew that white women were called madam but were not aware that they were due to see any madams. NaBeke had told them it was a yellow house and this was the only yellow house that they had seen.

Does this mean that I have to call mama madam too? Maybe Uncle Gabriel will have to as well, thought Beke with fear replacing the excitement that had been there up until then. Dade made the two children sit down on the yellow kitchen chairs and busied herself with stirring the pot of stew which was starting to burn.

Schlep, Schlep. Dade stirred the pot and turned down the knob adding a little bit of boiling water from the electric kettle that was plugged into the wall. At Luveve, boiling water was boiled from one of the wood fires outside near the chicken pen. When NaBeke came out of the bath with a towel around her Uncle Gabriel was relieved to know that they were indeed in the right house.

'How are you, how are you?' NaBeke screeched at the top of her voice, relieved to see that the children had succeeded in not getting lost.

'Are you hungry? Come, sit down? Are you hungry? Where is the suitcase?' NaBeke seemed to do a hundred things at once, kissing the children jointly and hugging them.

'Suitcase?' The children looked at each other. 'Where is the suitcase.' NaBeke asked again. 'The one with all your clothes, where is it?'

'It was on the bus with us?'

'Oh no,' NaBeke said.

'What happened to it?

'We fell asleep.'

NaBeke could not believe it. All those beautiful clothes, the bubble gum pink two-piece suits with large green flowers. There was the diaphanous turquoise pleated dress that NaBeke had bought from an Indian store. There was no point in getting angry with the children as they had done well. They had just lost a suitcase of clothes that cost the average African's monthly salary.

The children were surprised that NaBeke had not been angry. Dade served them hot mealie meal, vegetables and a stew with fiery red tomatoes, onions and curry spices. The children were pleased to be served in their own plates.

I am glad I do not have to fight with anyone for sauce or to have the smallest piece of meat because I am the youngest, Beke thought to herself as she ate just as fast as if she was sharing a plate with other children.

The children ate until they could feel the heat from their chests as their bellies expanded. The children could sit on special yellow chairs, eat as much as they like and then have cold Orange Mazoe poured for them by a nanny. The suitcase was soon forgotten.

At exactly half past five, a beige brown Vauxhall with a black stripe pulled up on the driveway.

'Haarrr-llo,' NaBeke said in a loud laughy-happy-lovey voice swaying her generous round bottom through the front glass door and greeted Mr Trenholm

52

with a kiss.

'Beke this is Uncle. You must call him Uncle.'

This man is very old and looks like the albino in Luveve, thought Beke. The old man had kind blue eyes and wore a sun hat to protect his head which was nearly all bald. He wore a short-sleeved beige striped shirt and beige safari shorts. His knees were covered in black grease. His bow legs had neat knee-length socks that were folded over and kept neatly by an elastic band. Uncle Trenholm knelt down and patted Beke on the top of her head.

'Hello,' he smiled from ear to ear showing perfect white teeth. Beke immediately felt comfortable with Uncle Trenholm.

Lesley Alfred Trenholm was born in Penzance in 1902 and had moved to Rhodesia in 1952, the year that Beke's mother was born. Uncle Trenholm, as he became known by everyone, was a friendly man with smiling, watery blue eyes hidden behind gold-rimmed glasses that sat on his perfectly aquiline nose. On his left cheek was a big brown mole the size of a five cent piece. As soon as Uncle Trenholm arrived Dade had put the kettle on to make a fresh pot of English tea. She poured two generous helpings of the dark leaves in the heavy, polished silver pot and poured enough fresh milk in the pure white delicate china milk jug that matched the cup and saucers. His evening tea always came with fresh scones and pure, creamy, dairy butter and sweet jam. Uncle Trenholm always sat down with *The Bulawayo Chronicle* and read the paper from front to back, ignoring the sports pages, which didn't much interest him.

It was clear to everyone that NaBeke despite her youth loved Uncle Trenholm very much and he loved her back. They spoke softly to each other in kind voices. NaBeke washed Uncle Trenholm's weary feet, soaking them in bicarbonate of soda and trimmed back his toenails before gently rubbing lotion and massaging them.

Uncle Gabriel was very quick to adapt to his new lifestyle chatting to Uncle Trenholm in English and sitting on the sofa with his legs crossed exactly in the same way as Uncle Trenholm. Beke decided to copy Uncle Gabriel and sit on the small sofa next to the two gentlemen.

'*Bhalu* four [write the number four] if you want to be English.' Uncle Gabriel instructed Beke to sit with her right leg over her left knee in the English manner that Uncle Trenholm crossed his. Beke got up and went out. Uncle Gabriel, puzzled and yet determined to continue to belong, picked up *The Chronicle*.

'Mr Smith says fifty–fifty,' Uncle Gabriel said in his best English voce imitating what he had heard on the bus. Uncle Trenholm looked over at Gabriel who was reading *The Bulawayo Chronicle* upside down and smiled to himself. Beke rushed back into the room with a piece of paper and pen.

'*Wenzani?*' (What are you doing?)

'*Ngibhala u four, uthe ngibhale u four.*' (I am writing the number four, you told me to write the number 4).

Uncle Gabriel was beside himself laughing and went to his sister in the kitchen.

'Sisi, you will never believe this, I was trying to educate your daughter into being a civilised English girl and told her to sit with her legs crossed like an English person. I told her to cross her legs like the number four ... ha ha ...' Uncle Gabriel could not get his words out.

'And, a ... and ha, ha, heee, heee, ha, ha ...' He was laughing so hard tears were streaming down his face.

'Then she came back with a pen and paper with the

54

number four written on it, ha, ha, hee, and heeh.'

NaBeke laughed, Dade the servant girl laughed, Beke laughed, and even Uncle Trenholm laughed even though he didn't quite understand the pen and the four part.

**

On her first day in Trenance, Beke was thinking what a strange and long day it had been. It felt like she had done what she would do in a whole week in her fantasy dreams. It was a fantasy dream that she was sitting watching her mother whom she hardly ever saw. The main light in the bedroom had been switched off so that only the side lights of the double bed were on. The big bed which was as big as the spare bedroom in Luveve was covered with a luxurious purple and gold quilt. Beke's mother wore a delicate mauve gown that had fine purple feathers on the edges that fell neatly above her knees. The trimming went all the way up and around her neck and back down and was joined in the middle by a silk bow. When mother moved, it opened to reveal a nightie that was tightly bunched in the middle hugging Beke's mother's bosom then falling away to meet with the fine feathers at the bottom. Beke was mesmerised by mother's matching purple slippers with matching feathers which hung over her mother's toenails which were painted a shiny red colour that matched her fingernails.

Beke had never seen anyone more beautiful than her mother, not even Mrs Sibanda and her nice perfume. Not even any of the teachers at school, not Cynthia's mother, none of the women in Luveve or on the bus or at City Hall. What made mother beautiful was her beautiful skin colour. Many people thought she was a coloured woman until she spoke perfect Ndebele. In her black and white photographs mother was so light-skinned that she could even be a white person if it was not for her nose, which was not straight like white people's noses.

Mother dabbed the left side of her neck with 'French Lace' perfume, which was in a square bottle and had a beautiful, light yellow colour that looked like weak tea. When her mother dabbed the right side of her neck under her ear Beke could then smell the hypnotic sweet smell of vanilla, bergamot and oak moss. The French Lace perfume sat on the three-mirrored dressing table with other perfumes with silver tops, red tops and pink tops. There was baby powder, face powder and powder for the feet. On the right-hand side mother had red lipsticks with shiny tops and a bottle of 'Ambi' and 'Butone'.

Beke picked up the tube of Ambi, which was red and white, and opened the tube to mimic her mother who was putting on the Butone cream. Beke's mother put a dollop of Butone on her flawless forehead and noticed Beke doing the same.

'Beke don't do that, this cream is not good for small children.' Beke's mother grabbed the tube away from Beke who was left surprised as she watched her mother put another dollop of cream on her right cheek then her left cheek. The white cream had a strong smell that Beke had not smelt before.

'I didn't say you can't touch anything, Beke, just don't put it on your face.' Beke's mother had sensed her daughter's sadness at being told off.

Beke was pleased that her mother was not upset, she hated upsetting her beautiful mother and would rather read the jar than put it on her face and upset her mother. There were so many strange words on the back of the jar that Beke had not seen in her life, they looked like a new alphabet.

V-I-T-A-M-I-N A
S-O-D-I-U-M L-A-C-T-A-T-E
H-Y-D-R-O-Q-U-I-N-O-N-E

Brown Blue Eyes

In Trenance, Beke's mother got to know the locals quickly. There were the Smiths who occupied the plot in the corner of the street. The Smiths were a big family with Mr Smith the head of the family, a short man of about 4 foot 11 who seemed to be always drunk or about to be drunk or suffering from a hangover. Mr Smith was married to MaNyoni, a tall statuesque woman who would have been beautiful if it wasn't for the missing two front teeth that formed an unexpected cave-like feature between her remaining long, white teeth. Mr Smith and his wife had several children who spent a lot of time arguing with each other and their parents. Lina, Debra, Charlie-Roy and David. Because her eldest child was called Lina, MaNyoni was called NaLina.

Beke's mother spent countless hours hearing stories about fights, drunkenness, parties and unpaid rent from the Smith family. NaLina spoke perfect Ndebele all the time to all her family who always answered her back in perfect English. NaLina always made sure she emphasised every word when she relayed the dramas leaving you perfectly clear of the impact of what happened. She had a habit overemphasising the first syllable in a loud voice then abruptly truncating the last syllable to a whisper then pausing after every word as if it was a sentence in its own right. It was a habit Beke found very disconcerting at 11pm on Friday nights when she was tired. She would be dozing off when Mrs Smith would knock on the door.

'*Qoki!*' Mrs Smith, NaLina, MaNyoni would be at the door, with a wide smile revealing the cave in her mouth. NaLina was always knitting. At first the stories would start off slowly and Beke would doze off and as time went on the disyllabic drama would start.

'U-LEE-na,' (pause, one, two,)

'YEEE-na,' (pause, one, two,)

'WA-hamba.' (pause, one, two.)

Today, it was the story of Lina (U-LEE-na pause, one, two), her daughter who was involved with an older man whose wife had discovered the affair and had come over to the house and had caused a fight with Lina at midnight. There had been broken beer bottles and the wife had to have stitches after someone had thrown a bottle at her.

As Beke dozed off in between the longer pauses, NaLina's tongue darted in and out of her mouth like a big pink knitting python. To the right of Beke and Uncle Trenholm's house was a new family who had moved in recently: Ken and Carol and their four kids. They were a quiet family who kept themselves to themselves. The big plots of land meant that neighbours did not need to be in each other's pockets although everyone knew everyone's business sooner or later.

The Cohens were a rich coloured family whose Jewish ancestors were part of the Sephardic Jews that had moved to Rhodesia in the 1920s. The Cohens owned a big house in the middle of the same street as NaBeke and Uncle Trenholm's house. The house was surrounded by a seven-foot wall with broken glass and barbed wire to prevent any thieves who might be tempted to jump over the fence. If they did jump over the fence, there were three ferocious Rhodesian Ridgebacks and an ugly black bull dog. The gate was always locked and opened only by the security guard who had a key.

Uncle Trenholm and Beke's mother did not socialise with the people in Trenance, not because they were unfriendly but because they were busy. If Uncle Trenholm was not working at Wards Transport the two of them would be working at their workshop in Botswana mending cars, fixing valves, changing tyres, selling parts then driving back to Bulawayo. Beke's mother preferred to spend her time making sure her daughter read and wrote well. Her daughter was already showing incredible potential in school. Beke could read better now, especially in English, and her handwriting had progressed from looking like a spider's waltz to a more rounded and disciplined affair. Beke picked up *The Bulawayo Chronicle* that Uncle Trenholm had left on the sofa. Beke could barely open the paper which was nearly the same size as her. On the top right-hand side of the paper was the headline 'Pieter's Dead' next to a small black and white photograph of a man in his thirties with a moustache and a frozen smile.

'*Mama Umuntu lo ufile?*' (Mum, is this man dead?) Beke was now fluent in speaking English and Ndebele as mother had instructed her.

Mother came over to see where Beke's little index finger was pointing on the paper and nodded without speaking. Beke knew what dead meant. Dead was a horrible thing that happened to very unfortunate people when a group of terrorists came with a gun. Dead meant people would cry loudly and make a lot of noise and then you had to climb into a box and live in the ground for a very long time.

'Mama …' Beke said quietly so as not annoy her mother. The pat on the head was a sign that the short question and answer was over but Beke was too curious.

'When people die don't they sleep forever?' said Beke, ignoring the sense of finality in her mother's gesture.

'Mama, so they must have forced his eyes open to take this picture?'

Beke's mother laughed out loud and hugged her

innocent daughter. Her only child.

**

The weekends in Trenance came and went too soon; before Beke knew it they were driving back to 3rd Avenue and Lobengula Street to catch the Luveve bus back to the joyous chaos of her Grandmother's house.

'How was it? Tell us, tell us,' everyone at her Grandmother's house wanted to know.

'We sat on cushions on sofas every day and the maid served us on our own plates.'

'*Iqiniso?*' (Really?) the other children shouted back with envy and the desire to know more at the same time. Uncle Gabriel told them about NaBeke's house, his stories getting more and more exaggerated with each minute.

'Never mind, I am going there myself next week to take Beke, I will see it for myself,' said Hetta. As time went on Beke was allowed to travel to and from Trenance by herself. She got used to the routine of waiting at the bus terminus on Fridays, then waiting at City Hall for the bus and the 45-minute bus ride from City Hall until the bus stopped and she got off and walked to her mother's house. She had even found out that if she waited 15 minutes longer she would get a bus that dropped her off in Trenance itself at the end of her mother's road. All she had to do was to walk down the main road and she would be home. She didn't have to wade through the treacherous thorns and bushes with the ever present fear of a snake or black *chongololos* (centipedes), which seemed to crawl out of the ground whenever it rained.

Matshayiskova School had accepted more and more children, which meant one week Beke's classes were in the afternoon and ended at 4pm. Mr Moyo had slowly reverted back to his old ways of leaving the children unattended. He would slope off unannounced to have discussions with the headmaster or go into town for supplies. Sometimes Samson and Cornelius would try their games again and bring fear back to the Grade 4 children but never to the same extent.

One Friday afternoon Mr Moyo had been absent from 1 until 3pm. Before leaving he had asked the children to prepare for a spelling test. It was February, the sun was belligerent and harsh casting iron shadows in the classroom making the children sleepy. When Mr Moyo returned he was furious with the children. It was obvious to him that none of the children had spent any time learning any spellings.

'Do you want to end up as garden boys and nannies?' he bellowed to the children, juddering some of them out their sleep. 'Well there is no one who was taught by me who is going to end up as a garden boy,' the sweat poured from his protruding forehead and slid down his cheek and beard. He didn't bother to wipe it off and this made him scarier to the children.

'Sit up!' Mr Moyo shouted banging his wooden ruler on his table waking up the dust and making the children who were already sitting up shudder with surprise. It was very rare that Mr Moyo would shout this way on a Friday. He would often let the children take turns in reading from a book until it was 4pm. It was clear that something else had upset him and the children knew they would never know what that something was.

Mr Moyo gave them the spelling test as he had promised. Instead of taking the books home to mark, he made the children swap their books and mark each other. Those who did badly were told to repeat the spellings again while the class waited. Tick, tock, tick, tock. The City Hall clock ticked. Mr Moyo's class was the only class that had a clock. Beke was not very good at telling the time yet, but she knew a little bit. The short hand was now on four and there were still seven people who hadn't done the spelling right.

Tick, tock, tick, tock, the long hand moved again. Beke dared not look at it. The last bus to Saucertown was at 5:30, that much she knew. She was always at City Hall by 5pm when the big clock sang its five o' clock song.

Ding, Dong, Ding, Ding, Dong, Ding, Dong-Ding, Dong, Ding, Ding Dong.

Five dongs meant it was five o'clock. If she got the five o'clock bus she could enjoy a deserted bus ride with only one or two people in the bus.

If she got the 5:15, she didn't have the long walk through the bushes. Clara was the last person to do her spellings while the rest of the class sat and watched, glad that they were not the class idiot. From the window, Beke gazed across the row of Jacaranda's that lined the school road which was now filled with Friday's schoolchildren with jerseys around their waistlines, laughing, singing and kicking their balls to each other.

Over and over again Mr Moyo made Clara repeat the words until she got them right. It was twenty to five when the children left the classroom group by group. The school was like a graveyard without a single teacher or pupil in sight. Beke's group was the first to leave and she ran to her Grandmother's house as fast as her little legs could carry her. Her white socks which were covered by fine particles of sand had migrated from her knees and sat by her ankles as if they also had been exhausted by the run. Beke dropped her school bag and wished she had packed her few clothes early in the morning or the night before. Aunty Hetta was surprised at how late Beke was.

'You can't go now, it's too late.'

'No mama will worry, I have to go.'

'OK you must run all the way.'

Beke ran all the way to the bus terminus. There was a bus already standing there so she ran faster and faster, her lungs filling up with dust and air making her cough.

She was the last passenger on the bus; the driver grabbed her 25 cent coin and impatiently threw the change of coppers in her sweaty little hands. The bus coughed and spluttered black fumes of diesel as it turned out of the terminus in a hurry. Beke's eyes were burning, her throat was burning, her chest felt like hot coals. All she wanted to do was sit down but she had to stand. The bus was full of people everywhere: mothers wearing colourful headscarves with babies on their backs, men smoking cigarettes, coughing and making small talk with strangers they had just met on the bus. Underneath every seat was a suitcase or a bed sheet carrying supplies, bags of mealie meal, tea, sugar and soap.

The heat and the smell of sweat made Beke dizzy but she was glad she had managed to get the bus. The smell of chlorine rose in the air from the swimming bath as dozens of children were piling into the Luveve swimming baths. At the nearby Fish and Chip shop, the wafting smell of vinegar and fried chips made Beke wish she was staying in Luveve to swim and watch the sun setting while eating hot chips.

'*Asambeni, Asambeni,*' (Let's go,) the bus driver shouted amidst whistles, smoke, dust and men hanging out of the bus holding down their hats. Inside the bus was already full and Beke held on tightly to the metal railing of the seat. An elderly woman saw the distress in Beke's eyes and asked her to sit on her lap to stop her from being crushed.

Beke was relieved and whispered a 'Thank you' to

the strange kind eyes, with her hair plaited in 'buns'. The woman continued to look outside the window and chat to the woman next to her. She held Beke as if she was her own child, keeping her safe from the sweaty bodies.

By the time they got to Renkini most of the people had got off the bus to get to the bus terminus to The Reserves. Beke was relieved to see them all go, even the kind woman and her sister. At least she could now have a seat of her own, a window seat at that and to look outside at the cars hooting, hawkers selling their wares, and people sitting underneath trees knitting and breastfeeding.

As soon as Beke got off she sprinted out of the bus, dodging in and out of the tide of people who seemed to be going in the opposite direction to her. She did not ever remember seeing so many people at once. The Indian shops on 3rd Avenue were starting to close.

'*Woza mama, Woza mama.*' (Come in ladies, Come in ladies.) Mr Naidoo's robotic voice was starting to wane like a tape recorder with low battery power. He would still let anyone into his shop as long as there were mannequins dressed and standing there. Beke waited to hear the sound of the City Hall Bell

'Ding-Dong- Don ...'

That was the sound in her head, wishful thinking. It always did that the minute she crossed the street from the Spar past the robot lights to the flower sellers. Today there were no flower sellers, they were all gone. No roses, pink, red, white or yellow. No buckets of fluorescent green ferns, no sunshine yellow dahlias, or the smell of carnations; the last of the hardy flower sellers were gone.

There were still buses at the City Hall; most of them were pulling off and queuing at the robots on 5th Avenue next to the buses going to Killarney, Montrose and Barham Green.

The long hand went to quarter past. Beke dared not look at the clock that was covered by the date trees as she climbed into the bus. Her bus was always the first in the queue near the 'whites only' toilets, which was next to the 'whites only' bench.

The bus was full but not as full as the bus from Luveve; the bus driver was less grumpy and even smiled as he gave her change. It might have been a smile, Beke didn't really know she was just so relieved to have caught the last bus, to top it all she had a seat all to herself and put her small bag with washing down.

'Last stop, last stop!'

Much as she had tried to stay awake, Beke had fallen asleep, but was determined not to leave her bag on the bus the way she had with her Uncle Gabriel. She ran out of the bus scared that the bus driver would start the engine and take her back to town.

Darkness.

What was the time? Beke had no watch.

When did it get so dark? How long was she asleep for? Was she at Saucertown near Garden Cash? Or was she at the top of her mother's road where she could walk through the main road for ten minutes and be home.

The darkness was confusing Beke. She looked around and did not see the Garden Cash store so she was not at Saucertown. There was a big house with a wall the size of the house that went round the perimeter of the house. This looked very much like the pinky-sandy house at the top of the main road that led to her mother's house but Beke could not be sure. She never paid attention to very much when she got off the bus. Everything looked so different in the dark and the street lights really did not help.

'This must be home, the house looked yellow in the

dark, the lights were on like the lights in her home,'
Beke said to herself.

'*Ngubani lapho,* who is there?' came a voice that
sounded like Baron's voice except it was older and
slower. Beke was dazed and confused. She had been
walking for more than two hours hoping after hope that
the next house would be her mother's house.

'*Ibizo lakho ngubani*? What's your name?'

The old man had big eyes which were brown with a
blue rim at the edge. This made his eyes look as though
he was a white man although she knew he wasn't. Beke
didn't know the name of the street where her mother
lived. She only knew that they had a yellow house with
a boys' *Khaya* where Baron slept. She told the old man
what her mother looked like but he did not know her.
She tried to describe Uncle Trenholm but the old man
had never seen him either. The old man gave her a
clean blanket to sleep on the floor near him.

**

The inspections started soon after Beke had been lost at
night; she couldn't remember how she had got home in
the end.

'Did he touch you?' Mother whispered with
concern. She pulled down her daughter's panties to
examine if her hymen was still intact. Beke's mother
was shocked to find her daughter had the body of a
teenager and was growing fine hairs in her pubic area,
and little circular breasts in her chest.

She was only nine.

1, 2, 3, four, five,6, 7, 8, 9.

'NINE, dear God, only nine.'

She had never seen anything like this before, a nine-
year-old with breasts. She had ignored the hairs she had
seen at the age of seven hoping they would go away.

Soon her little girl would have periods and maybe get pregnant early the way she had at 16 years old.

Beke's mother remembered reading an article in *Drum,* a South African magazine about a little girl of twelve who had become the youngest mother in the world. The little Zulu girl held her little bundle with a haunted stare of a lost childhood. She could not let her child lose her childhood. There would be no cameramen taking pictures of her nine-year-old daughter with a daughter.

'Are you sure?'

'Yes,' Beke said fearfully after her mother asked her for the second time, third time, fourth time … maybe the old man had touched her, she wasn't sure. The old man with brown eyes with the blue rim.

Wonder Woman, Superman and Spiderman

Bekezela was sitting cross-legged on the cold polished floor in the hallway listening to the wind outside. The wind in Trenance seemed to blow harder, faster and sometimes shook the shiny glass pane. Bekezela felt safe as she watched the overgrown clumps of lawn swaying chaotically. At times the wind would slow down with no warning and become a gentle whistle, its soft lullaby waking the leaves of the mulberry bush.

Bekezela decided to put together her puzzle of Wonder Woman. Wonder Woman, beautiful blue eyes with a golden belt, right leg with red boot, left leg with red boot, right hands and arms, left arms and left hands, one corner, two corners, beautiful blue eyes, golden belt. Ooops three pieces missing!

No left eye?

No right eye?

This was not Wonder Woman. Beke looked in the Superman box. There were no beautiful blue eyes, no mouth. This was not Wonder Woman without her beautiful eyes. Even if she had the star in her forehead, this was not Wonder Woman. Beke decided to dismantle the puzzle, and decided she was not interested in Superman or Spiderman but would look at her mother's recipe book *The Kitchen in the Bush*, written by Mrs M. Fletcher. She turned the black and white pages with garish illustrations to page 69, mulberry jam.

Beke stared at the mulberry bush, which was now in complete obedience to the dictates of the wind as it howled and hooted. The mulberry bush pretended that the wishes of the wind were its idea all along; its little black berries plopped to the ground. Beke stared at the title 'Mulberry Jam'; there were no pictures of jam, not even drawings of jam. Beke had never seen mulberry jam or heard of anyone making mulberry jam.

There were mulberries from the mulberry bush alright but no jam. The mulberry bush had black berries with juice that stained your fingers red forever. Red black berries with bumps, each bump with a small hair.

Mulberry Jam

To make beautiful mulberry jam you must make sure that the berries you use are not overripe or spoiled.

11 cups of fresh ripe mulberries

4 cups of sugar (add an extra half a cup if you want it sweeter)

1 teaspoon of yeast (to ferment it)

1/2 teaspoon peptic enzyme

1 package wine yeast

1 gallon water

Method:
Crush the berries and place in the primary ferment... Beke's eyes glazed over, tired of hearing the wind, tired of Mrs Fletcher and her invisible mulberry jam.

Did that man touch me? Or didn't he? Bekezela was sure that he didn't. He was a good man, a kind man with brown eyes with a blue rim. He had given her his grey blanket with a blue stripe and used a coat to sleep instead. He had woken her up very early and taken her to her mother's door at seven in the morning before they got worried. He had given her Tanganda tea with milk in a plastic cup so she wouldn't burn her lips. He had held her hand like any Grandfather would. The old man had wondered how a child of nine could be left to wander the streets alone. Beke's mother wondered whether the old man had touched her. Beke wondered who ate mulberry jam and whether Wonder Woman could live with parts of her missing.

**

The Rhodesian Broadcasting Corporation was based in studios in Montrose where they broadcasted programmes that came from England largely for its colonial population. In 1978 they decided to open its studios to the talent of African children for a Christmas Special. They commissioned a production and put out announcements on the television and the radio for dancers to audition for a one-off special for Bulawayo's best talent. Beke and her Aunty Hetta were sure they would win the audition and started to rehearse their dance with four weeks to spare.

You and me
Will go motorbike riding When the sun is shining
And the rain
I've got money in my pocket
Tiger in my tank.
And I think of the road again.

Beke and her Aunty Hetta decided that this would be the best song for them. They had found the 7-inch record amongst NaBeke's collection next to Elvis Presley, Don Williams, The Dooby Brothers and Roger Whittaker. The girls had loved the beat and knew all of the words of the song. At least some of them.

'*Kutshoni ukhuthi tiger in the tank mamomcane?*' (What does tiger in the tank mean, aunty?)

'I don't know; a tiger is an animal like the ones in Chipangali.'

'Like an elephant or a zebra or a lion?'

71

'Why does he have a tiger in his tank?'

'Maybe a tiger is another word for petrol in London.'

'OK yes I think so it's true a tiger is another word for petrol.'

They practised again.

'*I've got money in my pocket,*' tap right bum with right hand.

'*I've got tiger in my tank,*' turn left and pretend to put petrol in car while shaking left knee and hips.

'OK, I know, I have an idea when we put petrol and shake left knee let's also shake shoulders down to the middle,' Beke said to her aunt. The new routine looked good but Aunty Hetta did not want to be outdone by her short nine-year-old niece who had the advantage of watching more television at the weekend and seeing all the dances. Aunty Hetta went back to the hi-fi and picked up the needle from the record careful not to scratch it as it would never sound the same again. She placed the needle on the side and explained the next dance.

'*Lapha,* take the right hand and put it on the forehead and move it away to show the distance,' Aunty Hetta demonstrated shaking her hips and pointing to a distant place. Beke understood straight away. Their routine was nearly done.

'*You and me,*' right hand point out while shaking hips with left hand on hip.

'*We'll go motorbike riding,*' pretend motorbike, bend, shake hips and smile.

The girls practised every Saturday. Aunty Hetta stole away from Grandmother's house so she didn't have to cook for all the children. After all, big sister had a nanny who cooked for her. She didn't even have to wash a single thing, or dry the plates or put them away; her sister paid the nanny $10 to do that. Dade the nanny would use that $10 to send to her own family in The Reserves to buy mealie meal and vegetables or save it up to buy a cow, or send one of their brothers and sisters to school.

After the incident with the old African man with the blue eyes, Uncle Trenholm picked Beke up at quarter past five every Friday evening outside Bulawayo post office. Bulawayo post office was an unashamed symbol of colonialism, a building made of fiery red stone that shone like a copper monument. It stood proudly on 5th Avenue and Main Street overlooking the statue of Cecil John Rhodes who was looking over the city with his hands behind his back.

The streets of Bulawayo were generous and open like its people, allowing cars to park on either side, two lanes of cars going in both directions and ample space for cars to park in the middle section. The beige brown Vauxhall with the black line in the middle would park in front of the bench where Beke sat waiting and watching people going home. Uncle Trenholm got out of his car greeted Beke and let her into the passenger seat. Uncle Trenholm would then walk up the neat row of cold granite steps to the post office boxes to open box number 2-4-6-8 in the middle section of the neat row of shiny olive green boxes.

Electricity mail, mail for the TV licence, water bills and a letter from his daughters in England and Violet in the Orange Free State. Uncle Trenholm would spend the entire hour sitting in front of the television after the RBC news reading the neat, curved writing from his relatives overseas.

'How was school today?' Uncle Trenholm asked Beke politely.

'Very well,' Beke replied in the way her mother had taught her. At Grandmother's house the children sat on the floor and being quiet and obedient was what children did. Conversation, even polite conversation, was for the adults. Uncle Trenholm talked to her about England where he had come from.

'Penzance,' he said showing Beke black and white pictures of himself as a little boy with a thick black fringe. Uncle Trenholm was wearing a long coat that made him look like a little girl.

'Perrh-zz.'

'No, Pee-nza-nce' slowly, softly so the little girl could understand and show her Cornwall on a map, pictures of Queen Elizabeth, Big Ben, London. England, precious England.

Sometimes when Uncle Trenholm sat to watch the second dose of news mother would ask again about 'The Incident' and ask Beke again if she was sure that the man had not touched her. Mother would try to jog her memory.

'When you fell asleep … do you remember falling asleep? Did you feel a hand? Are you sure he was sleeping far away from you? … Take off your panties,' NaBeke instructed. For what felt like hours even though it was minutes, NaBeke was finding out whether Beke was telling the truth. She seemed satisfied after the inspections and Beke searched her mind and was sure that the man still had not touched her.

Uncle Henry

'Tummy?'

'What's wrong?' mother said.

'My head is sore,' Beke said clutching her stomach then her head in a disjointed whisper.

'What, speak up I can't hear you.'

Beke started to cry, thinking of the journey to Luveve, the two buses, Samson and Cornelius. She would have to go into her mother's purse to take 25 cents to give to them. The very thought of the bullies made the tears flow spontaneously from her ebony eyes.

'Gabriel, Gabriel lo!' Beke's mother shouted at her younger brother talking to Baron the garden boy instructing him on something that was none of his business.

'You will have to go back by yourself and tell the school that Beke is sick and will be back tomorrow.'

Beke could not believe how easy it was to get a day off from school. Uncle Trenholm drove away giving Uncle Gabriel a lift. Beke imagined them talking about the bush war. Beke imagined Uncle Gabriel nodding furiously with his brow painfully furrowed into an exaggerated 'w' on his forehead as they talked about Rhodesian politics.

Their voices drifted away with the wheels and the engine until silence could be heard all over the house and all over Trenance.

The trucks and cars all gone to work.

The children all gone to school.

Mother was all alone.

Dogs all quiet.

Beke thought how she never heard any trucks zooming away in Trenance. She never heard any children laughing or crying because the houses were so far apart. She never saw anyone except MaNyoni now and again. No dogs barked. It was so different to her Grandmother's house where she heard the Lobels truck at 7am revving loudly, followed by the milkman with the milk crates and the glasses tinkling away like a glass orchestra.

The three dogs in her Grandmother's street barked to provoke the dogs in MaKhumalo's street which chased the skinny ones near *emagrosa*. By 9am the sounds of dogs became background music. Only in silence did Beke contemplate the level of discomfort that was the silence which opened the gaps between her thoughts.

'What's really wrong?' said mother sensing that Beke was not really ill. Beke found herself pouring out the story of Samson and Cornelius to her mother. The role-playing, the staged fights, the party fund for the party that never happened, the slap by Mr Moyo.

'Phew,' Beke sighed and started to drift off into a sleep woken up by Baron singing as he washed the windows.

'Impi ngeyethu hayi, hayi.' (This is our war.) Baron sung washing windows first with soapy water, then vinegar to remove the smears. Baron was always singing war songs and always listening to the 'African stations' that were being illegally broadcasted on his radio. Drifting in and out of sleep, Beke was sure she could hear voices talking. *Had Uncle Trenholm come back?*

'Bulawayo yethu Hayi,' Baron's voice was going into a whisper; he was now washing the windows by the kitchen.

'Baron-lo,' mother shouted from the living room jolting Beke in the living room, did she have to shout?

'Hamba uye emagrosa.' (Go to the shops.)

76

Beke could not hear what her mother was saying, the sun in one corner of her face forcing its way through the drawn curtains like an unwanted intruder.

Baron left.

Mother continued talking to the man in the living room, Beke was sure it was a man. Suddenly mother laughed and Elvis started to sing through the hi-fi.

Kentucky rain keeps falling down.....

The man spoke loud enough for Beke to hear that it wasn't Uncle Trenholm, Elvis sang, mother laughed.

Elvis sang again.

A little louder

With the rain in my shoes, thinking of you....

Footsteps. Bang, bang the man was walking, Elvis sang, mother walked through the hallway carefully. Elvis kept singing in the living room, nobody was there.

Beke drifted back into sleep that wasn't sleep. Just pretend sleep, the sleep that if you pretended long enough became real sleep.

Quiet. No voices. Elvis sang again, wiping off the sweat pouring down his brow with a white handkerchief.

With the walky, talky, rain, walky rain, walky rain, walky talky rain ...

Beke's eyes closed tightly, sleep blinking to Elvis's bass in her chest, in the living room, the hallway, the kitchen, bathroom, and mother and Uncle Trenholm's bedroom.

Elvis stopped singing after girls' voices kept repeating walky, talky rain after him. What was walky, talky rain? Beke asked herself lots of stupid questions the way you do when you are off sick with pretend stomach pains.

Quiet. No voices. No footsteps. Elvis was now quiet probably sipping water after that performance. Baron was probably singing war songs, cycling on his bike to the Garden Cash store to get something that Beke couldn't quite hear before Elvis started to sing.

Someone was whispering, still someone in the house, it was mother's voice whispering. Kind, considerate mother knew that her only daughter was sick with a pretend stomach illness and didn't want to disturb her.

'Bye,' a man's voice, an English man's voice, an English man who didn't sound like Uncle. Beke got out of her bed, opened the curtains to see a green Citroen with a beige roof rising up from sleep like a tortoise, a tall man without the top of his head turned the steering wheel and drove off.

Elvis sings again, volume turned down so you can't hear what song he is singing but you know it's Elvis, only one Elvis.

**

Another Friday. The children were full of morning tea and Downings bread, which the children didn't like as much as the Lobels bread. Beke waited for her mother. Uncle Gabriel and Aunty Hetta had at first fought about who was going to take Beke to Trenance, each one of them giving reasons why they would be better for the job.

'*Last time walahla suitcase, this time bazakhu fica e Salisbury lo mntwana.*' (Last time you lost the suitcase, this time they will find you in Salisbury with the child.)

'*Manje khe, so what usisi katshongo lutho?*' (So what, it didn't bother our sister?)

'*Voetsek wena, wothi ngihambe lami.*' (Let me go

'*Malumesifuna Ukuprac-tiza thina.*' (Uncle we want to practise our dance.)

'Never mind, neither of you is going. Beke's

78

NaBeke is coming here tomorrow.'

Uncle Gabriel sat in the front of the house waiting for Beke's mother, his sister.

Beke knew Uncle Gabriel's plan: he would pounce on her mother and try to persuade her to take him instead of his sister. Beke wanted to practise with her aunt, besides her aunt was more fun. Most times she was fun. When she wasn't pulling hair into buns she was rubbing Beke's legs with Vaseline quite violently or she would be pushing down pullovers over her head too fast. Apart from that she was fun.

Through the thick dirty lace curtains which had become dirty from years of dust that nobody bothered to wash, Beke could see Uncle Gabriel standing on the wall by the veranda saying hello to every passer-by as they went: '*emagrosa.*'

'*Yebo Sabelo?*'

'*Uthini?*'

'*Salibonani Masire-nje?*'

'Makhona, where is my money?'

Uncle Gabriel knew everyone that walked past No. 203 New Luveve.

For five minutes the street was packed with people wearing *pata patas* (flip-flops) and tennis shoes making the dust cling to their Vaselined legs. Then suddenly everyone disappeared except for one beautiful girl sauntering past 203 swaying her hips from side to side. Uncle Gabriel wasted no time whistling so the girl could hear.

'*Sisi umuhle njani,*' (Sister you are so beautiful,) Uncle Gabriel said in a loud whisper. Beke wondered how her Uncle did this to every girl for hours day in day out.

'*Ende ngiyafuna mani, ende umuhle kakhulu ntombi!*' (You are so beautiful and I really fancy you girl!)

79

Uncle Gabriel kept on until the young girl walked into Mdamburi the grocery store to buy whatever her mother and father had sent her to the store for. Uncle Gabriel waited for her to come back and distracted himself with more salutations.

'*Susa iviri lelo usisi wami uyabuya kathesi,*' (Remove that wheel from there, my sister is coming in a minute,) he shouted to the young boys who had parked a massive wheel in front of his house and were planning to sit on it and relax for the rest of the day.

The children did not move.

Uncle Gabriel wasted no time in running after them.

'*Fusekhi, Fusekhi hambani, izinja lezi.*' (Go away, you dogs.)

The young boys, shirtless with torn khaki shorts, rolled up at the waistline displaying dry, grey, ashy bottoms. Uncle Gabriel wasted no time in throwing a stray shoe in their direction to move them away from his territory before composing himself and waiting for the beautiful girl with the swaying hips.

'*Suphendikhile,*' (You are back,) Uncle Gabriel said to the beautiful girl with the swaying hips.

Silence. Hips swaying left and right.

'*Ungithengeleni?*' (What did you buy for me?)

Silence, hips swaying, suddenly the Salvation Army church seemed very interesting to the swaying-hip girl. Uncle Gabriel could not bear the overt rejection and started to walk out of the seclusion of the veranda to approach the swaying-hip girl.

She started walking faster, almost trotting away towards Gwabalanda.

'*Aah fusekhi, umubi vele!*' (Piss off, you are ugly anyway!)

**

80

By the time NaBeke came Uncle Gabriel had given up, uGogo was drinking a bottle of Castle beer and talking to Mr Ndlela about the 'the boys in Zambia'. NaBeke looked beautiful in her denim bell-bottoms and chequered shirt. Uncle Gabriel looked at his sister with pride, she looked exactly like the American women Gabriel and his friends saw singing songs on TV. His sister had skin like Donna Summer with powder and red lipstick, blue eye shadow and hair like her too.

UGogo was proud of his eldest daughter too. When she came to visit, especially if she came in her car, she would call all the neighbours one by one to introduce them to her eldest daughter who was married to a white man from England.

Today NaBeke was late and could not decide who to take with her to her house in Trenance. She knew her youngest brother was dying to come to Trenance again. She wanted her younger sister Hetta to come instead to practise the dance routine with her daughter. God knows she had fought hard to get her that audition; it would be a shame if she could not make it. She was so proud of her daughter who was a natural performer who loved the limelight. Where other children shied away from the limelight her daughter would entertain swaying from side to side dancing exactly like the people she had seen on TV. She only needed to hear a song twice before she knew the words.

Besides, her daughter adored her auntie Hetta, she was like a surrogate mother. NaBeke was torn; her brother was such an accidental entertainer, she knew she would be laughing all day and every day. Mr Trenholm her husband liked her younger brother too. There also the small consolation that Gabriel would be good company for Baron. NaBeke felt sorry for him during his days off from 1pm on Saturday afternoon until Sunday evenings; he always seemed lonely. She didn't know what he did as he did not have any friends in Trenance. Baron's spirits always lifted when Gabriel came. Baron was always cloaked in an invisible cloak of duty and honour from the moment he woke up. It was easy to forget that he was only 15 years old. When Gabriel came to Trenance the old man in Baron went to sleep and the young boy came out.

Gabriel and Baron were very different; Gabriel was a Bulawayo boy, street-wise who could talk to anyone black or white about anything. He did not have the innate deference that most Africans had towards Europeans. Baron was painfully respectful to women, old people, small children and whites. His respectfulness robbed him of his spontaneity and this was where her brother Gabriel was an asset.

NaBeke decided that she would ask her brother to come after all. Hetta would be hurt but there would always be next week. Once Beke's mother made a decision she believed it was important to act on it and not waiver or dither so she walked into the spare third bedroom next to the kitchen and knocked on the door to tell her sister the bad news.

NaBeke opened the door to find not Hetta her sister but Nancy the third of the nine children in the family and the girl that came after her.

What was she doing back here? The two sisters exchanged a few civil words before Beke's mother stormed to the first bedroom of the newly extended section of the house.

'What is she doing here?'

'It's her home just like it's yours and you can come and go as you please?'

'I contribute to the house, what does she do?'

'She has just had a baby.'

'So?'

'Her third child mama and she is only 24,' Beke's

mother's voice was now raised and could be heard in the living room.

'So?'

'Her third child with three different men.' Beke's mother's voice could be heard in the kitchen. The kitchen was next to the third bedroom, where her sister could hear the argument. 'How dare she?'

Nancy put her new baby Sithabile down on the bed and stormed out to the first bedroom where her sister stood with her hands on her hips. Nancy had vowed she would never give her children 'white names'. *Sithabile* meant joy and *Siphiwe* meant gift in Ndebele.

'How dare she?' Nancy looked straight past her sister. She knew how much her sister hated being ignored or belittled so she decided to talk about her as if she was not there.

'How dare she? Married to a dirty old white man now she thinks she can tell everyone how to live their lives?'

Beke's mother had not come for an argument and did not want to fight. She just wanted her sisters and brothers to stand up for themselves and stop living at home and relying on their single mother.

Hands came off hips and went to hug her younger sister to let her know she didn't want to fight.

'Nancy you must go to the clinic to get pills you know.'

'Ha ha ha,' NaBeke's younger sister's laugh was so forced and unnatural that NaBeke knew that the fight was far from over. She had heard that laugh before when they were growing up playing in the fields in Essexvale.

There was more to come.

'You are jealous aren't you?'

'Jealous?' thought their mother confused.

Jealous thought NaBeke, wondering if her younger

sister would explain how she could be jealous of
someone who was lodging in one room in her mother's
house with three children while she lived in a plot of
fertile land with a house, servants and drove a car just
like any white madam in Bulawayo. She was as good as
a madam.

'Jealous of what, meeeh?' She overemphasised the
'me' spitting it out and pointing to her own chest with
her mouth snarling and her nose upturned as if she had
smelt something bad.

'ME, you bitch, jealous of me because *inyumba* like
you who cannot have children is always jealous.'

The two sisters fought with bare fists insulting each
other with each blow. Nancy's hair was pulled from the
lovely plaited buns that Hetta had spent a whole hour
on. Beke's mother's Donna Summer hair was on
uGogo's floor, top buttons were open, middle button
broken and showing bras. The noise woke the baby in
the third spare bedroom and the baby started to wail
uncontrollably. Siphiwe Nancy's first daughter shouted
at Beke because her mother was fighting her mother.

'*Fusekhi*,' the little five-year-old shouted loudly,
blinking hard and waving a fist that hit the invisible
person that stood between her and her cousin. Beke,
annoyed at the little girl's insult, hit the little girl on her
bare arm and she started to cry. Aunty Hetta hit
Sithabile on her head full of buns. Hetta knew that
Beke would have been less willing to hit a smaller child
if her mother was not here. Hitting a smaller child was
just rude even if you had a very pretty mother married
to a white man. Aunty Hetta would not tolerate such
behaviour from any of the children she looked after.

It seemed everyone was fighting: uGogo with
Beke's mother; Beke's mother with Nancy her sister.
The older women fought with each other, the children
with the adults. A few sofas were misplaced, doilies left

the top of tables and landed on floors, wigs were displaced, water was spilled.

Uncle Gabriel watched and smiled to himself knowing that his older sister Hetta would not be going to Trenance today no matter how much of an advantage she had. Hetta had made two unforgivable mistakes.

One. She had hit her sister's only daughter.

Two. By doing one, she had taken sides and with her sister Gabriel had learnt very early on that you were either for her or against her: there was no in-between.

**

Boob tube or jump suit? Beke and Aunty Hetta were not sure what to wear to the audition that was going to be at the studios that Saturday. It was Friday morning, schools had closed for the Christmas holidays and both Beke and Aunty Hetta were confident that they would make the auditions.

'Why don't you practise in front of us and we will tell you how good you are?' It was seven o'clock in the evening, the Bulawayo night sky was a deep, rich, velvety song with sprinklings of clear silver stars. The 'us' that Beke's mother was referring to was her two new visitors who they had met in Selebi-Phikwe in Botswana and were here for the weekend.

Beke didn't mind except that it meant she would have to sleep on the floor in the small space between the wall and her mother's bed and her Aunty Hetta would have to sleep in the slightly bigger space between the short end of the bed and the door. The visitors that made the 'us' that Beke's mother was referring to would sleep in Beke's ¾ bed that she used on weekends to sleep.

The nanny had put freshly starched sheets and clean blankets and fresh pillows for the visitors that were staying for two days. The visitors were Sarah, a beautiful, heavily pregnant Tswana woman with her boyfriend, an older white man.

Sarah seemed to be in a bad mood all the time and hardly ever smiled. Beke was even more surprised that Sarah didn't speak any Ndebele. How was it possible for an African not to speak Ndebele, she knew that some of the coloureds didn't speak Ndebele or pretended not to but as pretty as she was Beke knew that Sarah was not a coloured.

'*Dumela Ra,*' (Hallo,) NaBeke would say to Aunty Sarah in an exaggerated voice.

'*Tsamaya sinthle,*' (Good bye,) was all the Tswana she ever heard mother speak to Aunty Sarah, the rest of the time they spoke in English. Uncle Henry smelt of strong lavender aftershave that lingered in the house weeks after he had gone to Australia, wherever that was. Beke thought all old white men came from England in Cornwall.

The 'us' was Uncle Trenholm, Uncle Henry and Aunty Sarah who sat on the olive green leather sofas while Beke's mother switched on the hi-fi and put the record on. The girls waited with their hands on their hips ready to start shaking them when the music started.

Right hand on right bum, shake left knee.

You and me ....

Right hand to chest then out, shake left knee, shake, hips.

The 'us' audience clapped and smiled and sipped cold beer.

Clap, clap.

Dance routine over.

'Yeahhhhh,' clap, clap, clap, whistle, clap some more.

Aunty Sarah came to the girls and gave them a hug.

The girls were excited and confident that they had done well.

**

On the day of the audition, the December rain had poured out of the sky that had been cloudless the day before. Never mind, the girls were still going to 'stretch' their hair. Hetta put the heavy, black, metallic, hot comb on the electric rings of the stove. The circular rings grew hotter and hotter becoming the colour of orange fire making the hot comb hot enough to melt rubber. Aunty Hetta put sunflower cooking oil on Beke's matted hair. The hot comb sizzled and grey smoke rose from Beke's skull as her hair became straighter, softer and longer.

A little burn at the top of the ear was normal and Beke didn't mind having her hair straightened. It was better than having it plaited into buns even if it meant a little ear skin would melt into the hot comb leaving a black scab.

The smell of cooking oil and burning rose from the stove filling up the kitchen. Even though the two girls were almost suffocating they persevered knowing they would look prettier with straight hair.

Plaited buns in rows were out of the question, especially on TV. Especially since it was their first time on TV. Beke and Aunty Hetta walked the half a mile from the yellow house wearing matching green bell-bottom trousers and striped yellow boob tubes, a jersey each and an umbrella to hide from the rain. Green and white Gordon's paper bags covered the girls' hair to preserve their 'push back' matching hairstyles. Aunty Hetta had carefully wrapped the record in two plastic bags.

Fat, shiny rain drops danced on the shiny green

tshomoliya leaves, bouncing off the carefree green leaves of the new corn and disappeared into the drains that had been dug by Baron. The girls waited at the top of the road where they could see the seven-foot wall of the Cohens. They waited for the bus to take them to Montrose Studios to show off their dance.

The grey RBC Kombi pulled up between the edge of the road and the red muddy dip picking up the girls at exactly 10am on Saturday morning as they had promised NaBeke on the phone. Inside there were already four hopefuls singing and chatting away at the back. The kombi drove past Saucertown, past Baines School, now deserted without a single blue uniform or blue hat. The driver zoomed through Main Street and stopped at the Bulawayo post office to pick up the last five girls who would be hoping to broadcast their dancing skills.

In town, the sun had peeped out through the black clouds and white women were piling out of their cars near Haddon & Sly with their servants in their white uniforms in tow. The kombi driver revved up the diesel engine into the edge of the city. Once he had gone past the deserted industrial sites the Rhodesian Broadcasting which stood on a small *kopje* came into view. The blonde receptionist with steely grey eyes eyed the African children suspiciously.

'Whuu aaahr they? What do they want?'

'They are auditioning for the Christmas Special,' the African driver answered her in a weary tone.

'Oh … Arr-khay ahh whaz nhat to-ld about this Fredrick.'

Fredrick ushered the children to a corner and went back to whisper something to the receptionist who seemed agitated and confused.

'Look Nancy … ' He whispered something to her, a little too close for comfort the children thought.

88

'Oh arr-khay, ahh understand,' she said in an Afrikaner accent much stronger than the average Rhodesian accent. Whatever Fredrick had said had calmed her down. Nancy the studio receptionist was suddenly smiley, at least her lips moved to reveal small, even teeth. Her smile did not move to her eyes, which were still suspiciously eyeing the African children wearing boob tubes, jump suits and bell-bottoms.

'Oooh-kay now, your name plee-ze,' Nancy pointed to Bekezela.

'B-E-K-E-Z-E-L-A' Beke said slowly.

'Arr-khay sbp-ell that for me plee-ze'.

The studio receptionist wrote down all the children's names pleased that the rest of them were called Charlotte, Emily, Lucy and Hetta.

'Just wait.'

Nancy the studio receptionist with the blonde hair and now smiley grey eyes came back after what seemed like ages although it was only ten minutes.

'Foh-llow me plee-ze.' She smiled again and the children smiled back wondering what had made Nancy lose her suspicion of the African children. The children could not believe that they were standing in the very studio where Mr David Emberton read all about landmines at 6pm and negotiations with the obdurate Mugabe and his comrades.

Emily was the first to dance in her yellow sun dress, elasticated in the chest area with little bows going over her bony shoulders. Beke thought how beautiful Emily looked, almost as beautiful as a white girl with her straight nose and high cheekbones. Emily's dress was not appropriate for the rainy day and the cold studio and its shiny beige cold tiles. She danced in her white socks and yellow sun dress and was picked.

Next was Charlotte, a pretty chocolate coloured girl and her friend Rosie. Charlotte wore a red jump suit, with rainbow coloured stripes on the suit with a zipper in the front. Rosie's jump suit was blue with red and white stripes on the collar and an exaggerated bell-bottom.

Don't leave me this way, I can't survive I can't stay alive… The girls moved wildly when the song reached its crescendo, kneeling on the floor, waving their heads from side to side in a frenzy that made everyone in the studio clap.

Beke had never seen such amazing dancing, not even on the *Sounds on Saturday* show that showed The Jackson 5, Roberta Flack and The Commodores. These girls were good and Beke was not sure that she and Aunty Hetta would be up to scratch. Their outfits were great alright but Aunty Hetta was so much taller than Beke; Aunty Hetta was nearly nineteen.

The lights came on from this way and that, the studio suddenly warmed up and by 4pm when everyone had danced and done their dances twice with the camera on. When the children were driven back to their destinations, exhausted and uncertain about who was selected, Fredrick told them they would soon find out and the show would be shown on the Sunday before Christmas.

**

'Did you see me on TV?' Beke said to her friends at Matshayiskova School.

'*Nini?*' (When?) said Precious and Cynthia excited about Beke's news.

'Were you really on TV?'

'Yes, I danced with my aunty. They asked us to come on again and dance'.

Beke spent a lot of time telling Precious and Cynthia about her new life with her real mother.

'We have a television and I am allowed to watch all the films when I want to'.

'We have bacon and eggs in the morning with toast, do you know what toast is?

'What is toast?'

'Well it's just bread that they put in a thing called a toaster for a few minutes, then the toaster pops up after five minutes then you put this thing called butter which makes it very nice.'

'Do you eat *isitshwala*?'

'Sometimes, but with knives and forks on the table, which has a table cloth and napkins to wipe your mouth like this. Also I have my own plate that breaks and I don't have to share with anyone.'

The children listened with envy about her bed with white starched sheets, the nanny and the garden boy who mowed the lawn and cleaned the car.

'Tell us more about your mother's husband,' the children were curious to know about the white man her mother was married to.

'Is it true that white people eat their own snot?'

'My Uncle doesn't eat his own snot, he has tea in a cup that is breakable and eats potatoes with a knife and fork like this.' Beke demonstrated using an imaginary fork and chewing on imaginary potatoes.

'I heard that white people don't go to the toilet, is that true?'

'Is it true that they eat children?'

'Is it true that they don't wash because they don't smell?'

Beke loved telling the children about what she got up to in Trenance in her mother's big house. Every lunchtime it became a ritual for the children to ask her questions which Beke enjoyed because she enjoyed being the centre of attention. Word grew of her stories and her life and the group of girls that congregated around her at lunchtime grew.

'Is it true … that this?'

'Is it true … that that?'

'Do they … this?'

'Do they … that?'

'Is it true that your mother is a white man's prostitute?' said someone.

**

'Don't worry about what anyone says just ignore them.' Beke had found the courage to speak to her mother about what Cynthia had said. She was not going to keep it quiet the way she had when she was troubled by Samson and Cornelius. 'Tomorrow morning we will go shopping all day so don't you worry about anything'.

Beke forgot her troubles on Saturday morning when she and her mother and aunty caught a bus from Garden Cash store to the City Hall. At the corner of Selbourne Avenue before they could turn right to go to Gordon's, Beke and aunty were chatting loudly when they heard someone say '*Nangu*' (Here she is).

'Rhoda?' said Beke's aunt to a woman who Beke recognised as she had been one of the few visitors who had been to Trenance. Beke remembered that mother had said Rhoda and her daughter lived on the road between Garden Cash store and the turning to their house at Northlyn Place. Mother said they lived in a Motel, where they had different white boyfriends on different days and nights.

The next thing that Beke knew Rhoda was punching her mother with a fist. The two women were standing upright in pugilistic stance. Aunty Hetta picked up her handbag and hit Rhoda, whose daughter then made fists and hit Aunty Hetta. Beke felt confused and pulled at her mother who was now ferociously exchanging blows with Rhoda.

The stream of people walking behind them stopped to watch while some walked around them. Beke stood rooted to the same spot where she had stopped and started crying. Rhoda and her mother were screaming, shouting and pulling each other's blouses. Rhoda's shoulder-length black wig bounced from her head to her shoulders and onto the floor. An older man stood by the pillar in shock, his hand on his jaw and kicked Rhoda's wig to the side.

Beke's mother punched Rhoda in the face; a crowd suddenly developed around the fighting women. Beke's mother pulled Rhoda away from the crowd onto the main road stopping a car that would have driven past the robots which had just turned green. The car behind stopped in time as the robots changed to red. Beke's mother was standing up. Rhoda was now on the floor, defeated with her trousers torn and her wig lost beneath the spectators. Beke's mother rained blows onto Rhoda in the middle of the street stopping the traffic in both directions.

The police on the corner of Selbourne Avenue did not take long to send one of their constables to the fight scene and try to calm the women at the station. Beke's aunt collected all the shopping bags and tried to comfort Beke who was now sobbing quietly.

Queens Park East

In 1979 Robert Mugabe had been to London to talk to the 'evil' British. Bishop Abel Muzorewa had failed to successfully create a Zimbabwe-Rhodesia made up of whites and blacks. The rippling of an inevitable change was being felt from the winding Limpopo river to the Zambezi valley.

Broadcastings from Radio Mozambique crackled through makeshift radios. Marxist propaganda ripped fear into the white whites, the mixed coloureds, the pure blacks, and the invisible browns from India.

'*Pamberi ne* Zimbabwe!'

'*Pamberi ne* ZANU-PF!'

'*Pamberi ne* Hondo!

'*Pasi na* Ian Smith.'

'*Pasi ne* Rhodesia.'

The only change that Beke felt was the sudden move from Trenance to Queens Park East leaving behind the Smith family and their weekly scrapes and Mrs Smith's toothless smile. Leaving behind the yellow house with the boys' *Khaya* to the left, the rows of corn that grew on the plot of land to the left, the mulberry bush and the pots of jam that were never made. They left behind the Cohens and their seven-foot wall with the barbed wire.

The new home was number 54 Shetland Drive. At least her new home had a name that she could remember. If she ever saw the old man with the brown blue eyes again and he asked her where she lived this time she would say '54 Shetland Drive, Queens Park East'.

It was a windy but sunny January morning when the removal van moved all of Mr and Mrs Trenholm's belongings to their new house twenty kilometres away from Trenance.

94

Queens Park was a classier suburban area occupied by mostly whites and a few middle-class coloured people. A few of the more affluent Africans had started to slowly move into the 'white only' suburb which was being vacated by the whites. Following the victory of ZANU-PF and the acceptance of majority rule, many of the whites were starting to migrate to South Africa or to more expensive white areas that Africans could not afford.

Beke's new home had a huge garden in the front with a luscious freshly mown green lawn. In the middle of the lawn were three weeping willows, one of which hung over the neighbours' fence. In the middle was a pond with ten goldfish that swam in blissful tranquillity. There were two tall date trees with yellow fruit so high up that only the birds could reach them. White, red and yellow roses occupied the mid-section of the garden forming a border. The front patio was surrounded by a low wall. The garden had more species of flowers, ferns and shrubs than Beke had seen at the City Hall. A gravel path separated the roses and the sweet peas, chrysanthemums and dahlias whose heavy scent wafted in the air.

To the right of the flower garden and lawn was a short gravel driveway that led to the open garage covered in sweet grapevines where Uncle Trenholm parked his beige brown Vauxhall with the black stripe.

On the right-hand side of the drive a vine tree led to a fruit tree garden with juicy peach trees, bright yellow lemons, soft, sweet tangerines and heavy oranges with thick skins. Fat guava fruits hung thick and heavy next to succulent mangoes and miniature apple trees. The leaves of the trees joined together at the top to form a canopy of shade that almost completely blocked the sunlight. Directly in front of the fruit garden was the new boys' *Khaya*, which was covered with more black grapevines that twisted in and out, creating a shaded walkway. This was a fertile paradise with a bigger more fertile plot of land for the garden boy to grow more corn and more *tshomoliya*. Adjacent to the boys' *Khaya* were three steps made from Delft blue tiles painted with gabled houses, miniature windmills and little Dutch children in traditional dress. The steps led to a tortoise pen where mummy, daddy and baby tortoises indolently ate tomatoes and scraps of lettuce.

The streets in Queens Park East were wide and generously lined with giant swaying trees. Outside each yard underneath the comfort of the shadows, children walked and cycled up and down the streets. Dogs barked, cars zoomed by. Every afternoon the blue and white Dairy Board ice cream man rang his bell as he rode his cart full of rainbow coloured lollies and creamy vanilla cones with chocolate flakes. When the Dairy Board ice cream man opened his little square cart, nitrogen ice keeping the lollies cold always welcomed the children and their nannies.

In the three years Beke had lived in Trenance she had not made a single friend. In one week in Queens Park she had made three friends: Annette Cohen, Ruthie Payne and Yvonne Wilson. Annette Cohen lived at number 62, Ruthie at 58 and Yvonne lived on Orkney Road, a small close off Shetland Drive.

For weeks it was just Annette and Beke exploring their new neighbourhood. Shetland Drive was a very long road that took you from the main Bulawayo airport road all the way down to the railway track where trains went to Victoria Falls. All the names of roads in Queens Park East were named after Scottish places. The next road after Shetland Drive was Sutherland Road, a long road with most of the houses empty. Scared white madams and basses had left overgrowing lawns with weeds and no garden boys to cut them. Guava trees grew next to the orphaned flowers with squatter bees moving pollen here and there in a show with no audience. A stone's throw away from Sutherland was Cavan Road where the bus stopped every morning to take children to school. Cavan Road had more coloured people than any other street. Every Saturday loud music could be heard from the houses on Cavan Road.

It was 1979. Three years earlier, Ian Smith had said, 'I don't believe in black majority rule in Rhodesia … not in a thousand years.' The Marxist 'terrorist' had finally won; the whites were moving from Queens Park in their droves, headed for 'South' or 'Bots' or if they were lucky London, but most went to South Africa.

Bekezela and Annie spent their days after school looking through windows of the empty houses. Occasionally they would find half-empty swimming pools and throw stones and twigs for fun. Most houses had orchards full of juicy apples, sweet *naarjties* and bitter lemons. They climbed up tall trees until they could not see the sun through the leaves. By mid-afternoon they would pick up as much fruit as could fit in the makeshift pocket made by their rolled up dresses. MaSikhosana, Annette's nanny, always made sure she chastised them for stealing.

'It is NOT stealing MaSikhosana, there is nobody there,' Annette said emphasising the NOT angrily.

'You jump over gate?'

'Never mind THAT.'

'Annie I will tell Bass no must not steal, police bam, bam.'

'No police, no bam, bam.'

The children laughed at the absurdity of MaSikhosana's allegations and sat in the veranda. They cut a piece of the raw, green guavas and mangoes into slices and ate them with salt and pepper. They savoured

97

the bitter, sweet and sour flavours that stimulated their saliva glands. The warm rays of the sun poured through the pillars of the veranda. The children sprinkled more salt on their hands and watched MaSikhosana as she folded Annette's and Leon's school uniforms. She folded Bass's overalls and Madam's Meikles uniform in a neat pile.

On the days the girls were bored with exploring they walked to the shops in Queens Park East to buy pink bubble gum, sherbet and liquorice straws in little purple packets. Beke was intrigued by the sherbet, which she had never seen in the Luveve shops and gulped the whole packet in one go. Annette laughed as Beke almost choked with the white powder covering her nostrils making her cough and spit out the effervescing sherbet.

'Ag *sis* man,' said Annette in disgust. 'It's all over your nose, wipe yourself!'

Annie was Annette Cohen who was related to the rich family of Cohens from Trenance who were descendants of Joseph Cohen, a rich Jewish man who had moved from South Africa in the 1940s. Joseph Cohen had married a local Sotho girl who bore him sons that had created the dynasty of Cohens who owned more than 30 per cent of the businesses in textiles, jewellery and removals in Bulawayo.

When the sun started to go down, Beke and Annie had eaten more salty guavas than they could stomach. Soon afterwards Beke walked back home. At number 56 Beke saw friendly white neighbours moving out. At number 53 the neighbours had ten dogs that barked loudly all the time. Their owner was a white man who would have had blond hair was it not for his bald head. He told the dogs to shut up so often so that Beke's mother and Otheliya called him 'Mr Shatapu'. Otheliya was the new nanny they had hired when they moved to

Trenance. She was also Baron's sister. Baron had decided he wanted to join the Rhodesian Army to fight. Mother had agreed to let his sister take his place.

Uncle Trenholm had complained about the last white man in the street not being able to control his dogs. Uncle Trenholm was wrong. Mr Shatapu was not the last white man in the Street: there was John with his two sons, Paul and Shaun, only a few years older than Beke.

'In fact they were not only moving out,' said Beke cockily to Uncle Trenholm. 'IN FACT, they have just moved in, so there,' she said just like the little white girls from London did on TV.

In-fact Uncle-John-comes-here when-you-are-at-work to-talk-to-mummy while-Elvis-sings, Beke's thought waves shouted but her lips remained quiet. Uncle Trenholm wouldn't be happy to know that Uncle John came here sometimes but at least it wasn't the obnoxious Mr Shatapu with the obnoxious dogs. At least it wasn't the man with the green Citroen car. Beke remembered the pretend sick tummy day for a second and made sure the thought remained shut like her lips.

McKeurtan

Since the pretend sick tummy day, Bekezela's mother had walked into the headmaster's office and told him to stuff his school. She took her pretty daughter to a new school where teachers paid attention to their children and didn't slap them.

1979 became 1980. Beke loved 1980 more than 1979, she didn't know why. She did know why. She only needed to take one bus to school instead of three. Once Uncle Trenholm dropped her off on 3rd Avenue and Main Street she only had to walk ten minutes to McKeurtan Primary School. Her new school. No black Coca-Cola Samson, no Orange Fanta Cornelius, no ugly Clara with the number 11 scars on each cheek, no round Mr Moyo with his slaps.

The children were all clean: no torn shorts or shirts, everyone was wearing black, polished shoes with brand new white socks that were either folded at the ankle or up to the knees. The boys were handsome, all the girls were pretty.

At Matshayiskova I was the second prettiest girl, socks and black shoes and an ironed uniform, shoes with the least dust. Here I am the darkest, the one that is not coloured in blue, pink or yellow ribbon. No plaited hair to my shoulders, Beke thought to herself.

Mrs Doney was Beke's Grade 5 teacher who reminded her of Mrs Sibanda, her very first teacher. Mrs Doney wore a different perfume to Miss Sibanda but with the same comforting bouquet of floral notes mixed with lavender and sandalwood. The smell alone made Beke feel safe and she drifted off into the cosy world of Miss Sibanda and her A-line skirts.

Mrs Doney was older than Miss Sibanda. Mrs Doney was not black but not white, and she looked

Indian but didn't speak like the Indians who ran the shops in town. Mrs Doney wore dark red lipstick the colour of old tomatoes; her lipstick spent most of its time on her two front teeth.

Mrs Doney greeted the children in a voice that didn't betray whether she was going to be very kind, just kind or kind but sometimes hard. After Mrs Doney said good morning she wanted to see if everyone was present. The children all answered by saying 'Yes Miss' while sitting down instead of standing up and proudly shouting 'Prezzzent' the way they did at Matshayiskova School. Beke couldn't help but notice how the children spoke English differently to the children in her old school. They said 'Yes Mass' instead of Miss. Miss Sibanda had always stressed the importance of pronunciation.

All the children are clean, smart with ironed uniforms, white, white socks everywhere. Black, shiny shoes with not a single barefoot, dust or ugly faces. The girls have soft skin, not shiny and greasy with Vaseline, soft, coloured and superior. Cheeks like ripe peaches, Bekezela thought to herself.

'Caroline Davies'
'Yes Mass'
'Revonia Hanson'
'Yes Mass'
'Mary Herbert'
'Yes Mass'
'Sonia Jeffries'
'Yes Mass'
'Beauty Millen'
'Yes Mass'
'Bekezela Ntuli'
'Pr, yes Miss, yes Mass.'

Bekezela that is my name! Bekezela's nerves and loud thumping heart drowned out everything else after she heard her name. Two voices had said yes to the same name, all brown eyes looked at the extraordinary coincidence of two people having the same name in the same classroom.

'What is your name?' Mrs Doney asked both girls.

'What is your surname?' Mrs Doney asked Beke.

'It seems that your name is not on the register,' Mrs Doney told Beke.

Beke wanted the ground to swallow her, how could her mother make such a foolish mistake.

Maybe mother enrolled me somewhere else maybe… at Robert Tredgold School instead? Bekezela now embarrassed and sweaty stood up, her chair making a noise that she was sure could be heard by the whole school.

If mother has made a mistake it would not be so bad as Robert Tredgold had exactly the same uniforms as her old school, Matshayiskova: bottle-green with the yellow collar and stripe on the sleeve. Bekezela tried to look on the bright side as she sat outside the headmaster's office waiting for Mrs Doney and the deputy headmaster Mr Pretorius.

Bekezela sat silently on the hard wooden bench outside the deputy's office watching the cold black shadows flooding the quadrangle. Mr Pretorius was a tall, thin, sinewy man who looked like what Beke imagined Scrooge would look like if he lived in Bulawayo. Mr Pretorius spoke kindly and smiled a lot and seemed very concerned about the mystery of the child who was not on the register. Beke stood outside Mr Pretorius's office as Mrs Doney explained how the two children had strangely answered to the same name.

Mr Pretorius came outside and asked for Bekezela's home phone number.

'Was everyone present and correct in your register?' Mr Pretorius asked Mrs Doney.

'No, there were two children not present: Cecil Madonga and a Rebecca Trenholm.'

'Hello,' Mr Pretorius said after a dialling Beke's number on his black phone, his horsey voice betraying that he was heavy smoker. 'OK, OK,' Mr Pretorius laughed uncontrollably, taking off his glasses to look at Mrs Doney who was now seated on the chair opposite Mrs Pretorius.

'Kam in, Kam in,' Mr Pretorius motioned to Beke, who was still sitting outside the door looking at the sunrays intruding into the classrooms with the children sitting down quietly on their first day of school.

Kam, Kam... the coloured teacher speaks different to the teachers in Matshayiskova Beke thought silently.

'Ah jest spow-ke to your maather,' Mr Pretorius said with a knowing smile and his startling hazel-green eyes melting into the creases of his deep-set eye sockets. Mr Pretorius paused and fiddled with his glasses that were now on the table.

'Miss Trenholm,' Mr Pretorius said rhetorically. Beke stared blankly and answered 'Yes' not understanding that it was not a question.

'Reee–becca Trenholm,' Mr Pretorius exaggerated the R and E and making him sound like a distressed bee. 'That's your name, my girl,' Mr Pretorius said proudly.

My mother changed my name from an African name to make it easier to pronounce. Bekezela suddenly understood but didn't know whether to thank Mr Pretorius or to cry. As she walked back to the class she thought about her new classmates. New school, new name, new identity.

Bekezela.

Beke.

Rebecca.

Becky.

Becki.

Becki with an I

In Queens Park, Beke was now Becki. She had new friends who spoke English with a different accent. Her new friends were Annette, Ruthie, Yvonne and Barbara. Ruthie Payne had a brother Denzel and a sister Anita. Ruthie's mother was a short Indian looking woman, pretty but with slight buck teeth that spoilt what could have been flawless beauty. Ruthie's father was an almond-skinned coloured man with a big afro. Ruthie inherited her father's almond skin and her mother's straight Indian hair, which she plaited into two neck-length plaits that she tied with different coloured ribbons in the middle.

Her youngest sister Anita had inherited her mother's nearly flawless face with buck teeth and her father's thick hair which went all the way to her waist. Denzel the middle brother looked exactly like his father with nothing of his mother and kept himself to himself.

Every day the girls explored the neighbourhood, argued, broke off friends, became friends again and explored again. They played rounders on the road, glassy-glassy Ouija boards in the dark, climbed every tree and teased each other. When the sun was too hot they sat under the trees and had penny colas, peeled oranges or bit into juicy mangoes to pass the time.

First Becki and Annie were best friends, they fought, then Becki and Yvonne were best friends and of course that meant including Barbara. Barbara was Yvonne's youngest sister. Some days the girls played with dolls in Annie's house. Some days they went to Becki's house. Occasionally, they played at Ruthie's house but Ruthie's mother wanted them to go by 3pm so she could cook in peace. They never went to Yvonne and Barbara's house because Yvonne and Barbara had two nasty brothers Ken and Trevor.

'*Jorl here ek se,*' (Come here,) Ken pointed to Becki with disdain in his voice, his unruly afro blowing over his blood shot eyes.

'*Jorl here ek se.*'

Becki had heard that language at school. Neither white nor black but a mixture of Afrikaans, isiNdebele and English and a few colourful made up words. Mrs Doney and the headmaster had banned coloured slang language in the school area saying it was dirty and common and not English and was not to be spoken anywhere in the school.

'Wotchu bring that focking *Kaffir* here for?' Trevor the middle brother shouted.

'She is not a *Kaffir*; you are a *Kaffir* with your horrible black skin,' said Barbara to her brother.

Becki was sorry that she had caused an argument between Barbara and Ken.

'Of course she is a fock-ing *Kaffir hoti*, what's your name you?' Ken pointed at Becki aggressively. Becki didn't answer but stared at Ken who brought back memories of Samson and Cornelius.

'Tell me now or I *klep* you!'

Becki ran out of No. 16 Orkney Drive and refused to play at Yvonne and Barbara's house.

'Her name is Becki, Becki with an I,' shouted Yvonne to her brother who was lighting a cigarette. On the way out of Orkney Drive past Annie's house Barbara, Yvonne and Becki decided to forget the unspoken rule that said you couldn't freely go to Ruthie's house and decided to visit her.

Knock, knock.

Ruthie's mum was wearing faded jeans and a blue shirt with huge yellow flowers. She was standing over the electric stove pouring oil into a battered aluminium saucepan.

The children were careful to stand by the door

unless they were invited in. Mrs Payne was friendly but didn't invite them in. Who could blame her, she really didn't want to clean the house again. Mr Payne would be home by half past five.

'Whatchu cooking?' said Yvonne meaning can we come in.

'Would you like to know?' Mrs Payne replied with a smile on her face, her eyes looking tired with black half-moon crescents under her eyes.

The girls strained their necks and saw that Mrs Payne had already prepared a mound of chopped carrots and a mound of fine green beans. The stove had been turned up to number 5 and glowed, the orange rings heating up the yellow curry base. Mrs Payne chopped green chillies and chopped red chillies.

The children moved closer to look at her silver pots of spices. First she put the fiery chilli into the hot oil forming syrupy hot lava. Then she added the cumin from India which was a brown yellow fine powder which smelt liked dried mango leaves. When she added the powder mixed with the angry chilli it tickled the children's nostrils making the hot oil sound like a rushing river. Next coriander, which smelt like late summer orange groves soothing the chilli and cumin.

'Chilli, cumin, coriander, the three Cs, those are your main ingredients for this pickle,' said Ruthie's mother proudly.

'Then of course turmeric for your colour,' she said softly and Becki noticed her slight lisp for the first time. 'My mother used to call it Achar,' Ruthie's mother continued in her soft voice now almost a whisper.

'Achar,' the children chorused, pleased to have learnt something. Ruthie's mother stirred and stirred the kaleidoscope of colours and spices.

'You can make Achar from anything girls, mango,

lemons, garlic, you must try it.' In their distraction the children had forgotten that they had come to find Ruthie.

'Where's Ruthie aunty?' said Yvonne as Mrs Payne removed the pan from the hot rings and added a generous helping of white vinegar to the saucepan.

'She should be back soon ...'

'You know Becki. Achar is delicious with pap.'

Pap. What is pap? Becki's blank face told Mrs Payne that Becki did not know what pap was.

'Pap, *sadza*, you know what you people say isi-tsh-wallah,' Mrs Payne strained the 's' through her slightly buck teeth. *Isitshwala*, yes pap to the coloureds, was the maize meal that they ate lunchtime and evening with gravy and *tshomoliya* with clean washed hands. Becki learnt very quickly that living in Queens Park East meant changing from being African to being coloured. It meant going from eating isitshwala to the same thing called pap. From being simply called Bekezela to being called Becki. Yes. Becki with an I.

**

Visitors always came to Becki's house every Saturday for braais, sometimes parties that lasted till late at night. Becki thought that there were definitely more visitors since they moved to Queens Park. Maybe it was because they had one less bus to get from City Hall. The bus stopped on Cavan Road and the walk was only five minutes from the bus stop and not one hour.

Becki's mother had more friends in Queens Park, not just Mrs Smith and her toothless grin. The Queen's Park visitors were sophisticated and elite. There was Mr and Mrs Conceicão. Mr Conceicão was from Lisbon in Portugal, a short man with a bushy beard and a strong accent that was different from Uncle Trenholm's. There was Mr and Mrs Harris. Mr Harris was an old Yorkshire man with pure white hair and his wife with tribal scars on her cheeks. Sometimes Becki had heard people call her an uneducated Kalanga woman as if to say they did not understand how a 'white man' like Mr Harris, especially one from England the best country in the world, could be with a black woman of the lowest Matebele tribe, despised and vilified by both Ndebele and Shonas alike. At least that's what Becki thought she heard people say at braais where Mr and Mrs Harris could not attend. There was also aunty Jane and her husband from Scotland, aunty NaVeronica who didn't have an Uncle but had three coloured children with a Greek man from Athens.

The women, their husbands, their children, and their dogs if they had any, all met every Saturday. Aunty Mrs Davies and Mrs Lee also came even though they both didn't have husbands. Mr Davies had died of illness but Mr Lee had been killed by a convoy of terrorists when he was on his way to South Africa. They had cornered old Mr Lee in his caravan, beaten him with the back of their rifles and then set fire to him and his belongings. It was a terrible day when Mrs Lee had to identify him by the wedding ring on his finger that had mysteriously survived the fire.

Sometimes the braai would be in Queens Park then in Hillside at the Conceicãos. The Conceicãos' house with its warm swimming pool was a favourite. Then Mrs Davies the widow in North End. If they were desperate they visited the uneducated Mrs Harris in Morningside with her old Mr Harris. Sometimes new couples came and went but it was always the older white men with the younger black women.

Spicy boerewors would be grilled with big eland steaks with pap for the African women and potato salad or chips for the white men. Castle or Lion beer was drunk by some of the men and a few of the women. There were a few women that drank and sometimes smoked. African women generally did not smoke. This was normally the behaviour of coloured women who were well-known for their yellow nicotine fingernails, dark brown nicotine lips and eyes that were either bloodshot from alcohol or *dagga*. The African women who drank and smoked had crossed that invisible fine line which made them outcasts.

'Is that your *Old Bali*?' said Ruthie Payne's mother to Becki on the Monday after the braai after she had cooked Achar.

'Yah,' Becki answered wishing Ruthie and her mother would not ask any more questions.

'But, you … you are not coloured are you?' Ruthie's mother asked the question making Becki feel embarrassed.

'He is my stepfather, not my father,' Becki avoided the question of whether she was a coloured or an African. Her name was now Becki instead of Bekezela; her surname was now Trenholm instead of Hadebe.

Becki Trenholm = coloured.

Beke Hadebe = African.

She was Becki Trenholm even if her skin was dark like an African, even if her hair was not straight and could not have two plaits that she tied together with a pink ribbon.

'How old is your father then?' said Ruthie, making sure she would not let Becki get away with not answering the question.

'My father?' said Becki, surprised to hear anyone refer to Uncle Trenholm as her father.

'Yes, how old is he?' said Ruthie, readily showing that this was a discussion her family had had many times before in the quiet of their kitchen while eating hot mixed Achar pickles.

'50!'

'50?' Ruthie and Mrs Payne laughed uncontrollably.

'He is more than 50.'

It was the first time that Becki had ever thought about Uncle Trenholm's age. He was old, he moved slowly. He took a long time to read the paper, he took a long time to do everything but he was 50.

NONE of YOUR business! The thought waves in Beke's head rose up to the apex and back down again to their trough forming one complete thought before saying absolutely nothing.

**

Sometimes visitors came from far away on planes. England, Australia, South Africa, New Zealand to visit 54 Shetland Drive, Queens Park East. When the visitors came, Becki's mother expected good behaviour from Becki and good behaviour from Otheliya the nanny.

Good behaviour for Becki meant extra quietness during the news when Mr Emberton talked about the planes being brought down by anti-air missiles from China. It meant no reaction when she heard of the killing of little white babies. Good behaviour for the nanny meant that she bathed in the morning and in the afternoon when the sun became hot. Good behaviour for Becki meant that she did not bring her friends Annie, Ruthie, Yvonne and Barbara to play in the house, or in the garden or on the road. Or anywhere else for that matter. Good behaviour for the nanny meant she gave visitors Kellogg's cornflakes with hot or cold milk with their breakfast.

Cornflakes were what you ate when you had visitors from England, visitors from South Africa, visitors from Australia. Cornflakes were like boring crisps with no

111

taste, no salt, no vinegar, no tomato sauce. Cornflakes were eaten first thing in the morning with ice-cold milk and sugar. Sometimes the cornflakes were crunchy, if you left them long enough they got soggy. In the time that Uncle Henry came to visit, Becki started to understand all about cornflakes.

Uncle Henry Mitch was one of the visitors who came to eat Kellogg's cornflakes for breakfast. Becki remembered him from the time he had come with his pregnant girlfriend Sarah. The baby must have been big now, was it a boy or a girl? Was the baby milky coffee coloured like NaVeronica's half-Greek children.

'Where are Aunty Sarah and the baby?'

'Shhh,' Becki's mother put her middle finger over her mouth.

'How long is Uncle Henry staying?'

'Shhh hey wena,' Becki's mother frowned the kind of frown that Becki recognised because it said 'the next question will be followed by a slap.'

No more questions.

Becki was not enjoying Uncle Henry's visits. It meant she could not play with her friends or climb any trees.

Becki didn't like Uncle Henry much.

Becki felt that Uncle Henry was a nasty man. He had a big nose that looked like Pinocchio, glasses that turned black in the sunshine, funny knobbly knees and hands behind his back like Cecil John Rhodes. He didn't talk to children very much; he talked to Uncle Trenholm about war, money, diamonds and gold. Becki had overhead him call her a *pikinini,* a word which had made her mother angry.

On the day after Uncle Henry arrived, a strange man had visited 54 Shetland Drive, Queens Park East on a bicycle.

'*Qoki,*' the small stranger shouted from the gate. He

talked to mother for a minute before she opened the gate to let him in.

The small man was wearing something that was too short to be trousers and too long to be shorts tied with an expensive but battered leather belt that was too big for him. The man held himself with the nobility of an Ndebele chieftain. Becki's mother had welcomed him and made him sit on the blue Dutch tiled step next to the tortoise pen under the shallow shade of the weeping mulberry bush that didn't bear any fruit. Becki's mother gave the man Mazoe crush mixed with cold water from the fridge in an aluminium cup.

The man had come to see Otheliya. Becki made small talk with the small stranger about the sun, the heat, the crops, the cattle and everything else until Otheliya came back from the shops.

Baron was dead. That is what the man had come to tell Otheliya, Baron's older sister. Beloved Baron, Otheliya's youngest brother, the only boy in the family was dead. He had been killed ironically at the end of the war by a hand grenade thrown in a village twenty kilometres outside of Lusaka.

Otheliya wailed so loudly the neighbours dogs in number 52 barked. The dogs went to the gate so that the dogs opposite started to bark and woke up Mr Shatapu's dogs. Mr Shatapu must have been out because they did not stop barking. Even the tortoises in the tortoise pen were alarmed by such a loud noise and moved slowly away to hide under the small bushes in their pen.

'*Maye babo!*' Otheliya was inconsolable, swaying from side to side hugging herself, her hands on her head then on her neck then hugging herself again then beating the walls. Otheliya's grief brought back memories of the war songs Baron sang day in, day out while cleaning windows or mowing the lawn. Tears ran down Becki's mother's face. She walked up to Otheliya and tried to hug her. This made Otheliya wail even more, a haunting, eerie, piercing shrill.

'Maye babo o o o o! Maye babo! Maye babo!'

Rivers of tears merged until she coughed and hiccupped at the same time.

'Maye babo! Omama ma-ma ma a a a …'

Her heart-wrenching soliloquy continued for hours.

Becki's mother packed Otheliya's brown suitcase and gave her some money before driving her 'e-*Renkini*' to catch the next bus to Lupane.

By the time she had left, Otheliya had calmed down sitting in the front seat of Becki's mother's white Mini, something Becki had never seen Otheliya do. Becki felt powerless and knew that the best she could do would be to help mother around the house. She hated washing clothes especially bed sheets. That would have to wait until Otheliya was back.

'Is Becki here?' Annie was addressing Henry the visitor as Becki clambered over the sink to wash a bowl which had been stuck with flakes of browny-orange sugary corn flakes.

'I am here Annie,' Becki shouted to her friend. Annie looked pretty with her hair plaited into two pony tails which were joined by a pale blue ribbon that matched her pale blue summer dress with little pink flowers. Annie was on a bike. A shiny silver and blue Chopper that everyone at school wanted.

Annie wanted to show off her new bike which she brought to the back of the house and parked it against the pillar of the washing area.

'Brand new, my daddy bought it in town.'

Waves of envy came to Becki like unwanted visitors. Annie went to some length to describe how she had chosen the blue-green shiny colour herself.

'My cousin has one just like it, blue-green 12

114

inches, coz she's bigger.'

'Really?' Becki was fascinated by the wheels and the noise they made as they turned.

'Do you want to try it? Come on.'

Annie beamed from ear to ear reminding Becki of the adventurous bond that they shared.

'Stand over there and catch me if I fall.'

Becki ran to the top of the gravel path, holding her hands out, not sure whether to save Annie or block her. As Becki turned to face the house she saw Mr Henry Mich looking at her and Annie through the window.

'Hope he doesn't tell my mummy that I was playing more than I was working?'

'What's he doing here?'

'He is our visitor, he is always here.'

'I am going to tell my mother to buy me a bike also,' said Becki forgetting the audience looking through the window.

'OK buy a 10 inch or a 12 it's just the right size, my daddy knows people that sell bikes.'

What a good idea. The children walked through the gravel pathway on to the main road chattering with the bike between them. Becki forgot the layer of grief and sadness that clung over the house since the death of Baron had been announced.

'Lemmeshowyou!' said Annie eager for her friend to join her new world.

Becki tried to ride the bike again and remembered when Baron had tried to teach her on the black bike that he ran errands on. Dear Baron. Becki missed their daily after-school rituals in the sun eating mulberries or raw guavas with salt.

'Guess what?'

'What?'

'We are going to South for school holidays.'

'Waaah wu,' said Becki with exaggerated

excitement that hid the waves of green envy that came from nowhere.

'Everyone's going away for holidays man.'

'Where?'

'Ruthie is ill so I hear she is not going anywhere. Denzel told me today.'

'Yvonne and them are going to the farm.'

'The farm' was where coloureds went to during the school holidays. To see the 'Old Queen' and 'Old Bali' and other African relatives.

'What's wrong with Ruthie?'

Ruthie was ill; nobody had seen her for a while. But did Becki know that Ruthie's dad hit Ruthie's mum quite often. Becki thought of Ruthie's mum standing over a hot stove cooking. Thinking of Ruthie's dad hitting Ruthie's mum made Becki sad, but not as sad as knowing Baron was dead.

By the time mother came back from dropping Otheliya, Annie and her new shiny bike had gone, the dishes were washed and dried.

'Annie's going to the farm and Yvonne and them are going South,' Becki said to her mother getting it all wrong but determined to get the point across.

Everyone was going somewhere these holidays and she wasn't.

Becki was surprised at her own temerity. Gone was the shy little girl who had tossed and turned before she could open her mouth to tell her mother she was being bullied.

The new school full of colourful, confident coloureds had raised her confidence.

Mother lost her patience with her daughter. Becki always knew when her mother had lost her temper, she spoke in Ndebele.

**

116

'Baron was dead.

Didn't Becki know?

Was she selfish?

Did she only ever think of herself and no one else?

Did she remember Baron and all that he did for her?'

The telling off exhausted Becki slowing her down so that she didn't even enjoy the curried oxtail stew that mother had cooked in her pressure cooker. The telling off made her want to spit out the English mashed potatoes even though she liked the melting butter that mother put on them. She missed pap and wished she was eating Aunty Hetta's *tshomoliya* or *delele* with her hands. The telling off drained her joy so that she missed sitting on uGogo's kitchen floor eating with her hands, licking one finger after the other then the palm of her hand.

Aaah.

She didn't like the boring way you had to chew with your mouth closed then talk about Mr Smith, the Queen, England and wait and listen. Sometimes it was so quiet all you could hear was the silver knives and forks clinking against the china plates.

Mummy, Uncle Trenholm, Uncle Henry and Becki.

Clink, clank, clink clank, silence.

Becki's mother was tired after dinner, exhausted she said. Baron's death had exhausted her. After supper Uncle Trenholm and mother always watched the news. Becki always sat on the carpet far too close to the television with her little legs crossed, back hunched with both hands on both cheeks sighing as David Emberton the boring news reader said what sounded like what he said yesterday.

The news read by David Emberton.

'Terrorists, Mozambique, terrorists, ambush,

117

terrorists, grenades, terrorists ...'

Becki's head would start to get drowsy.

'Terrorists, Nkomo ...' voices trailing away, eyes closing, lids too heavy to do anything but close.

'Convoys, terrorists, Ian Smith ...' head going forward, loops then back, hands on cheek to secure head again, eyes open slightly, close slightly.

'Terrorists, terrorists and now for the weather ...' Becki's eyes, now wide open like a spring fountain, turned around to see if the adults had noticed her sleeping. Mother had gone to sleep and Uncle Henry was sitting next to Uncle Trenholm. Uncle Henry was wearing khaki linen shorts and bush sandals.

Uncle Henry, legs wide open, pink thingy peeping through the khaki shorts. Look away and pretend to sleep.

**

Annie had a new bike and was exploring farther and farther out before going to South Africa on her holidays. Becki felt jealous and couldn't hide it and spent more time with Ruthie and sometimes Yvonne and her sister Barbara.

Uncle Trenholm was starting to show his impatience with Uncle Henry who had been a visitor for six weeks. Shortly after that Uncle Henry announced that he was going to move to North End to be a priest at the Roman Catholic church. Father Pearce had accepted him at last after a few complications here and there. Uncle Henry was going to be Father Henry Mich.

Becki felt a mixture of relief and sadness when Father Henry Mich left. The house was quiet although he was not a noisy man. The bedroom had the faint smell of his cologne which he always left when he came to visit in Trenance with his girlfriend Sarah.

'Father can't have had a girlfriend that's not true,' said Ruthie with horror etched into the furrows of her brow.

'Yes he did.'

'No he didn't.'

'Yes he did.'

'And she was pregnant also.'

'She can't be.'

'You are a liar and you are not even Catholic.'

'So?'

'So?'

'So what?'

After the argument between Ruthie and Becki, Annie and Ruthie spent all their afternoons together as new best friends. Yvonne, Barbara and Becki played with dolls. Yvonne and Barbara thought climbing trees and stealing fruit from empty houses was very childish and their days were spent being the 'Three Investigators' investigating important criminals driving through their streets.

When the afternoon sun had beaten them, the children lay down on Becki's freshly mown lawn and stared at the faraway wispy white clouds. Occasionally droning aeroplanes moved through the curvature of the sky, leaving a long straight trail of engine smoke. The children looked up at the giant trees which seemed to want to fall down but never quite managed it. They closed their eyes and thought it was funny how you could still see the aeroplane and the trees with your eyes closed.

'What do you see?' said Yvonne.

'Nothing,' said Barbara.

'I wonder where all those people in the aeroplane are going?'

'Maybe they have already have been.'

'How strange it must be so high in the sky hey!'

119

said Barbara.

'So close to the sun. So you think it's hotter there?'

Saturday Braais and Visitors From Overseas

There wasn't time to worry about friends, especially lost friends. Uncle Trenholm announced that his grandson Matthew would be coming all the way from England. Matthew was the son of Audrey, Uncle Trenholm's eldest daughter with his first wife who still lived in England. Somewhere.

Matthew was erudite, handsome and charming. Matthew was Becki's and Becki's mother's favourite overseas visitor. He was not as good as Uncle Trenholm's daughters in South Africa who always brought exotic second-hand dresses and divine chocolates that made the days more enjoyable. Matthew did not bring many gifts but always took the family on very interesting trips.

Matthew arrived at Bulawayo airport on the 16th April 1979. Uncle Trenholm had driven to the airport by himself while mother and Becki put on freshly starched sheets, polished the floors and cooked curried ox tongue with buttered squash, roasted potatoes and sweet potato fritters. Preparing for new visitors always took days, sometimes weeks. Uncle Trenholm was annoyed that his grandson Matthew had only given them five days' notice.

Matthew was 24 years old, tall, muscular with piercing blue eyes and Uncle Trenholm's aquiline nose and chiselled film star good looks.

Matthew was very different from all the white Europeans that came by to visit. He was very interested in all the intricate details of Becki's schooling, he didn't smoke or drink very much and was always polite and helped mother and Becki to clear up the plates after dinner since Otheliya had not come back after Baron's death.

On the first day of his visit, Matthew and his Grandfather sat under the willow and date trees drinking tea and reminiscing about England. Uncle Trenholm would start off by talking about good old Penzance, the mines, St Anthony's gardens and Lescudjack Castle. Matthew always listened to his Grandfather attentively without interrupting once. Eventually, after Uncle Trenholm had finished talking about Penzance then Redruth, then Falmouth then Padstow he would pause and ask Matthew questions.

'How is granny Lois?'

'Fine with a bit of a cough that won't go away these days.'

'How is your sister Vera?'

'Drinking too much!'

'How is your brother jack?'

'Also drinking too much and now gambling too.'

Oh dear wasn't there any good news from back home, Uncle Trenholm wondered wishing his grandson was more positive.

'I don't like him, he reminds me too much of Tony.'

Uncle Trenholm came to the kitchen to whisper in Becki's mother's ear while getting the Port wine that he kept for special occasions.

Tony was Matthew's father, a dandy who had wooed Uncle Trenholm's eldest and most favourite daughter born just before the Second World War. Uncle despised him for his laziness; Tony spent all day wearing a waistcoat, a monocle and sipping whiskey from crystal glasses and talking about Descartes or Dostoevsky or Dante.

'I have seen pictures of Tony, he doesn't look like him at all.' Becki's mother tried to make light of the situation. After Matthew's father's premature death from cirrhosis of the liver, Matthew had tried hard to

122

win his Grandfather's affection. Matthew had enrolled into a prestigious mining school to demonstrate his allegiance to Cornwall.

Matthew was always very eager to take his extended step-family to interesting places. On Friday evenings Matthew took Becki, Yvonne and Barbara to the Nite Star Drive Inn cinema in Uncle Trenholm's Vauxhall. Yvonne and Barbara were always pleased to get away from their nasty brothers Trevor and Ken. On the way Matthew would treat the children to ice cream at 'Eskimo Hut' before taking the children to watch the popular movie *American Werewolf in London.*

During the break Matthew would order steaming hot chips, hot dogs and colas for the girls. Scared and tired after the film, the girls slept all the way back to Queens Park East. Yvonne's mother and father had agreed that the girls could sleep at Becki's house. It was that night that they decided that they were 'cousins'. From now on wherever they went they would tell everyone they were related, after all they had slept in each other's houses.

The next day Yvonne, Barbara and Becki were going to go home and change clothes and come back to help Becki and her mother to prepare for a braai. From Orkney Drive into Shetland Drive Yvonne and Barbara saw Annie and Ruth dressed in white wedding dresses. The girls were not sure whether to ignore their new enemies or to make them jealous of their visit to the Drive Inn.

Barbara suddenly said, 'We went to the Drive Inn last night.'

Yvonne was irritated, it's what she would have wanted to say, after all she was the older one.

'We are getting confirmed today,' Ruthie said missing the cue to be jealous.

'Is that what you are wearing those white dresses

for?'

'We are going to see *Grease* afterwards with my cousins,' said Annie responding directly to Barbara's provocation.

'We went to the Drive Inn also,' Barbara repeated herself in case anyone hadn't heard her the first time.

'Yes, we heard you,' Annie said.

'Me, I tell you, I have been to the Nite Star so many times it's boring,' said Ruthie

'No you never,' said Barbara.

'Your father hasn't got a car,' said Yvonne.

'We went with my Uncle, you stupid,' said Ruthie, angry that her father had come into it.

Barbara noticed that the mention of her father had made her angry.

'Your father always *kleps* your mother.'

'No, my father does not,' Ruthie said emphasising each word with her big eyes bulging out.

Anita, Ruthie's little sister started to sob.

'You child, look what you did,' Ruthie poked Barbara on the forehead with her index finger.

'I am going to tell my father you made my sister cry.'

Barbara and Yvonne, scared of being involved with Ruthie Payne's father, turned their heels and hurried away.

'Tell your father I don't care, Becki and us are cousins now and her cousin from England and my brothers will sort you out,' said Barbara. The thought of the braai, food, music and dancing quietened Barbara's and Yvonne's nerves.

Annie's mother's shrill voice could be heard telling Annie to get into the car to drive to the Catholic church reminding Ruthie and Annie that they had more important things to do today. Becki, Yvonne and Barbara hurried away to Becki's pretty garden with

124

burgundy and yellow roses, manicured lawn and sizzling braai. Most people at the braai had come to see Mr Trenholm's grandson.

Mrs Conceicão was the first to arrive in her new red Volkswagen wearing a beautiful vibrant pink and green kaftan with tight green bell-bottoms and platforms. Her afro was tied back with a pink translucent shiny scarf. She wore bright red lip gloss and big sunglasses that covered two-thirds of her beautiful face.

Mrs Conceicão had brought Sema her nanny to help with the braai. It was going to be a big one to celebrate Mr Trenholm's grandson's visit. The sun was blazing through the date trees, The Jackson 5 were playing in some distant hi-fi. Most houses had hose pipes and sprinkler fountains watering lawns and rose bushes. Most garden boys and nannies had knocked off for the weekend. In town the shops were shut, the town was deserted and braais were being lit.

The fridge was full of food, beers and cold sweet Mazoe orange for the children. Becki's mother had made redcurrant jelly in a jelly mould; her step-daughter had told her how much the English loved jelly since Victorian times. Some of the African wives loved to eat traditional food in the corner with their hands so Becki's mother made delicious, tangy okra with tomatoes and onions. Becki's mother had asked Uncle Trenholm to buy a long list of meat from Athlone Butchers.

4 Kg of fresh boerewors for the braai.

Thick, juicy steaks for all the basses.

1 ½ Kg of *amathumbu* for the African wives, half of it boiled with salt and tomatoes the other half would go in the braai after the steaks and sausages. Chicken for the curry with rice for the coloureds. The children would love that too. Ruthie Payne's mother had volunteered to cook the secret recipe she had learnt

125

from her Grandmother.

Mrs Conceicão busied herself helping Becki's mother with the cooking. Yvonne and Barbara helped to put together all the garden chairs and put the glasses, knives and forks ready for the guests. Matthew watched everyone and took photos of the girls, the nannies, the dogs, the food and the sprinklers in the garden.

By three o'clock most of the guests had arrived and the bottles of Castle and Lion were being opened. Laughter could be heard all the way down to Annie's house drowning out Mr Shatapu's dogs and any cars going by. Most of the visitors' cars parked in the gravel driveway. Once the drive way was full of cars they parked under the weeping willow. Some of the visitors even went past the weeping mulberry bush waking up Mr and Mrs Tortoise as they took their nap. Different pockets of conversations were going on everywhere.

'I killed a kudu with my own bare hands in ... yaah, it's true.'

'The children go to Kariba on school camp holiday; they say its sooo *lekker* you know.'

'Stay away from the Germans and their businesses in Namibia if you can.'

'So and so's 15-year-old daughter was pregnant.'

The African wives laughed loudly every five minutes. They always laughed so loudly the men would stop their conversations to see if something else was going to happen. Nobody talked of the war, the fighting, racist tension or anything that was going to upset anyone. No politics. No race talks. No religion.

That was until Annie, Ruthie, Denzel and Anita stood at the gate with Father Uncle Henry. They were all wearing pure white silky dresses with big 'Just been confirmed' smiles. White socks to their knees and black shoes.

'Come in, come in.' Father Uncle Henry beckoned

the four plus one uninvited guests into 54 Shetland Drive, Queens Park East. It was very common for Bulawayo get-togethers to double or treble in numbers because of 'drop by' visitors.

'Come in, come in,' said Becki's mother with Castle beer induced ebullience.

Father Uncle Henry was still wearing his Catholic black and white dress and looked very silly to Becki and Yvonne who laughed.

Father Uncle Henry apologised for the impromptu visit but had forgotten some books and socks in his bedroom. The children who were being confirmed lived nearby and he had agreed to drop them off.

'Have some food, have some food, Sema get some food,' Mrs Conceicão shouted at her nanny Sema who was sitting down for the first time after cooking all afternoon.

Annie eyed Becki, Becki eyed Barbara, Ruthie scowled at Yvonne and Denzel went to play with the other boys. The girls stared at each other in silent defiance until Anita the youngest one giggled uncontrollably.

Ruthie glared at her younger sister but gave in to the fits of giggles, then Barbara joined in. In seconds all the children were laughing.

'Truce?'

'Truce.'

They shook hands. They were all friends again thanks to Ruthie Payne's baby sister's giggles.

'Where you from?' Mr Harris who had MaNcube his wife on his lap asked Father Uncle Henry.

'Well I have been living in Australia but was born in Ireland in Galway,' said Henry sipping his beer.

'Galway. I am from County Antrim,' someone said.

'Oh I knew someone in Belfast,' someone else said.

'How long have you been a priest?'

'Not long,' said Father Uncle Henry.

'I see.'

The little girls played with dolls; the brave boys stripped off their shorts and dived into the sprinklers to cool them down. Mothers chastised the over-excited children, the boys played their games in the front and the girls hid from the boys in the back, boys who always seemed to cause trouble.

The day eventually cooled down and gentle shadows fell on the granite gravel pathway. The girls sat on the Delft blue *stoep*. They watched the tortoises stretching their yellowy brown elastic necks in slow motion.

'They are so cute,' said Annie as the other children watched and Ruthie put water into their pen.

'There are three of them you know,' Becki said proudly.

'Do they eat the mulberries?' Anita picked a green, raw mulberry from the weeping mulberry bush and threw it at the tortoise before anyone could answer.

Father tortoise spent five minutes waking from his slumber, his neck slowly stretching out. His beady brown eyes eyed the green mulberry that Anita had thrown onto the rustling carpet of brown, yellow and grey leaves. When he eventually got to the mulberry, he paused and eyed it suspiciously, twisting his head from side to side before opening his toothless mouth.

Silence.

The children were transfixed and looked at father tortoise as if waiting for a daunting verdict. After the teeniest bite, father tortoise's back legs moved first followed by his right-hand front leg as he moved away from the mulberry towards the a patch of sun. No one liked bitter mulberries, not even tortoises.

'I am going home,' said Anita sounding like father tortoise's rejection of her mulberry was the ultimate insult.

'Let's just get some ripe mulberries from the other tree. Come on,' said Annie trying to cheer up the other children.

'OK, let's go,' Ruthie the oldest and tallest girl led the children followed by Annie in her Sunday dress, then baby Anita then last Becki. Becki felt like she should lead the troop since it was her house and her mulberries, her tortoises and her garden.

Across the way the children could hear someone playing Smokey Robinson.

People can change.
They always do.
Haven't they noticed the changes in you.

'I just love this song,' said Annie rolling her eyes to the sky and lifting her hands up. 'I know all the words also.'

I don't care if they try to avoid you.
I don't care what they do.

Annie made a fist with her hands that became a microphone and swayed from side to side.

'Me, I hate this song, it's boring,' Anita said loudly and Annie lost her first audience member, followed by Becki who loved the song but didn't know the words and hated anyone showing off.

'Let's go eat some mulberries before they all fall off,' said Becki putting Annie's microphone hand in hers.

Within two minutes the children's mouths were covered in purple, juicy mulberries from the big weeping tree in the corner of the garden. Many of its ripe berries lay on the floor, oozing thick black sweet

129

juices.

Teeth changed from white to black, mulberries covered the palm of their hands and fingernails. Ruthie tried to stay clean. Annie didn't care; MaSikhosana did all the washing and never complained. Becki was proud of herself for changing from her smart Sunday clothes to something she didn't mind getting dirty. Baby Anita didn't care, Ruthie was worried what her mother would say if they came back home with dirty clothes, their mother did their own washing, there was no nanny.

'Nita look at your dress you have dirt everywhere.'

Little Anita looked at her big sister Ruthie with scornful defiance, her eyes locked into Ruthie like hot black coals. Little Anita's mouth carried on moving in stark contrast to her eyes and the rest of her body. Becki thought it was fascinating how little Anita could carry on chewing and enjoying the mouthful of mulberries while her eyes prepared for war, her hands folded in defence as she had not decided whether to attack or cry.

'I have had enough, no arguments you two, I can't eat any more anyway,' Becki said, determined to be the first to lead the pack. Becki waded through the mud in the garden knowing that the other children would follow and opened the gate that would lead back to the tortoise pen and into the front garden. The sun had mellowed into the late afternoon sky, the temperatures were lower and the trees were starting to cast their shadows onto the dusty gravel.

Anita surprised everyone by spitting her mouthful of mulberries and taking Ruthie's hand. Becki was annoyed about the little spoilt Anita, who did she think was going to clean the mess? Ruthie and little Anita followed Becki and Annie and her clean dress without a single mark followed behind them.

'Oh look, what's that?' said Anita whose eyes were

level with the bottom of the window pane if she stood on tip toes.

'Aaah you!' said Ruthie, annoyed about being pulled back by her little sister's never-ending distractions which meant everything took twice as long to do.

Ruthie crouched slightly and looked through Becki's window.

Becki who was the same height as Annie crouched to look through the window wondering what little Anita had seen. Annie who was the same height as Becki crouched in the tiny space left in the corner. All the children had their hands cupped against the window and their eyes strained to see a man sitting on the bed without his trousers on playing with his thingy.

Up and down, up and down his big hands stroked his big thingy that looked like a pink snake with hair. Becki noticed it was much bigger than the boys at the school.

Up and down the man played with his boy thing; his hand moving steadily up and down. The children could not see his face.

Faster and faster, his hand jerked the big tube in his hands.

'Do you think he can see us?' Ruthie whispered. Nobody answered. The children knew that they should not be watching this man doing whatever he was doing; if the adults found out they would be in trouble.

'Let's go,' Annie whispered.

The man with the white legs kept playing with his thingy until thick, white sticky wee wee came out of the top and poured all over his thick fingers, knuckles and nails.

'*Sis!*' little Anita said a little more loudly so that the man stood up holding his hand and kicking away his jeans and something black on the floor.

The children scurried away, five heartbeats beating faster than before.

'*Sis* man,' said little Anita, 'your cousin from England is dirty' she said with the same defiance she had before, eyes locked straight into Becki, her lips all twisted showing big teeth that looked like dried winter maize with big black gaps where her two front teeth should have been.

'That wasn't my cousin?' said Becki, her hands pointing to the window where they had seen the white man playing with his penis.

'It was so,' Anita said pushing away her plaited pigtails and making it clear that it was Becki's fault that they had seen this disgusting, sticky play.

'No it wasn't, you can't see you are so short.'

'No I am not, I could see his face. You couldn't because you are tall and can only see his feet.'

'Yes I could,' said Becki getting annoyed at little Anita's never-ending cheekiness.

'Shhh, I know who it was,' said Ruthie.

'Who?' they all chorused at once knowing Ruthie always told the truth.

'Promise not to tell,' Ruthie looked at Annie, Becki and little Anita with wide eyes. Ruthie tapped her fore finger against her thick brown lips so that her almost buck teeth stuck out.

'Promise,' the girls replied in a loud whisper.

'Cross your heart and hope to die,' Ruthie's eyes grew wider showing that this was serious.

'Cross my heart and hope to die,' little Anita said very fast, eager to know who Ruthie thought was the man with the sticky, white cream coming out of his thingy in the middle of the afternoon.

'Cross your heart, Annie?'

'Cross my heart,' Annie said motioning a cross near her heart.

'And you Becki?'

'Cross my heart.'

'It was Father Henry.'

'No way,' Annie said.

'Yeah,' said Ruthie nodding furiously, 'I saw his face.'

'Did he see us?'

'I don't know.'

**

It was the school holidays. Otheliya was still away to comfort her family and Titus the new garden boy was working half days helping with the garden. Cousin Matthew had gone back to England and Uncle Henry had returned because the church was being renovated and he had nowhere to stay again. This meant that Becki had to do everything that Otheliya would have done. She had to lay the table with the red and white table cloth for the morning, make sure there was a cup and matching saucer, the best silver spoons for the fine china sugar bowl. Because Father Uncle Henry had stayed for so long he was no longer being fed bacon and egg every day. 'Don't worry about bacon and egg Ma' he had said to Becki's mother one morning when she got up early to make him breakfast. 'No, no, no,' Becki's mother had protested, it was Ndebele tradition to make sure that your guests were fed well until they decided to go. For your white guests you always gave them bacon, eggs and cornflakes and Becki's mother would have it no other way.

Eventually, Father Uncle Henry had persuaded Becki's mother that she really needn't do that.

'Sit here,' Father Uncle Henry said to Becki as she washed Uncle Trenholm's early morning cup of tea cups. Becki obeyed and sat next to Father Uncle Henry as he slurped his cornflakes with a little golden flake straying to his chin and a slither of milk sitting parallel to the flake. Father Uncle Henry's glasses always went dark in the house so that he looked like he was wearing cheap sunglasses.

'Eat some cornflakes.'

Becki was too shy to say she didn't like cornflakes. In Ndebele tradition children never disobeyed adults; if an adult said sit down, you sit down. If an adult says get me some water, you get some water. If an adult says 'Eat some cornflakes' you eat some cornflakes.

Becki pulled the lemon kitchen chair which made a loud scraping noise against the black and white tiled floor. Becki found she enjoyed the cornflakes much more than she thought she would.

After breakfast Father Uncle Henry went to the Catholic church while he was waiting to get his house.

'Three more weeks and I will be out of your hair.'

'On no, please, you can stay here as long as you like.'

'No, no I am sure you want me to go and have your house to yourself,' said Father Uncle Henry to Uncle Trenholm smiling so that his bulbous nose sat like an awkward piece of wood on his white face and brown eyes.

'Anyway, the little *pikinini* will be able to have her room back,' Father Uncle Henry smiled patting Becki's shoulder and pulling her towards her.

'Thank you young lady, I wouldn't have been able to do it without your kindness.'

Mother's car arrived much later than Uncle Trenholm, which was very rare.

'Ha-llo,' mother shouted from her car. Titus and his long insect-like legs and flip-flops ran to greet mother as fast as he could so that she did not suspect for a minute that he had been lazing around. The truth was

Titus had spent all day working, sweeping, raking and even washing dishes but he still thought his employer would think he was not good enough.

'Hello madam,' Titus said with a slight curtsey and holding out his hand. In Ndebele tradition you would normally curtsey when you met your elders and betters, but in Ndebele tradition it was normally girls that curtseyed. It always baffled Becki's mother why Titus insisted on curtseying.

'Yebo Titus, come and help me with these things.'

'Hello mummy,' Becki shouted from the washing area doorway.

'Hello my child, put the kettle on and make some tea.'

Becki loved to please her mother and went straight to the kettle to make a strong cup of Tanganda tea. It had been a while since Becki had seen her mother drinking tea by herself; she mostly had her tea with Uncle Trenholm. Titus came around with something metallic, a bicycle.

'It is yours,' Titus said to Becki.

Becki yelped. Mother had bought her a bike, her own bike just like Annie's. She could cycle to Annie's house, cycle to the shop by herself and even go as far as the railway line. Becki could not remember being this happy and could not wait to tell Annie the next day that they could cycle together to wherever they wanted to. Annie and Becki would be best friends; the other children would envy them.

'Yeah but your bike is not even new, look at the wheels,' said Barbara when she saw her bike.

'You are just jealous,' said Becki who had anticipated her answer.

'Look at the colour, Annie's bike is shiny and blue, yours is dull red, looks like it was painted with shoe polish,' said Barbara laughing at her own amazing observations.

'Barbara stop it,' said Yvonne unconvincingly.

'It is going to fall apart in two weeks.'

'My girl, you are jealous because you can't afford one,' said Becki with her hands on her hips. This is exactly how she thought the nasty Barbara was going to respond, she was just like her nasty brothers.

'Who, me jealous of an old bike, you must be joking.'

'OK, I am going.' Becki got on her bike determined not to hear any more of Barbara's jealous nastiness. This was the beauty of having your own bike: you could get up and go when you wanted to, you didn't have to hang around.

'My bike is not old, you are old, you old bitch,' said Becki getting on her bike not believing the words that had just come out of her mouth.

'Who you calling a bitch my girl?' Barbara suddenly screamed at Becki as she started cycling away.

Becki started to ride away, shaking and shivering.

'I said who are you calling a bitch my girl? Who? Who? Tell me?' Barbara screamed spontaneously closing her eyes in anger, stamping her foot and pulling Becki's plaited bun and pulling her towards herself.

'Barbara shut up!' Yvonne said, pulling her fiery younger sister away.

'Don't you also tell me to shut up, the little *Kaffir* just called me a bitch.'

'Leave me alone you!' Becki shouted back with a hint of fear in her voice as she pulled Barbara's hand away from her hair leaving pins of pain.

'I'll *klep* you,' Barbara opened her eyes revealing black eyes that had become marbles of shiny, black fire, her forefinger pointing at Becki and then immediately clapped her on her right cheek. The smack

136

on Becki's right cheek was more intense than the hair pulling and made her right ear immediately hot as if somebody was pressing hard against her head.

'Your mother is a fockin' bitch, everyone knows your mother is a focking bitch,' Barbara shouted at Becki who was now scared.

'Barbara stop it, stop it!'

Becki pedalled away standing up, her chest tightening as she tried to breathe more oxygen into her lungs. An uncontrollable stream of hot tears raced down Becki's cheeks. By the time she was home Becki was sobbing uncontrollably sounding like a choked up broken tractor.

'What's the matter?' said Father Uncle Henry.

'Bah, Ba, ba, Bar-bara ...'

'What happened?'

'She, she, she he he hee,' tears and snot ran down Becki's face.

'She hit you?'

'Be, Be, Bah, bah-she she,' more tears, more snot. Father Uncle Henry wiped the snot from Becki's nose and the tears from her eyes.

'Naughty girl this Barbara, I will have to talk to her mother and father, don't cry, don't cry.'

Father Henry pulled Becki to his chest and patted her between the shoulder blades so that she could smell the whiff of lavender.

Closer, closer, Becki felt Father Uncle Henry's lavender-flavoured heartbeat, his muscular arms stroked her hair buns and neck.

Swing, swing, quickly up and down put me down. Becki wanted to say out loud but had been taught to never speak first to a big person.

'Don't worry, don't worry,' Father Henry said to Becki. 'Let's sit here.' Father Uncle Henry sat on the faded white garden chairs. 'Sit here,' he tapped his

137

knee and Father Uncle Henry let Becki sit on his knee until her tears had stopped. 'Thaaaaa-aat's better.'

Father Uncle Henry swayed Becki back and forth until he was sure she had forgotten the incident.

Just like a fast car, swing, swing, I feel like vomiting. Mama, Uncle, Miss Sibanda, vomit, vomit she thought to herself silently. Sitting on Father Uncle Henry was not comfortable; it reminded Becki of the time she and her aunt had seen two giant snakes rolling in the dust, sideways crossing their path. The two snakes were a shiny, rusty brown colour and had made them run home as fast as they could. Becki wanted to run from Father Uncle Henry's grip.

'Tell me about school?' sway, sway. 'What's your favourite subject, English?' sway, stroke, sway.

'Yes I love English, I love the stories, my favourite books are *The Three Investigators* ...' Father Uncle Henry stroked her neck, slowly, softly, '...*The Famous five,*' Becki whispered looking down at her knees. 'I used to like *The Famous Five* last year but I read them all now.'

'Oh really,' said Father Uncle Henry shifting Becki from the top of his knee to his upper knee. She was much heavier than before.

'*Nancy Drew*?' said Father Uncle Henry, so that Becki could smell the faint smell of beer on his breath. Becki always knew the smell of beer as it reminded her of all the visitors to the Shebeen.

'Yes I like *Nancy Drew* but not as much as *The Three Investigators.*' Becki was not going to be persuaded to like anything else but *The Three Investigators* that she had swapped with Pricely, Algernon, Sonia and Gary at school. Becki's feet swayed back and forth, hardly touching the ground.

I want to get off from Uncle Henry's knee; I don't like feeling his thingy through his khaki shorts she thought to herself, wondering how she was going to get off. Something inside her told her that this was not a good thing for her to feel. It reminded her of 'mummies and daddies' in her primary school; she did not want to feel another boy's thingy.

Boys' thingies are sis, she thought, wiping away an invisible tear. *I don't like how this feels, let me down, I hate you* were the words that stuck in her throat.

Father Uncle Henry sensed that Becki wanted to get off and pulled her off his lap.

'Tears all gone now, no more cry cry now.'

Becki was relieved to not have to sit on Father Uncle Henry's lap. She ran with the same speed she had used when she had run away from the two brown snakes.

Rounders and Hula Hoops on April 18th

It was February 1980. Dark clouds covered the Bulawayo skies, deep thick menacing, dirty grey cumulonimbus, cotton wool balls. Early morning rush hour cars rushed down Main Street to the industrial sites at the edge of the city. Uncle Trenholm dropped Becki off at the corner of Third Avenue just outside Main Court. Becki always picked up her friend Caroline Davies from the first floor of Main Court.

Becki and Caroline Davies always had a lot to talk and laugh about. Becki thought how Caroline looked so pretty in her blue McKeurtan pinafore. Her blouse was so white it looked like it came from the Surf ad on TV. Matching her white top were pretty, fine, crotchet white socks and black shoes so shiny you could see your face. Both girls carried brown size two school suitcases with a pencil case, a spare hat and sandwiches.

'My brother Gerald has a new LP by Kool and the Kang, we have been playing it all weekend.'

'I like *Get down on it.*'

'Me too.'

'I kept rewinding the record and writing down the words.' The two ten-year-old girls talked incessantly until they arrived at the gates of McKeurtan Primary School.

Becki loved school and Becki loved Mrs Doney, Mrs Doney was just like Mrs Sibanda. Today Mrs Doney was teaching them a new dance. Becki was so excited that she did not even mind that she was called Becki and not Bekezela and that her mother had forgotten to tell her. Becki did not even mind that she was not talking to Yvonne and Barbara and that when she came home there was no one to play with but her two dolls.

Mrs Doney's game involved red, yellow and green hula hoops. This made Becki happy as she just did not like any of the boys except for Algernon Pillay who was very handsome, very shy and quiet. Best of all, hula hoops meant that Becki didn't have to go home and be with Father Uncle Henry. Becki just did not like him touching her thigh on the day that he bought her the pink dress. It had reminded Becki of the mummy and daddy games that Samson and Cornelius used to play.

'OK, make a line,' Mrs Doney said putting her gold glasses between her teeth which had the usual red lipstick. 'OK, you, you, you and you,' Mrs Doney pointed at Revonia Hanson, Mary Herbert, Pricely Jones and Charmaine Shirto. 'Then you, you, you and you,' Mrs Doney's arthritic index finger pointed at Sonia Jeffries, Becki, Beauty Millen and Antoinette Potgeiter who stood next to each other looking at the remaining girls. When Mrs Doney was doing the third group of girls, two of the strongest boys Gary Shirto and Melvin West were carrying red, yellow and green hula hoops. The colour of the new Zimbabwe flag.

Mrs Doney demonstrated how to hula hoop with the waist. Within seconds all of the girls were going round and round with the different coloured hula hoops. Hula hoops were falling left, right and centre and then being picked up and rolled round and round the waist lines. Next the girls learnt how to hula hoop with their arms, which they all found much easier to keep steady. When Mrs Doney saw that they found the arms much easier she made them roll the hula hoops around their necks so that they all looked like graceful ostriches. Mrs Doney was pleased with how enthusiastic the girls were at learning how to hula hoop with their knees as well as their ankles.

'Well done, children, we will practise every day after school so make sure you tell your parents.'

Becki was excited about the new hula hoops exercise; Mrs Doney was always full of fun things. Becki enjoyed the singing and dancing lessons she gave the children, the drama classes and the swimming trips. Becki was deeply absorbed in her own hula hoop thoughts wishing Mrs Doney had allowed them to take the hula hoops home.

'*Howzat* Becki, do you want to play rounders with us?' It was Annie on her blue and silver Chopper. Becki was so happy to see her friend that she even forgot to be jealous of her blue and silver Chopper that still looked as though it had just been bought.

'How? Just me and you?'

'We'll ask Yvonne and Barbara.'

'No I am not talking to Yvonne, she's a bitch.'

'OK, we'll ask Angie Sweetman.'

'But that's not enough.'

'OK, we'll ask Ruthie and Nita.'

'Nita's a *lighty:* she always cries and wants to go home too much.'

'Me, you, Angie and Ruthie and Nita can catch the ball for anyone she wants.'

'She won't want to but we can ax her.'

'OK come and eat lunch with me,' said Annie.

'OK thanks Annie.' Becki was pleased that she did not have to go home to eat bread and butter and talk to Father Uncle Henry who always seemed to be home these days. Becki was pleased also because Annie always made nice lunches but this was the first time she had asked Becki to come home for lunch with her.

'Titus, I am going to Annie's house OK?' Becki shouted across to Titus who was raking the lawn which he had just mowed.

'Yebo mama,' said Titus in siNdebele, Becki hated

it when Titus spoke to her in siNdebele. It made her feel too 'African'. Whenever Titus spoke to her in siNdebele Becki wanted to pick up the hose pipe and strangle him. Becki was sure Titus did this on purpose, he was full of mischief.

Becki walked near Annie who was trying hard to not cycle too fast so that Becki could keep up. Annie cycled to the right in a quarter circle then to the left in a quarter circle then one pedal forward then back then stop to let Becki catch up.

'What are you having for lunch; is your nanny cooking it for you?'

'No, I cook for myself.'

'I cook for myself also at home.'

'Can you cook pap?'

'Yes I can even cook pap, can you?'

'No, MaSikhosana cooks pap but I don't like it and we don't eat it very much,' said Annie getting back on her bike and then stopping again deciding it was better to push the bike instead.

'I don't like it and we don't eat it very much,' lied Becki. Eating pap was like talking in isiNdebele. Too African. Too *Kaffir*.

'Hallo Madame Annie,' said MaSikhosana, Annie's nanny as Annie and Becki opened the wrought iron gate. As soon as the gate creaked, the dog at No. 60 Shetland Drive started to bark. Nobody ever saw the dog through the wild bushes and trees in the front garden of the house where an old European man with a kind smile and his handsome young son who went to Milton High School lived.

Annie cut some potatoes making them look like fat Willards chips. Annie asked Becki to cut some onions. Becki hated cutting onions but was so glad that her aunty had taught her a special way of cutting onions so that she didn't cry. The way to do it was to simply

143

make sure that you did not cut off the roots of the onion, peel off the top layer of skin then cut the onion one way without cutting through the root. Turn the onion around and cut the other way. Turn the onion on its side then slice through without tears.

Annie poured the *Mazola* oil into the frying pan and put another frying pan for the onions. When the frying pans were heating up, Annie put salt onto the raw chips and asked Becki to butter the sliced Downings bread. Becki was impressed with the evenly sliced bread. Uncle Trenholm preferred the bread not to be sliced, he said it tasted better. Annie fried the onions in the frying pan and turned on the silver kettle to make tea with their lunch. The smell of the onion and fresh tomatoes made Becki and Annie hungrier especially after Annie added the hot *Rajah* curry. When the quick lunch was cooked, Annie poured it over the chips and gave a plate to Becki. Both children scoffed their lunch in silence. Becki was so glad to have hot chips and relish in the afternoon it was not as boring as the plain bread she had every afternoon.

'Hello Bass,' said MaSikhosana to five-year-old Leon, Annie's younger brother. It always amazed Becki how much little Leon looked like a white boy with his golden syrupy skin and straight hair and straight nose. He looked exactly like Annie's mother who could also easily pass for a white person. Annie looked more like her father with her darker skin and less straight hair.

'Come and eat, where have you been Lee?'

'School,' Leon answered putting down his school satchel.

'Why are your shirt buttons all open, Lee? Have you been fighting?'

'No,' said Leon, quickly tucking his shirt in his trousers, putting his finger in his mouth and looking down.

144

'Come eat now,' barked Annie sounding more like a mother than a sister.

Leon sat down next to Annie on the kitchen table, his feet which were 10 cm from the floor swinging backwards and forwards.

'It's *lekker* Annie,' said Becki.

'Yah it's *lekker* Annie,' Leon repeated to the two girls making Becki insecure about whether Annie was making fun of her or not.

After eating, Becki and Annie left the dishes for MaSikhosana the nanny to wash. MaSikhosana never really complained about having to wash dishes after Annie, after all she was paid ten dollars a month for that. Leon disappeared into his bedroom at the back of the house to play with his toy cars and trains without Annie shouting at him.

Annie decided to leave her bike behind and walk first into Orkney Drive to look for Angie and then come back to find Ruthie or Anita her little sister. Angie Sweetman was older than all the other children and Ruthie had guessed that Angie was fifteen years old although Angie herself did not want to talk about her age. Angie lived at number 8 Orkney Drive with her mother (Mrs Sweetman) and her brother Stephen Sweetman, who all the girls thought very handsome and funny. Angie's father was not Mr Sweetman but a white man that Mrs Sweetman had had an affair with. Mrs Sweetman was herself quite a light-skinned coloured woman with bone-straight hair who spoke fluent Shona. Angie Sweetman was often mistaken for a white girl with her long torso and flat backside, green eyes and blonde hair that she dyed now and again to make it blonder. Angie too could speak fluent Shona but relished being thought of white a lot more.

Annie shouted louder as she thought Angie might be at the back. Yvonne appeared from her house which was No. 16.

'Hi Annie.'

'Hi Becki.'

'Howzat?' the girls replied in one chorus .Becki looked at her shoes hoping to avoid Barbara if she was there.

'Barbara is not here,' said Yvonne sensing Becki's nervousness.

'Hey, we are playing rounders, now, do you want to play?'

'Of course,' said Yvonne.

'Let's go get Angie then …'

'Angie!'

The gate to Angie's driveway was locked so that the children had to shout her name from outside.

'Angie.'

'Angie.'

'A-N-G-I-E.'

Becki decided to not shout as she did not want Barbara to hear her voice. Becki was still worried about the fight that she and Barbara had and did not want to see Barbara for a while.

'AAAAA-NNNNN-G-EEEEE'

'Angie!' The three girls shouted louder and Becki joined in knowing Barbara was not around. Mrs Sweetman came out of her front door with big blue and red curlers on her head.

'Why are you shouting like mad people?' Mrs Sweetman, who might have been in the middle of fixing her hair, seemed annoyed.

'Sorry auntie, is Angie here?'

'She's gone to the Comic Exchange I think.'

Angie was always going to the Comic Exchange and did not miss a single week if she could help it. She always exchanged comics and magazines for 10 cents. Angie's favourite character was Tess. Tess was a detective from South Africa who spent most of her time doing detective work in a bikini and nothing else. Tess was beautiful with pouting, big lips that looked like she had had Botox injections before Botox was being used. As well as straight long blonde hair Tess had big bulging breasts and deadly karate chops that she never hesitated to use on the villains that she met every day. Inevitably Tess would fall in love with, kiss or go to bed with someone for that week and she was not afraid to use her feminine powers to get what she needed from men.

'OK, let's see if Ruthie and Nita can play with us,' said Annie.

'Nita is a lighty man I tell you,' said Becki.

'No but we can still have a *gas* with Nita even if she is a lighty,' said Annie.

'Annie you got the items?'

'Yah one tennis ball and this stick, that's it.'

The three girls walked back to Shetland Drive past Annie's house and its evergreen hedge and past the overgrown house to number 58 where Ruthie and Anita lived. The children were not sure if Ruthie's father was there and decided that it was better if only Annie went in. Ruthie's father did not want lots of children in his backyard and had shouted at Ruthie many times when her friends had asked her to come out and play.

Becki and Yvonne sat waiting outside peering through the gate of number 60 to see if they could see anything more of the barking dog. In the driveway was the white Datsun that belonged to the kind old man with the son and the dog.

'You child, what are you doing?'

Yvonne jumped up in shock when she looked up to see her sister Barbara in her maroon jumper. Barbara had missed the first bus home and had had to catch the second bus. Becki's heart beat faster. She had spent so much time hiding from Barbara that she did not plan for how she would feel when she saw her after the fight.

'We are waiting for Ruthie, want to play rounders? Don't even call me you child, I am older than you!' Yvonne said in one fast sentence not thinking how it would affect Becki.

'It's mine and Annie's game; if she plays I am not playing.'

'Well if my sister can't play then I am not playing and two of you can't play rounders.'

'Let's ax Ruthie,' said Annie with the same authority she had had all day.

'Three people will be boring, Annie.'

'Me, I won't play.'

'Don't then, my girl, I won't cry.'

Annie came out with Anita but no Ruthie and saw the argument between Yvonne, Barbara and Becki.

'St---o----p edd you two girls. Just stop--ped. No more fighting.' Annie shouted at the top of her voice.

'Let's all play, you just say sorry to her, what you said was not a nice thing calling her a focking bitch so just say sorry and let's forget it.'

'OK, soz man,' Barbara said too quickly to be sincere.

'And you? Do you take her sorry?' said Annie pointing at Becki and sounding more mature than her ten years.

'Yah, OK,' Becki said not showing how pleased she was that there would no longer be a fight.

'Aww-kay,' said Annie clapping her hands and leading the group of girls to play outside Becki's house.

The children always played outside Becki's house. It was easy to see the cars coming all the way from the main road behind. Just enough time to jump away from the road if any cars came from the top of the road.

Ruthie's house was only three doors away from Becki's house, exactly where the road suddenly curved. Annie's house was two doors away from Ruthie's and suffered from the same problem but also the sun always seemed to shine in the children's faces when they batted and bowled. If they went to Barbara and Yvonne's house they had to deal with their horrible brothers and also the Orkney Road went up slightly which made running up the hill tiresome and made rounders not enjoyable.

Annie put a rock in the middle of the road, parallel to Becki's gate. The first and third bases were at the edges of the tarred road opposite each other and parallel to the pond in Becki's front yard. The second base was opposite the home base and parallel to the perimeter fence between No. 54 and No. 56.

Paper.

Scissors.

Rock.

The children always chose their teams using paper, scissors and rock. Annie with Barbara. Becki with Yvonne and Anita was going to pick up any short balls that went behind the bowler. Becki was pleased to not be with Barbara; she had not really forgiven Barbara and her big frog eyes.

'It would be nice if Ruthie was here then someone could pick from the side,' said Barbara at the top of her voice.

'Where is Ruthie, Nita?'

'Oh well Ruthie is very sick. They think she is deaf, she can't hear and she has to go to King George School.' The children did not believe Nita and decided to carry on playing.

'OK, let's play,' Annie shouted at Anita and Barbara.

'Annie stop, hear this, Ruthie has gone deaf,' Barbara said with her a loud whisper that seemed to get caught in the back of her throat.

'What? Please don't lie.'

'What happened,' Barbara said with horror in her eyes.

'I du-nno,' Anita shrugged her shoulders in a slow exaggerated way.

'Is she at home?'

'Yah.'

The children threw the bat and Annie picked up the third base brick away from the road and threw it at the dip between the road and Becki's house. Yvonne picked up the home base stone and threw it at the flame lily plant just outside Becki's gate which landed a few centimetres away from it without harming it.

'Is your daddy home?'

'No, he is at work,' Anita said picking up the first base brick, walking back and throwing it next to the flame lily. Anita was disappointed that the game had been stopped.

'Tell her to come and see us.'

'Tell her we miss her.'

'Tell her hi.'

'Please tell her to come out.'

At Ruthie's house, Barbara decided to go in with Anita and Annie. Yvonne and Becki sat outside the gate even though they knew Ruthie and Anita's father was not there.

Ruthie came out after a shorter time than the children had expected.

'Hi Ruthie,' the children said in unison, not sure how their friend would respond. Ruthie was wearing a red dress with elastic on the sleeves and waist and three big frills that went from her waist to her knee, another frill went from her left shoulder to the right. She had three of these dresses in red, blue and green: her mother always bought their clothes in threes.

Ruthie stared at the girls. Anita took Ruthie's sleeve and pulled it and said very loudly, 'they say Hi. You have to speak loud otherwise she will not hear you.'

'Hi,' Ruthie replied and everyone was happy to hear what Anita had done had worked. There was an awkward silence and no one knew what else to say next.

'Are you going to play,' Ruthie said pointing at the girls.

Everyone was relieved that Ruthie herself had broken the silence.

'Yes, are you coming? Are you allowed to play?'

'Of course,' Ruthie answered.

Ruthie went back to tell her mother that she was going to play and Anita followed her.

'If she is deaf, how come she didn't hear the first thing but heard the second thing?' said Barbara looking mortified.

Trade Fair

Right in the centre of Bulawayo, Matopos Road and Hillside Road meet, with Hillside Road going to the big houses in the suburbs and Matopos Road going to Cecil Rhodes's tomb. The two roads meet at the Bulawayo Trade Fair, which is sandwiched between Gifford High School for white boys and Coghlan Primary School for little white girls. Beyond the Trade Fair was the vast white only golf grounds and the Ascot racecourse where the only black faces would be wearing white uniforms serving beer and . The streets nearby the Trade Fair had names like Doncaster, Luton, Manchester and Edgware.

The streets were lined with date palms next to pristine lawns with sprinkling fountains gushing white foam vertically and sideways while making hissing sounds. Inside were colourful buildings with architecture that could not be found anywhere in the city. There was a red and white flamboyant art décor building with a wavy concrete appendage on the roof. In the middle was an old replica Victorian building that looked like a highly decorated cake with flags from countries all over the world. Opposite that was a small semi-circular bridge where miniature trains went to and fro, past a sign that said 'Beware of Trains'. Beyond the buildings were all the fair rides and displays with horses, army cadets and drum majorettes. From all around the Trade Fair was the spire, a tall, imposing obelisk which guided people back to the gates.

Everyone went to the annual Trade Fair at the show grounds. Anyone who was anyone that is, would be there to enjoy Fanta, chips, rides, shows and at the end of the evening be exhausted with all the fun that was possible.

'Are you going to the Trade Fair?' Father Uncle

Henry asked Becki.

'I think so but I am not sure. I haven't asked my mother.'

'Don't worry, I will ask her for you.' This is why Becki always loved having visitors from overseas. Visitors meant they ate nice food every day at the big table with silver knives and forks. Visitors meant new clothes and favours; Mother found it difficult to say 'no' to anything when visitors came. Things changed when the visitors left but for now Becki was happy that visitors were here as it meant they could visit the Trade Fair.

'Your mother said yes.'

'Really? Are you sure?'

Becki knew Father Uncle Henry was always sure. He was hardly ever the type of man to not be sure.

'But first …'

'Yah … but first?'

'You must have a nice dress, mustn't you?'

'Yes, but I am scared of asking mother. I think she will say no.'

'No, don't worry. I will buy you a dress. We will go to town tomorrow or Friday after school.'

Perfect thought Becki, she could not wait to show off her new dress to Ruthie, Annie, Yvonne and Barbara. She was always so jealous of Annie who always had the latest of everything: shoes, bikes, records, hair slides, sweets. This was Becki's moment and she couldn't wait to show them all what Father Uncle Henry was going to buy.

The next morning could not come sooner as Becki sat staring outside. The sun sat lazily at an angle in the milky blue sky. Becki sat back looking at her desk feeling the sun's warm blissful presence presenting an unpredictable drama of curves, lines, squares and swirls catalysing a million memories of times past. Mrs

Doney, her Grandmother in Luveve, Samson and Cornelius.

Grade 6 was more difficult and Becki was distracted all day and could not do her 8 times table in the morning and was happy when the school bell rang for the morning break. During the morning break she had a fight with Beauty Millen; Becki had decided to give her a piece of her mind.

'Yah Beauty, don't think we all don't know.'

'Don't know what?' said Beauty.

'That you only play with Sandra because she is rich.'

'No I don't.' Beauty turned on her heel and walked away and Becki was annoyed as she had always liked Beauty and wanted her to be her friend and could not understand why Beauty did not want to be her friend. The only reason Becki could think of was that Sandra's family were rich even though they were Africans. They owned a hairdresser, a butcher in town, a farm in the farm area, trucks and a very big car. Sandra was not a show off but everyone knew she had money and she could buy Beauty sweets from the tuck shop and hot chips with vinegar, salt and some piri piri from the Indian shop on Third Avenue.

Becki hated Grade 6; it was harder, she missed Grade 5 and Mrs Doney and her crooked piano playing hands. Mrs Esat her new teacher was a tall thin Indian woman with short boyish hair and glasses. She always wore colourful chemises with matching kuta trousers. If she wore a chemise with blue and pink designs her kuta would be blue with a matching shawl. If she wore a colourful kuta with green, yellow and brown designs then her chemise would be a plain green or yellow design. Mrs Esat had short unpainted nails and never wore any lipstick, perfume or eye shadow, just simple diamond studs that bounced against her flawless golden skin.

Oh how Becki missed Mrs Doney and wished she could replace her with the boring Mrs Esat. Becki wished she hadn't started the argument with Beauty and was annoyed that she was walking away rather than answering back.

'Yes everyone knows you only like Sandra for her money!' Becki threw caution to wind and spoke loudly and immediately.

'I heard you Becki,' said Beauty with a frown on her face.

'I wanted you to hear me.' Becki could not understand why she was causing trouble with Beauty and was glad to go back to the class and listen to boring Mrs Esat talking about *Gulliver's Travels* or generally paying attention to Antoinette her little pet.

Becki could not wait to go home or to be in Grade 7 next year and maybe be the Head Girl. Being in Grade 6 was too in between. Becki remembered the excitement of the Trade Fair and lost herself while Mrs Esat read from her book.

Brobdingnag? How silly, what a silly place thought Becki. Last week Mrs Esat read about yet another silly place 'Lilliput'. That sounded a bit better but still a silly place with silly small people. Becki drifted off as Mrs Esat read in her soft cotton wool voice.

The bell rang, it was Friday, no more *Gulliver's Travels* until next week, just Friday and a trip to buy some new clothes. Goodbye to McKeurtan Primary School with its blue walls that went a third of the way and then became white the rest of the way.

At the front gate, little blue and white pinafores turned left to get the buses to the European suburbs; some turned right to go Thorngrove and a few of those at the boarding school crossed the road to go to boarding school.

Someone hooted their car horn loudly. Becki turned and noticed it was Father Uncle Henry. Becki was confused but happy to see Father Uncle Henry in his rented blue car. It meant that she could save her bus fare and buy a Cadbury's Flake from the store.

'Hello pretty lady. I am going to treat you today and buy you a nice dress, I think you deserve it after all the hard work you do,' said Father Uncle Henry patting Becki's head. Friday, lunchtime Bulawayo, the sun was now a violent beast that roared its heat against the tarred roads, heightening the smells of stale sweat and silencing the air. People on the streets of Bulawayo slowed down with the heat and sat under the cool shades cast under Burkea and Jacaranda trees.

Becki was excited about going to buy a dress at OK Stores of all places. OK Stores was already full of mothers with their children buying clothes to wear for the Bulawayo Trade Fair. School girls from the Dominican Convent in their blue dresses and caps milled outside talking to the boys from Milton eating bags of chips chattering and laughing loudly.

Becki felt the stares of the shopping assistants looking at her with Father Uncle Henry. Becki wished her mother was with them and quickly walked away from Father Uncle Henry to look at the pretty dresses. There were pink dresses, little red riding hood tops, white blouses, denim trousers and pleated dresses.

'I think this one is nice.'

Becki chose a candy pink gingham cotton dress with a white waistcoat joined in the middle with two matching strings. The top and waistcoat were then joined to the soft, frilly, cotton skirt.

'Do you like it? Well it's yours.' Father Uncle Henry took out two fresh crisp notes from his bundle and handed it to the young blonde shop assistant who looked bored and distracted.

'Thank you,' said Father Uncle Henry smiling as the young shop assistant gave him the change. Father Uncle Henry kneeled so that he was at the same level as Becki, his glasses had become less dark since they had been in the store and Becki could clearly see his grey, brown, hazel eyes clearly. Father Uncle Henry was wearing his khaki shorts that he always wore with his brown sandals. Becki was relieved that he didn't kneel or crouch any further down as she was worried about everyone in OK Stores seeing his something they shouldn't. Becki could not understand why a grown man would forget to wear underpants and let his thingy escape from his shorts. Becki remembered the time she had seen it and hated it.

In the car they drove down Main Street and past the City Hall which was full of children from different schools: blue and white dresses and hats from Coghlan Girls' School, green and white uniforms from Montrose Girls' School, maroon uniforms from Founders, light blue hats from Milton Boys' School. Father Uncle Henry and Becki went past all the buses and turned left and stopped at the corner of Selbourne Avenue and 6th Avenue. Father Uncle Henry bought Becki a big bag of fat chips with tons of salt and vinegar. Becki wolfed them down while Father Uncle Henry ate his and they chatted about the Trade Fair the next day.

'Good girl, you have an appetite,' said Father Uncle Henry who was watching Becki, his glasses had gone darker as the sun's rays had become more intense. Becki thought he looked a bit like Roger Ramjet from the cartoons.

'Good girl.' Father Uncle Henry leaned over and put his hand on Becki's knee and left his hand on top of her blue pinafore.

'Do you like your dress?' he asked, with his face leaning very close to hers. His hand had now moved to her pinafore and her panties.

'Yes Uncle.'

Becki quickly pulled down her dress and smiled nervously. 'I like the dress and hopefully I will wear it to the Trade Fair.' Becki was not sure she wanted to go with Father Uncle Henry. She had enjoyed the fish and chips and the dress but did not enjoy Father Uncle Henry making her show her panties. She hated seeing his boy's thing, but maybe this is what priests did and there was no harm since he was a church man who wore a black and white dress on Sunday. By the time Becki and Uncle Henry were driving away from Bulawayo city centre she was sure that there was no problem with what Father Uncle Henry was doing. He probably did it with Annie, Anita and Ruthie when he took them to church sometimes.

Becki gazed out of the window to where the Lunar Park used to be. On the quiet streets near Baines School, a little boy with a satchel on his back walked slowly down the dusty path with a piece of wire. The little boy used the wire as an instrument to play each wire square that formed the primary school fence. At the corner of North End, teenage boys and girls were walking towards North End swimming pool. Becki turned the handle of the window to smell the distant smell of chorine and wished she was going to swim today.

The wind started to get stronger and Becki put her head out of the window when they got nearer to Paddonhurst and watched a man in blue overalls filling the cars in the garage with petrol and diesel. Becki always loved the smell of petrol and could smell it as Father Uncle Henry drove towards Queens Park. Queens Park East to the right and Queens Park West to the left and in the middle the funny looking Assemblies of God church.

By the time Becki and Father Uncle Henry arrived at 54 Shetland Drive, the sun was less oppressive: maybe it was the droplets of water that were carried in the air from the sprinklers in all the front gardens. Ice cream men wearing blue and red uniforms and hats cycled through the road ringing their bells. Titus was ploughing the back and doing his best to protect himself from the harsh afternoon sun by spending most of his time under the shade made by the trees. Father Uncle Henry had to immediately go to the church in North End and Becki felt an immediate wave of relief coming over her.

Becki stopped close enough to watch the sprinkler on the lawn with its myriad of droplets with miniature rainbows in the centre bouncing off in different directions. The water trickled down to water the red roses, the pink ones, the yellow ones, mother's dahlias and the little border plants with no flowers.

Becki strained her eyes to see a daddy-long-legs perched on the weeping willow tree at the top of her garden. Becki was frightened of daddy-long-legs with their funny green heads that looked like giant green pin heads. The daddy-long-legs seemed to stretch its long neck, looking from side to side before moving its long arms making it look like a witch doctor carrying an axe. The little creepy-crawly looked like he was wearing a green tuxedo. Becki did not want to move closer to the creature but was fascinated by it as it wilfully moved from a weak branch to a stronger branch.

In the corner of her eye she noticed that the daddy-long-legs had a guest to his party. The guest of honour also wore a tuxedo, dark, luxurious green with a beautiful, even texture. Daddy's guest sat lazily away from Mr daddy-long-legs as if embarrassed to be too early for the party. His sunglasses, red like the soles of Mr daddy-long-legs' wooden dance floor soon reflected

159

the light of his suit and he moved closer. The guest closed his eyes as if tired. He seemed to have a problem with one of his eyes and yawned, and when he yawned his tongue and throat were revealed making him lose his aloof sophistication and show who he really was.

Becki saw a long pink tongue move from the chameleon hiding behind the stronger branches grab the daddy-long-legs' neck, which snapped in one piece, the axe, the tuxedo and pin head disappeared into the guest of honour's mouth.

Goodbye Mr daddy-long-legs.

Becki was not sure whether she felt sorry for him or not; all she knew is that she had never liked daddy-long-legs, nor chongololos, nor the sly chameleons or the snakes at Chipangali.

Kieran

Kieran O'Connor

The wisdom and power of the planets is known and understood by a few people and ridiculed by many. It was not something that the Irish were known for but Kieran O'Connor had found a splendid joy in the subject from the first day his Grandfather had sat him down and told him the wonders of all different planets.

Kieran's Grandfather had set him his first exercises, which were designed to help him to understand how the planets so far away had affected his own parents' fate. Grandpa was always pragmatic and did not try to hide the truth about the reasons why he was not with his parents. He tried to teach him how fate was nearly always in the hands of the planets and Kieran hated to disagree.

'Does fate contradict free will, would you say Grandpa?' Kieran curiously enquired from the mountain of books. Grandpa was normally a laconic, gentle soul but to have such an eager student made him happy.

'Fate doesn't contradict free will my dear boy.' Grandpa spoke softly and slowly with the timeless wisdom of a man who has made mistakes and learnt from them. 'Free will was and is the ultimate gift that God gave to mankind. It is the freedom to explore the breadth of God's own infinite intelligence, the freedom to go beyond that even. Free will is the opportunity for God to discover himself through man.'

Kieran blinked and listened quietly; he always knew when Grandpa had more to say.

'Fate, however, is the path of the human soul on its journey to unite with the authentic source and the activities of the planets create a blueprint or a map that guides the soul back home.'

Kieran nodded silently.

Grandpa knew Kieran understood. Kieran was an old soul himself. Grandpa had tried to explain to Kieran that the horrible troubles that had marred his parent's union had been the act of fate and free will. Grandpa had told Kieran that he had chosen his mother. Every soul chooses the maternal human soul that would assist their journey back to the source.

Fallen Angel

Grandpa had been sitting in the warm breeze for what seemed like an eternity, watching the curvature of the sky reflecting every subtle tone of the sun's golden shadows. The clouds moved slowly and silently like giant cotton balls.

Grandpa sat quietly, humming gently to himself, listening to his own heartbeat beating in time with the universe. Kieran sat quietly watching Grandpa in his stillness and peace. Then Grandpa smiled with the love that Kieran found comforting. It made his demise feel less traumatic. Why he was here and not with his mother and father? How long would it take before he was with his beautiful mother looking into her chocolate brown eyes? Kieran couldn't hide from the ache he felt when he thought about his father: tall, handsome, funny. When could he sit with them both at the dinner table eating one of Papa's amazing suppers? His Ma and Pa always competed in the kitchen. Kieran's mother made amazing puddings while Pa was always king with the savoury dishes. Meals at home were always the best as Ma and Pa always strived to please Kieran.

Grandpa sensed Kieran's yearning and desire for his mother and father who meant everything to him. There were so many questions that were unanswered.

Grandpa tried to steer Kieran from his mood, which he sensed was dark and could get darker if he did not intervene.

'Son, one of the most beautiful things that can happen is when the sun is trine the moon in any relationship. This means the two bodies are 120 degrees apart and energy flows positively between the two.' Grandpa always seemed to sound like he was whispering; his sagacious baritone voice seemed to always command Kieran to listen.

Kieran always smiled attentively and wondered whether Grandpa had deliberately called him 'son' because he reminded him so much of his own son or whether his memory had faded.

'Oh really, what does that mean then?'

'It gives the relationship significance Kieran.'

'Do you want to know how Ma and Pa met?' Grandpa whispered to Kieran. 'This will explain fate to you.' Grandpa wanted to take his time to explain to Kieran how fate worked. 'There was a strong feeling of belonging to each other when they first met …' Grandpa stated almost to himself.

'Who did? Ma and Pa?' Kieran whispered back to Grandpa in a tone that let him know he wanted to hear more. May 21 was when Kieran's mother and father had met. It was an ordinary sunny day in Plymouth. Kieran's mother was still yearning to meet her soulmate. After weeks of blindly corresponding with Kieran's father they had decided to meet at her house for coffee. If he was half as beautiful as his picture, Kieran's mother knew she would be delighted. In his pictures, Kieran's father looked tall with broad shoulders and tanned skin. He had heart-stopping blue eyes that took centre stage on his captivating face, which was framed with thick movie star eyebrows and a lazy dimple on his right cheek.

'You have a beautiful soul' she had written to him when they first corresponded to each other. He had been flattered by her audacity and she knew she wanted to meet him and see if her intuition had been real or imagined. It was a Wednesday when they were going to meet. She had decided to take a day off and bravely meet him. She couldn't tell any of her friends that she was inviting a complete stranger into her home for an afternoon drink.

'Do you mind if I drink?' he had asked her on the phone the night before they met.

'Of course not.'

At 12:00 she had begun to get ready washing her face with the apricot scrub then putting on a face mask and waited for ten minutes before washing it off and drying her skin with a cotton wool ball. She hadn't eaten all morning and was unlikely to as the nerves had got the better of her. It was a warm day and she decided to wear a deep red polka dot dress reminiscent of the post-war fashion. Would he appreciate her Uranian quirkiness or simply think she was not sexy. She decided to leave her dress on and complement it with the burgundy platforms that automatically made her taller and accentuated her frame. She decided not to worry too much about her clothes as she had had two compliments about how alluring her dress was.

Kieran's mother decided to wear her new fragrance that she had bought in Assisi. It had the fresh, unusual appeal of an apple orchard in the summer infused with a secret pheromonal amine middle note that all men seemed to notice. They never noticed enough to want a date and that is why she had made the decision to find someone who she wanted. Looking in the mirror she decided that she looked as good as she could get: he would have to take her or leave her. If he didn't like her in the flesh it would be a case of nothing ventured nothing gained. A silver Mondeo pulled in front of her road at exactly 2pm, the time they had agreed. She avoided looking through the thick curtain and waited instead for the doorbell to disturb the wave of nerves in the pit of her stomach.

She opened the door with the type of salutation that would have made a passing stranger believe that they had known each other a lifetime.

'Hello,' he said looking at her with a beaming

dimpled smile. He was better looking in the flesh but thinner than his pictures. He was a little below 6 foot and wore a summer shirt and a pair of bleached denim jeans that were slightly too baggy. In his hands he carried a supermarket carrier bag and headed straight to the kitchen.

'How are you?' he said hiding his nerves. Without waiting for an answer he asked her the next question. 'Do you like Orangina. I know you don't drink but do you like Orangina, I brought some Orangina for you.'

'Oh, yes please,' she said unfolding her arms to reach for a glass from her top shelf cupboard.

The heat and buoyancy of summer was blazing against her whitewashed back wall although her north facing garden hardly got much sun. He unscrewed the bottle of vodka and poured it into his glass.

'Shall we sit outside for a bit?' Kieran's mother was instantly comfortable with his natural confidence. She didn't want the Orangina, it didn't really help her nerves and despite his confidence she knew that he was nervous too.

'So what do you do exactly?'

'Well I am looking to start my own exhibition, I am a photographer, I worked in media all my life ...'

'So who are you mentors?'

'Ansel Adams, have you heard of him?'

'Er no, should I?'

'He is the guy who said "A great photograph is one that fully expresses what one feels, in the deepest sense, about what is being photographed, and is, thereby, a true manifestation of what one feels about life in its entirety".'

'Do you like that?'

'Yeah, if I knew what it meant.' They both laughed.

His glass was full of Orangina and vodka and he talked for what seemed like ten minutes and time flew.

Kieran's mother had an instant attraction to the stranger she felt she had known all her life. 'One day my pictures will be known all over the world.' Kieran's Pa said confidently.

**

'Pa is very ambitious.'

'Grandpa, is it bad to be ambitious?'

'God was ambitious Kieran; he created the world, its creatures and the Planets in seven days.'

'Do you see the world? Take a look, Kieran. Do you see how big it is? God created ambition, it's not dirty, it's an expression of him.'

'But Grandpa, God also created the Devil, is Lucifer an expression of God? Grandpa, does this mean Lucifer and God are the same being?'

'No, no, young man.'

'Well ...?'

'Sometimes, Lucifer is expressed in certain aspects of man, but we can't speak of Lucifer himself. I am not sure that God himself has decided what to do with him Kieran. At times, Kieran, I pray for Lucifer. I can't help but feel sorry for the fallen angel.'

**

Grandpa was crying uncontrollably, he couldn't hide it from Kieran.

'What's wrong?'

'My son, my son ... I weep for my son and all that I could have done.'

'What do you mean?'

'Your Pa, Kieran, I made mistakes, I didn't protect him when I could have done.'

'What do you mean? Was Papa in danger? I am

169

confused. Is that why I am not going to see Papa and Mama, is that the truth?'

'I should have been there to protect him from the evil Henry, the man who wanted to protect God, he took away your Pa's innocence, in the blink of an eyelid he took away your Ma's innocence. That's what made them one. Yes, you see Kieran, that was it. Your Ma and Pa ... well their meeting was fated.' Grandpa continued.

'Do you believe in fate, Grandpa?'

Moon Square Venus

'Is love at first sight possible?'

'I don't know, Grandpa. Is it possible?' replied Kieran smiling knowing his Grandpa did not like questions being answered by questions. This is not how Irish children behaved at least. Even if Kieran was half-Irish.

'Are you saying Ma and Pa fell in love at first sight?'

'They met on a summer's day, your Ma was wearing a red and white polka dot dress like the ones they wore in the fifties,' Grandpa paused. 'She wore high heels that made her look taller, your Ma is a small girl you see, no more than yay high.' Grandpa demonstrated Kieran's mother's height by tapping the top his shoulder. 'Well it was love at first sight for your mother I must say.' Grandpa tilted his head to the left and pulled his upper lip down.

'So Pa didn't love Ma?'

'He loved her but not as immediately as she loved him. Ma was captivated by his blue eyes, his Irishness. There were many women who found him captivating and alluring.' Grandpa's voice rose softly. Kieran suspected that Grandpa was talking about himself more than his Pa.

'So they met on a summer's day ... as I said,' Grandpa corrected his posture and tone noticing that Kieran was drifting away into himself.

'The second day, your Pa even though he was drunk at the time, knew straight away that she was a soulmate, someone who would help him along his path.'

'How did ...?' Kieran was inquisitive but Grandpa cut in.

'Even though your Pa was half-cut at the time, he

called your Ma and said "I know that you are the one that is going to help me to get well". "Are you drunk?" your Ma had said as your Pa fell on the floor? "No I am not drunk at all?" your Pa said. Your Pa always denied when he had a drink.' Kieran's Grandfather chuckled to himself a rich, belly chuckle that made Kieran smile. The two of them stopped smiling when Kieran's Grandfather realised he had to explain to his grandson why he was laughing.

'Well I used to deny it with your Grandma, my Pa was the same, none of us ever wanted to admit we had a drink problem you see. Like father like son and maybe like grandson,' said Grandpa pointing his index finger at his grandson. 'No, no, no. Your mother will come for you Kieran and you will be her keeper and I think you are more like her, more studious, more of a philosopher, she will need you to be straight and dependable.' Grandpa seemed to take on a more serious tone all of a sudden.

'They fell in love very quickly after that second night he came over drunk and the third night he cooked her an amazing meal. Thai I think. That is daddy's speciality, they are both lovers of travel you see.' Grandpa continued his tale to a serious Kieran.

'Where did he go and where did she go?'

'Well your Pa went to Thailand many times, Japan, China, Cambodia, you name it he went there?'

'And Ma …?'

'Well Africa obviously, she had been to the United States, most of Europe, she loved India and had been there many a time.'

'Was Pa a good cook at the time, what did he cook?' Kieran asked as if he could not get enough of knowing about his parents.

'Pa did Pad Thai, Thai curries, Massaman curries, noodles, sushi that sort of thing.'

'What happened after their third meal?'

'It was June the 2nd, a few days before your Pa's birthday. Ma was very excited that she had met her opposite. A man that excited her and she wanted to make him happy on his birthday. She spent hours looking for a special card and gifts that said exactly what she thought of him.'

'Sounds like something happened, Grandpa,' Kieran said to his Grandpa when he noticed his body language wilting.

'On Monday night your Pa was babysitting your cousin Mary and could not talk to your Ma. On Tuesday when she called, he was drunk in a pub, maybe excited about his birthday, after all he was nearly 40 or maybe he just wanted to get drunk. Anyway she could not get any sense out of him whatsoever,' Grandpa continued.

'Was he in an Irish pub?'

'He was in an Irish pub for sure. He loved all things Irish, he always went back to County Mayo as often as he could to reconnect to his Irish blood.'

Then there was silence as though Grandpa had forgotten what he was going to say.

'And then what happened …' said Kieran in a loud over-excited whisper designed to wake Grandpa from his nodding mood without scaring him.

'It was his birthday …' Grandpa said softly looking as if he would fall asleep again.

'What happened?' Kieran's mind raced, wondering what awful thing could have happened.

'She couldn't get hold of him.'

'Is that it?'

'All day, on his birthday, she rang every 15 minutes. She was frantic; what had happened to this beautiful man she had just met.'

'Why didn't she call auntie's house?' said Kieran.

'Wellll … she didn't want to bother her, she didn't want to seem like she was a desperate soul.'

On Thursday, the day after his birthday at about 3pm, she had decided she would call his sister but only if she could not get hold of him before 5. She called and he answered.

'Where had he been Grandpa?'

'He had been with his best friend, his oldest school friend who he had not seen for a few years,' said Grandpa looking directly at Kieran.

'Now there is a story with his best friend. He was Spanish I think, he is called Rafa. Rafa was half-Spanish, half-English, his mother was from a rich family in Thurlestone in Devon. Rafa was very much bullied in school because you see when he first came he could hardly speak any English. So your dad you see, bless his heart, took him in and they became friends.'

'That was nice of Pa,' said Kieran with unyielding curiosity.

'Apart from the bullying at school and not being able to speak good English his mother and father had divorced and his Grandparents had cut her off from their will when they died so they were dirt poor. They lived in poverty and although we were not rich we often fed Rafa when his mother had gone to work in central London.'

'My Pa is great,' said Kieran smiling from ear to ear.

My Pa is great Kieran said to himself as if the greatness in his father's imagination was also his greatness.

'So that was his best friend Rafa. Rafa was damaged by all this and at one point in his life had tried to commit suicide, drank heavily and it was your Pa that came to his rescue.'

40, Softshell Crabs and Dreams

June, the month of golden sunshine and exams, seemed to bring warm rays and gentle winds into Kieran's mother's living room as she sat down making a list of what she wanted to prepare for his father's 40th birthday.

Today she believed in dreams, in holding on to dreams. He was exactly what she had dreamt of, his warm, crystal clear blue eyes, his golden brown skin, his smile.

It is important to stay true to your dreams and stay true to what you feel regardless of what anyone else says, she thought to herself sighing and enjoying the sun. The day was perfect. Kieran's father took away all of the heaviness of life, he made life what it was supposed to be. What it felt like at the beginning of time before karma's bitter lessons fossilised joy making it a relic.

She looked at tonight's shopping list which made her hungry and excited at the same time. The list had all her favourite food. How did he know she loved South East Asian food: galangal, ginger, kaffir leaves, coriander and coconut. He had insisted she get softshell crab, this was his favourite. He was amazed that she had never eaten it.

'Wherever I go, The Hilton in Tokyo, Four Seasons in New York, Thailand, whatever, you name it, I must have softshell crab.' She remembered him gesticulating wildly, his mouth forming an invisible 'o' to emphasise the exquisite taste.

Thinking of him made her stomach ooze with joy itself, seeing him felt like the first day when God said, 'Let there be light'.

The two of them drove through Exeter Street with its old and new buildings standing side by side. The old forlorn Charles Cross church had stood for over 50 years, naked, sepulchral and full of shame. Its Gothic edges were jagged and saw-like, its insides disembowelled and skeletal. She imagined the sound of six bells that were erected in 1709 tolling in synchronicity. It was hard to imagine the church packed full with over 1,000 people waiting to hear Dr Hawker's charismatic, lively sermons from his pulpit. She imagined little babies in their pure white smocks being baptised. The church had been violated by incendiary bombs during the war. The new buildings supported the weary, grey frame with its stoic, unscarred edges giving life to the tired St Charles church. Hidden in the coves of the industrial estate near Cattedown roundabout was PJ Foods, which she had discovered two weeks before. The shop serviced all the Chinese restaurants in Plymouth with an exotic oriental jamboree of things she had never seen before. Andy held her hand as they walked into the shop which smelt of aromatic Jasmine rice and star anise. The top of the open commercial fridge had colour-rich fruit and fresh vegetables all neatly stuffed in clear plastic bags. Pak choi, Chinese broccoli and pale green guavas in little white vests.

The bottom layer of the fridge had dozens of different varieties of tofu: vacuum-packed tofu, plain tofu, firm tofu, silken tofu, flavoured tofu, all kinds of tofu next to more tofu and fresh noodles.

'Hello there,' she said to Mani the Hong Kong Chinese lady owner of PJ Foods. When she said 'hello' she made sure that the Chinese lady owner of PJ Foods noticed the beautiful Andy next to her carrying an empty basket. She felt the Chinese lady's eyes following them as they sauntered to the first aisle with dried noodles. The Chinese lady was working hard unpacking boxes next to the till as if her life depended on it. In the freezer were frozen squid, frozen scallops, frozen prawns, frozen fish but no softshell crab. They decided to ask the owner, aware that she was trying to pretend not to notice them.

'Where are your softshell crabs? If you have them that is. I am obviously assuming that you have them,' he said looking at the shop owner as he oozed with charm and sweet handsomeness that made her proud. She wanted to parade him in the middle of Plymouth and shout 'He is with me, he is handsome isn't he?'

The shop owner carried on packing, unimpressed by his sweet handsomeness and shouted 'Hui' almost too quickly. At the same time she said something in Chinese that must have been to ask Hui the younger man crouching behind a box of glass jars full of different varieties of soy sauce. Soy sauce with low salt, light, brown, dark, soy sauce from China, Hong Kong, Vietnam or Japan.

'Here please,' Hui the Chinese worker in PJ Foods obeyed his boss with military precision. Andy followed him to the fridge freezer to the left of the store. As Andy followed Hui, she decided she was going to hang on to talk to the shop owner who seemed to be working like a robot.

'Busy today?'

'Not too bad, Saturday is always hard with every restaurant wanting something,' the shop owner said as her mercurial eyes darted about from the boxes to the floor, to the till and making eye contact with her for a second.

'New boyfriend?' the Chinese shop owner said, suddenly with a crooked , sly smile that unnerved her.

'Newish,' she replied twisting her mouth with her hand flat, horizontal and moving up and down to show her uncertainty.

'Very good-looking,' the Chinese owner said

continuing to pack, casting a glance at Andy and Hui deep in conversation about softshell crabs. She was glad that the Chinese owner had noticed Andy's startling blue eyes that sparkled like the diamonds against the backdrop of honeysweet tanned skin. She was glad of the affirmation and glad that her intuition was right. She knew that the Chinese shop owner had been eyeing them while pretending to pack and unpack boxes.

'Where did you meet him?'

'A friend of a friend,' she lied.

Silence.

Her brain tried to fill in the gap.

'He is a photographer and he took some photos for paintings that I was selling online.' She blinked, glad that her brain had worked fast enough. The only true words were 'photographer', 'paintings' and 'online'. Yes he was a photographer, yes she did sell paintings and yes they had met online. She left out that she had answered his ad for a 'No strings attached encounter' when she had had enough of her five-year celibacy. She left that out when she told the story to the Chinese lady owner.

'Too good to be true,' the Chinese shop owner lady said looking at her straight in the eye without a flinch of emotion.

'Sorry?' she said, she thought she had heard the Chinese lady owner say 'Sue gone too.' Who was Sue and where did she go?

'I said he is too good to be true in' he?' she said in a Cornish-London-Chinese blended accent.

'What do you mean?' she asked innocently.

'Well he is good-looking in' he? Too good to be true,' she repeated.

How dare she say that she thought, her thoughts forming a chaotic bombastic baritone, clanging hostile noise. Why burst her bubble?

Jealousy.

That's it, just jealousy, she thought to herself but didn't say that to her.

'We'll see,' she suddenly didn't want to carry on the conversation with the Chinese lady owner and walked towards Andy who had chosen a box of softshell crabs for £12. She told him straight out what the Chinese lady owner had said.

'You won't believe what that woman said,' she said picking up a box of softshell crab her eyes seeing the black and white plastic labelling but not focusing on it as she quickly put it back. Her interest was in making sure that Andy dispelled the sudden insecurity that she felt thanks to the Chinese lady owner's bubble-bursting antics.

What did she mean? What did lady Dim sum chi cho mean? Did she mean that Andy was too good-looking for her and that she was not good enough for him? Or that she was too ugly for Andy.

What did she mean?

Andy made her feel better by grabbing her hand and taking her to the till making sure that the Chinese lady owner saw his chivalrous actions. As the Chinese lady owner was serving two customers in front of them, he put the heavy shopping basket down, pulled her face to his and kissed her in full view of everyone in the shop.

When his statement had been made, Andy shuffled in his pockets and said to her, 'I am sorry I don't have any money, if you can pay for this one I will get the next one, it's just that my giro has not come in yet.'

She was not sure whether Dim sum Chi cho woman had heard Andy mention his giro. The Chinese lady shop owner looked disinterested and somewhat insulted by Andy's theatrical kiss. They paid for the shopping and drove through Cattedown roundabout with the sun

179

now cooling behind them as they turned right past St Jude's church.

By the time Andy was chopping garlic, galangal and preparing his coconut milk the Chinese lady had been forgotten. She was now looking forward to spending a blissful night with Andy with candles and softshell crab and dreams. Andy opened a bottle of Chablis to accompany his culinary art and played Stevie Wonder's greatest hits while heating a wok and singing at the top of his voice.

'*For once in my life I have someone who needs me.*'

He looked so handsome, the complete package, for a second she felt sorry for the softshell crab. Andy crushed white opaque crystals of sea salt and garlic in a grey and white pestle and mortar.

'*Someone I needed so long, for once unafraid ...*'

She watched him rip open the softshell crab, pulling its soft, cotton wool thread like insides. He looked like he had done it before. The kitchen smelt of fresh garlic, pungent and inviting, the aroma of ginger softened the garlic, fresh red chillies and chopped coriander made her hungry.

'*I can go where life leads me and somehow I know I'll be strong.*' Stevie and Andy sang an impromptu duet that sounded like the version that had been sung by The Temptations in 1967.

'*For once I can say this is mine you can't take it, long as I know I got love I can make it,*' he screeched theatrically knowing that she was watching him. He was on stage for her. She loved that song which was as old as she was. The song had been sung so many times by different artists starting from Jean Dushon, then Stevie Wonder, then The Temptations, Tony Bennett and even Frank Sinatra. Anyone who was anyone had done a cover of that song but none could do it the way Steve the Wonder. She looked at Andy dancing away, fleetingly losing himself. He carefully chopped some spring onions to go with the garlic and ginger. She could not remember the last man that had taken such control of the kitchen.

Irfan her first love always brought home his mother's keema with peas. While Juan Carlos her six-month fling from Andalucía sometimes cooked the fish they had caught in Cadiz. Daniel from Cameroon had made her a lamb stew that he had learnt from his French mother. Then there was Giles who was supposedly a chef at one point in his life, did he ever cook for her? If he did she did not remember. It didn't matter Andy cooked, Andy cooked exotic stuff from all his trips in South East Asia, Australia, Europe and that was all she cared about. Andy drank the rest of his wine and sang softly the way Ella Fitzgerald had sung live in Berlin in 1968.

'This is sho nuff mine, you can't take it, long as I know I got love.'

It wasn't long before Andy beckoned her to sit down in her dining room. The softshell crab was salty. Very salty. She did not say anything, he was too busy telling her about a meeting he had once had in Hong Kong where he had had the best softshell crab. He opened another bottle of Chablis and she sipped her ginger beer.

'Anyway it was the most amazing suite in the whole of the Hilton in Hong Kong ...' She ate what tasted like a cube of salt with a molecule of softshell crab in silence. 'They have so many ways of dressing it, the best way was with chilli and this sauce done by this amazing chef. He was the best chef in the world who had apparently cooked for Prince Charles and Di ... well royalty in general.'

She could not believe how he could talk such long sentences without pausing for breath.

181

'Is the softshell crab salty?' he asked her at the very moment she thought that it was too salty but could not tell him.

'A little bit.'

'Don't eat it then, don't worry, I won't be offended,' he said looking straight into her eyes to show that he meant it.

'Really?' she said surprised that he had even noticed.

'Yeah of course really, I think it's salty too anyway,' he said and picked up his glass of wine to neutralise the saltiness in his mouth.

She was glad that the main course was less of a Shakespearian tragedy or even a Dostoevsky feast but a simple Thai red curry with coconut milk and sticky rice. Suddenly out of the blue in a whirlpool of silence Andy said, 'Do you want to have children?'

She looked up, shocked and unprepared.

'What?' she said her heart beating with gooey, thick, sweet syrupiness.

'You heard me,' he said looking straight into her soulmate's soul with the same seriousness he had had a few minutes ago.

'Do you mean with you?' He didn't answer but tilted his head, his hands untightening from their steeple clasp. 'It would be an honour to have your baby,' she said, emphasising the 'You' in a suddenly bold whisper that came out unfiltered. He stared at her like he had just seen a ghost; she could not decipher his expression. Did he think she was insane? For once she did not regret *not* editing her truth but stated it with pride.

'What would you call our child?' Andy asked her.

'If it's a girl she has to have an Irish name like Sinead, or Siobhan or even better Niamh,' she said, her anxiety dissolving when she realised that he was not thinking she was mad.

'I like Niamh,' he said his smile revealing even teeth stained a little by the tannins in the Chablis.

'Did you know that Niamh is spelt N –I –A –M –H even though it rhymes with eve,' she proudly showed off her knowledge of Celtic names.

'Really? No way, how do you spell it?' he asked genuinely curious. She spelt it again.

'N –I –A –M –H.'

'Cool, I should know that I am Irish,' he said sipping and then gulping his wine and quickly filling it up before it was empty.

'What if it's a boy?' he quickly filled the small gap that would have made her notice that he had almost finished his second bottle of wine.

'I don't know another Irish name. I like Kieran, I always have.'

'Kieran?' he asked making it sound like a question that was uncertain of its identity. 'Kieran,' he said suddenly as if he had discovered the whole point of his existence.

Birthday

Andy was born on the 6th of June and today he was turning 40. He was a true Gemini: exciting, intelligent and witty. To celebrate his birthday, Kieran's mother thought of a million beautiful ways to let him know she loved him. She had spent three days in Cornwall finishing off coastline canvasses that had been commissioned by a wealthy Cornish family in the Cayman Islands.

A sudden breeze made her look into the distance, her eyes now mesmerised by the green, grey moors that stretched as far as the eye could see into Dartmoor. She could understand why the mysterious timelessness had inspired Sir Arthur Conan Doyle to write the *Hound of the Baskervilles*. Dartmoor had a mixture of beauty, danger and seduction in equal measure.

To her left she could see the expanse of the shimmering sea extending into Cornwall. How she wished she was with Andy. She wanted to show him St Mawes, Fowey, Tintagel but she especially wanted him to hear the thunderous waves of Bude.

She loved Bude and its romantic grey igneous rocks and layers of almost black lichen forming an unruly thick blanket that hugged the coastline. A sudden gust of wind forced her to focus on the bold brushstrokes of burnt yellow sedimentary rock with layers of ancient iron protruding through.

She remembered the first time the coastline had revealed its frightening beauty which had spontaneously made tears flow from her heart. How could such a sight make her cry, it was not beauty as we knew it. It had no symmetry, no clean lines, perfect circles, 90-degree angles or pure colours. This made her question all that was beauty? Why were humans brainwashed into believing that beauty was an aspiration and an absolute. Beauty was everything she was sitting in the middle of: chaotic, rugged, compulsive, exhaustive and yet infinite at the same time.

The rugged coastline made her fearful. Humans often fear that which is not perceived as beautiful. It goes back to Adam and Eve and the serpent and the first day that fear became an enemy of love.

What if she fell behind the great rocks? What if she met a dead body? What if she met a serial killer? What if the slimy black green seaweed turned into venomous snakes with only the desire to kill and destroy?

From that moment on she decided she would always walk towards fear and look it in the eye. The rocks ahead looked menacing, the path behind looked more even and less daunting. It might be easier to take one step at a time towards her fear or one step back and never taste victory. As she walked one step in front of the other each hard rock behind her became even, surmountable and less daunting. The further she walked she saw more beauty, God's own canvas of colours and interpretation.

For now she was in love with Andy and packed her paintings in the studio and drove as fast as she could to buy him something that would hopefully help him to realise that she loved him. He was going to be the father of her children and she knew that from the first time she met him. In her car she played a CD by Luther Van Dross that put her in the mood.

If this world were mine
I would place at your feet all that I own
You've been so good to me.

That song made her weep from the first time she heard it. She had never met anyone else that loved that song as much as she did until she met Andy. The only problem was that she liked this modern contemporary version which he felt violated the original that had been sung by Luther Van Dross and Roberta Flack. She could not deny that he may have a point but what mattered to her is that they both loved the same song and she had never met anyone else who loved that song as much as he did.

She rushed to the main department store to get Andy's present. The canvas of love had led her to the fragrance counter. She was glad that the sale of masculine scents was back. She was not sure that she enjoyed the proliferation of androgynous aqua scents that blurred the line between the Ying and the Yang. The new Gucci for men with its signature blue was exactly the mixture of smells that celebrated all that Andy meant to her. The only smell that muted all the other smells was sandalwood; every time she smelt it she was taken away into the middle of North Cornwall and its rugged coastline and healed by the waves of the Atlantic. She found her mind cleared, her purpose purified by the smell of sandalwood like no other smell that she had ever smelt.

She found a beautiful shirt by Paul Smith; she knew he loved Paul Smith. It was casual, with blue chequers that she knew would match his eyes. It took her exactly 15 seconds to spot the shirt just as the shop was about to close. She hated browsing in shops and loved it when it was just about to close and force her into a crisis that would make her find a solution. Within the last announcement that the shop was closing she found a beautiful handmade card in black and white made from velvet and silk material glued on to shimmery white paper. The image was of a silhouetted, vaudeville dancer wearing a black lacy dress and feathery headgear. Her dainty hands were covered in velvet gloves holding a white fan with the left hand and lifting the voluminous dress with the right hand. She had never seen such beauty in such a short space of time and her heart sang. She knew that he would be as happy as she was about this amazing find; she wouldn't tell him that she had waited till the last minute.

She wanted to write him a poem and the only one she could find was by Oscar Wilde, 'The Ballad of Reading Gaol'. She loved the poem but was not sure about the words.

Some love too little, some too long
Some sell, and others buy
Some do the deed with many tears
And some without a sigh
For each man kills the thing he loves
Yet each man does not die.

She thought about a poem by Sylvia Plath and contemplated why she was so attracted to such tragic writers and poets. She put down the heavy book on Oscar Wilde's work and picked up the complete works of Sylvia Plath which had a haunting black and white picture of the poet with sad penetrating eyes.

She stumbled on the poem 'Never try to trick me with a kiss', which had a promising title but didn't convey the tender love that she wanted to put into his birthday card. She had never related to Sylvia Plath's work at school but related to the depth of feeling for Ted Hughes. She shut her eyes and the words came to her like a waterfall.

But I, being poor have only my dreams;
I have spread my dreams under your feet
Tread softly because you tread on my dreams
WB Yeats.

How could she forget those words that she had studied and been mesmerised by. She had always had romantic fantasies about Irish authors and remembered

187

fondly her school trips to visit the James Joyce museum and debating with her friends about the meaning of *Ulysses* and *Finnegan's Wake*. From that time she had developed a mild obsession with all things Irish and could distinguish different Irish faces at a glance.

She found the only poem that could fit as easily as she had found the sandalwood scent and Paul Smith shirt. She knew he would be pleased when he got the poem, the scent and the shirt. She tried to call him again and got the answering machine. Where was he? She was tempted to call his sister. She had met his sister only once and did not feel comfortable enough with her to intrude on their privacy. When she called for the sixth time he did pick up and sounded a little drunk.

'Where are you?' she enquired speaking loudly to compensate for the noise in the background that she could hear. It was obvious.

'Harrr-lo,' he sounded happy to hear from her.

'Where are you?' She shouted again.

'My sister has organised a surprise, my best friend is here from London, are you at work?'

She felt a little embarrassed to be gatecrashing his party but at the same time happy that he was celebrating.

'Oh that's nice ...' she said wanting him to know she really didn't mind that he had not included her. She was happy that he was happy.

'Hello.'

'Hello.'

'You there?'

'Hello!'

The phone went dead. Maybe he had a bad signal. She tried to ring him again and the phone went to voicemail. For the rest of that evening she could not get him on his phone. She tried several times all evening and gave up at 10:30pm.

She cancelled the reservation at Edmund Davari's *Zuccha* restaurant which she knew he would love. The staff at *Zuccha* were always friendly and warm and cancelled the reservation without incident. She eventually fell asleep after tossing and turning for three hours.

In the morning at work she tried his phone again. No doubt he was asleep after spending his 40th with his sister and best friends. She decided not to try again. For some reason she felt ill and rung work and told her boss she would take a day off. Her boss understood. She knew exactly what she would do, she would get her hair done. Braids were all the rage these days and she knew a kind African lady called Merci from the Ivory Coast who had plaited her friend's hair.

Merci was free and was able to come over to braid her hair. Kieran's mother was always pleased about what she achieved at the last minute without too much planning. Merci was not very talkative and after a few conversations about her college course and her 16-year-old son she gave up.

When the hair was finished the two women were both pleased by the long curly streaked extensions that made her look glamorous and tall and complemented her skin tone. She felt beautiful and hoped that Andy would love it as much as she did. After she paid Merci a measly £60 for six hours of hard work she knew that she had got away lightly. In London the same time and effort would have cost her double that. On her way from dropping Merci at her home near Devonport she decided to try Andy again. Surely he would answer; surely he would have woken up from his hangover by now.

'Hi.'

'Hello,' he answered sounding a little tired.

'Did you have a nice birthday?'

'Yeah great, I was with my friend that I was telling you about, you know my best friend, remember? Well I just couldn't believe it. He flew down from London and surprised me.'

'Wow!' she said with a little too much enthusiasm that hid the disappointment that she could not spend his birthday with him.

'I have told you about Vernon right?'

'Think so.'

'Well he is my best friend ever, I have known him all my life and when last year I saved his life in er, er ... near Utrecht when a boat we were on capsized and he couldn't swim you see.'

'Wow, that's heroic.' She wished she would stop saying wow but found herself saying it every time he said anything.

'I think he thinks he still owes me, no matter how many times I say look man you would have done the same if it was me…'

'Did you have a good time?'

'FAN-TA-STIC.' He overemphasised all the elements of the word fantastic leaving her in no doubt that she had no room to complain about her not being able to get hold of him.

'I am glad you did. Is Vern with you? Do you call him Vern?'

'Oh God he hates that. Only Vernon. When you meet him don't call him that, he will kill you.'

'OK Vernon then, has Vernon gone back?'

'Yeah he had to go back today, he is going straight to work can you believe it, he has a meeting with a bank manager.'

'What does he do?'

'He is a painter and decorator and a rebel.'

'Really?'

'He comes from a very wealthy family. They own quite a bit of real estate in Chelsea and Mayfair, he went to Harrow, his brothers went to Oxford, one of his sisters married a Sheikh, so quite a well-heeled family.'

'Wow,' she couldn't believe it, the wow had come out so spontaneously.

'You didn't ask why he is a rebel.'

'Why is he a rebel?'

'He is a rebel because he is the only one in his EN-TI-RE family who did not go to Oxford or Cambridge,' he overemphasised the word entire again like he had each syllable of fantastic.

'The black sheep of the family then,' she said nonchalantly.

'Well I didn't want to be racist.'

'That's not racist.'

'Well what I wanted to say is that he is rich so he can afford to pay for an expensive hotel at the drop of a hat to show his gratitude.'

'That's nice. Where did you go?'

'Where are you right now?' he asked after telling her about the wonderful food they had had in the Kitley House Restaurant.

'At home, where are you?'

'Mutley, Vernon just dropped me off. Can you come and pick me up, I am at the bus stop.'

'Which bus stop?'

'Mutley, you know, just opposite the Quaker house.'

'I know where it is …' she said happy that she would see him again soon.

'OK see you in a few.'

She loved it when he said 'See you in a few'. On the way she couldn't help but worry about what he was going to think about her new hairstyle.

'Buongiorno,' he said in his fake Italian accent reminding her of his many travels to Italy.

'Wow,' he said as he banged the door shut looking at her.

'Wow what?' she said looking in the rear view mirror narrowly missing Bus No. 62 going towards West Park. He looked her hair up and down to the side and raised his eyebrows.

'Just wow,' he said.

She noticed that he had the same quizzical look that he had when she told him that she wanted to have his baby. She did not know what that look meant. A part of her wanted to believe that it was a look of admiration though another part thought that she was way off the mark. An awkward silence followed them as they turned past the newly refurbished Hyde Park pub.

'Lovely suit,' she decided to break the silence. The suit was a dark navy blue with thin pinstripes that screamed of quality and finesse.

'Paul Smith, cost £1,000, beautiful isn't it?' he said in one breath and with great pride.

'It is beautiful,' she said. In the back of her mind she thought how ordinary she must look, all that effort and she hadn't even managed to look that great for him. He looked so beautiful, stunning in fact, his startlingly clear blue eyes now sharpened by summer light and the reflection of his corn blue shirt.

The same haunted look came back to his face when he opened his presents. He thanked her and eased her ubiquitous insecurity by making love to her. This was a part of him that made him irresistible: his beauty mixed with his passionate love making made her love and want him more than ever.

**

Andy had fallen asleep by 10:30pm, the earliest he had fallen asleep since she had met him three weeks ago.

While he snored gently she turned on her computer to look up Kitley House hotel in Yealmpton just outside Plymouth. The picture on the website showed a luxurious building in an expansive estate surrounded by manicured gardens and magnificent trees. It was used for weddings, events, theme nights, casino nights and performances. She clicked on the link for Accommodation, which showcased Four-Poster Rooms, State Rooms, Club Family Rooms, Doubles and Singles. She then clicked on the link under the maroon navigation bar which said 'Kitley House Restaurant' in a verdana font in white. The menu took a while to load and she wondered if Vernon and Andy had slept in a twin room or two separate rooms. She expected to see a menu but all it had was the different prices for a three-course meal, £29.50, or a two-course dinner for £21.95. Eventually she came across a list of what they served:

Stuffed quail
Confit pheasant leg
Dartmoor venison loin
Blackberry essence
Creamed celeriac

The picture on the top of the page was a trio of South Devon game which was next to what looked like the blackberry essence or perhaps a pool of blood.

She sighed, resenting the tapping noise that had woken her up from a deep sleep, it was only 2am. Sometimes she wondered if there were spirits in the house. When she had told her father about it he said that's what old Victorian houses did. They breathed and most stupid people thought it was ghosts. He did not believe in ghosts or God or any paranormal activity. As she crept downstairs she tried not to make any noise. She didn't even know what she was going downstairs for. It's not as if she was going to make a cup of tea or coffee. It was probably the too many cups of tea and coffee that she drank that had kept her up.

She had lost a day, his birthday, but hopefully they would make up for it by going to some of her favourite places in Cornwall and meeting all her friends. She couldn't wait to show all of them that she too could find a man. Not just any man but a gorgeous, handsome, passionate and artistic man.

The kitchen was clean and tidy and the ginger and white cat did its catwalk across her back wall as soon as she lit the kitchen light. On the grey and black marble worktop was the usual bottle of wine that Andy always had when he came over to her house. Next to the bottle a lost cork smeared with faint red marks from the wine, a thick gold paper foil and a corkscrew. Next to the corkscrew was Andy's old phone. She picked it up and wondered why he did not get a slicker more modern phone.

She turned the phone over, flipped it open to see all the icons for Applications, Calendar, Address Book, Clock, Call History, Settings and Messages. Before she knew it her fingers had clicked, clicked, clicked up and down to see the same name.

Imp.

Imp.

Imp.

The messages went all the way down and she decided to click on the most recent one which said.

'I am home safe now, Gatwick was a nightmare.'

The next message said.

'A little hungover but OK.'

She felt guilty for spying on him but wondered who 'Imp' was.

She remembered the telephone number for Kitley House and found herself automatically dialling, not caring that it was 2:30am in the morning.

'Hello,' a young girl answered sounding as though she was sitting right next to the phone which made her feel less guilty.

'Hello,' she answered her heart beating fast and making her voice slightly shaky.

'Hello, my name is Karina Short, my brother Andy was at your hotel on the 6th but is in hospital after being mugged and hurt. He apparently left his passport and wallet in his room.'

'Do you know what room he was in?'

'No I am not sure, he doesn't remember, can you check against his name.'

'OK, hold the line.' She was surprised how easy that was. She waited for a few minutes while the receptionist checked her list.

'I am sorry there is no one by that name?'

'Did you use Andy or Andrew?'

'I typed in the name Short and that name didn't come up.'

'Oh, his friend booked silly me, his surname is Hoyt.'

'How do you spell that?'

'H-O-Y-T.'

'H-O-Y-T,' she repeated and went silent again for a few minutes. She heard a noise as the receptionist came back on the line.

'No Hoyt, sorry.'

'He was definitely there; he had dinner at the restaurant, he told me had a steak or something, he was definitely there.'

'I was working that evening, it was busy but I might be able to remember if he was here.'

'Tall, slim, good-looking, blue eyes with a slight tan, he might have been wearing glasses.'

'Hmmm it was busy though but I don't remember

two men.' She paused and then said, 'tell you what why don't you leave me your number I will ask my boss to check the safe and let you know if there is a passport or wallet.

She was now very puzzled. What reason would Andy have to lie about going to Kitley House? This didn't make any sense at all. She went back to the kitchen and wrote down the phone number that corresponded to the name 'Imp'. Who was Imp? She tossed and turned all night and woke up to her phone alarm at 8:00am. Andy didn't have the keys to his sister's house and had wanted to stay while she was at work. She was not sure she could trust him and decided to drop him off at his sister's work place.

She watched his beautiful graceful silhouette in his Paul Smith suit that made him look like he meant business. He carried a leather briefcase with clothes from his Kitley trip. Anyone looking would imagine this handsome man walking down the road with a briefcase had business papers and an Audi or BMW in the car park. Inside his briefcase she knew there was a litre of vodka that he would drink later.

Tread Softly

She couldn't remember exactly how she became addicted to nicotine but she had never been able to stop smoking successfully. She hated being a nicotine addict just marginally more than she hated nicotine itself. During the day it made her drowsy and lethargic and she only smoked it when she was stressed. Most of the smokers in the smoking 'bus stop' were pathologically miserable, with a grey, sallow pallor to their skin, unruly hair and untidy appearances. She hated being associated with them; most of them had very little to say and often stared at the ground while puffing their cigarettes. It was a tribe of 'no hope' people who seemed to have submitted to the fact that life had no joy so why bother.

Sometimes she tried to make conversation but found it futile. It was either one-word answers or they would simply give you their expert opinion on what you had asked and then turn their backs to smoke in peace. Occasionally you had the talkers who would talk endlessly about changing the engine on their car, or their new kitchen or their nasty boss; she often got the sense that they didn't notice that she was there. She might as well be a tree stump. If she stood on her head or simply walked away they would carry on talking and puffing nitrosamines, benzene, carbon monoxide. Smokers. She hated them. She hated coming to the miserable smoking bus stop but it was the only way to stop thinking about Kitley House and 'Imp'.

When she got back to her desk she found a message from Andy saying that he had got home safely.

Look at this email I sent to Vernon telling him all about your poem.' She read through the email thread.

Andy>>Hope all's well mate, would like you to

meet her soon when you come.

Vernon>>Would love to man.

Andy>> Check out this poem she wrote by WB
Yeats.

But I, being poor have only my dreams;
I have spread my dreams under your feet
Tread softly because you tread on my dreams.

FWD:>>> He is looking forward to meeting you
babe. He is my best friend ever. I was thinking of
cooking you a nice 28 day hung steak and snuggling up
to you.

She was proud that he was telling his best friend all
about her. Maybe Vernon was Imp. She typed in 'Imp'
in Google and the words 'Interface Message Processor'
and a description for folklore creatures came up. None
of this made any sense. She remembered a model in the
sixties called 'The Imp'. Was this a play on the word
'Nymphomaniac'. She felt like she was going mad.
This was all she had thought about all day.

She didn't reply to his email and decided to go
home early at 3:30pm. It was dishonest of her to be
sitting at work while her brain had checked out and she
was Googling irrelevant rubbish now and again. She
knew that if they were eating a 28 day hung steak she
was likely to be buying it. The last thing on her mind
was a 28 day hung steak on Wednesday. Her head was
thumping when she got home; she switched off her
phone and unplugged her landline. This was that time
of the day when cold callers called non-stop and she
was not in the mood for screaming obscenities at them
which sometimes gave her some satisfaction. If she felt
better she would think about the steak and buy it from a
supermarket. She promised herself she would not be

buying any wine for Andy. She had done that too often and she could not imagine him having his steak without a bottle of quite expensive red wine.

She closed the thick burgundy curtains in her bedroom. She tried to forget Andy and sleep but couldn't. Within five minutes she got up and rang the number on her post-it note.

'This is O2's messaging system, the person you have called ...' She rang off before she could leave a message, relieved that the other person had not picked up the phone. She went downstairs and decided she was going to cook her favourite food, tarka dhal and aubergine sabji with rice.

She soaked and washed the pink lentils and sliced potatoes to go with the aubergines. She never bothered to peel the potatoes, it always took too much time. In the potato pan she added some turmeric which she never measured, just enough to give the potatoes some colour. She had learnt to cooked sabjis from her best friend Jyoti, a Gujarati girl she had met at university.

While the potatoes were boiling she soaked a cup full of basmati rice. It was amazing how white the water was and the number of rinses it needed. Her father had always said to her that the problem with basmati rice is that it was caked with clay and additives. As she rinsed it out she realised she didn't care about clay, it was the best rice in the world with or without clay.

In her pestle she crushed two whole cloves of garlic; she had stopped trying to crush the cloves with their jackets on and take them off afterwards, it just didn't work. She couldn't be bothered with onions in her sabjis, they just didn't add anything, so she just covered the aubergines with olive oil and put the gas hob on. The problem with aubergines is that they are greedy for oil but it is better to put more oil than less and strain it afterwards if the aubergines decided they had too much. As the aubergines were heating up in not too hot a heat she peeled a little ginger about the same amount in weight as the garlic or perhaps just a little more as garlic tended to like to hog the limelight while ginger was happy to play the supporting actor with grace and dignity.

As the aubergine heated up and became intimate with the vegetable oil, she added a mixture of mustard seeds, ajwon or onion seeds, and fenugreek seeds. She simply followed her heart as to what was enough. While the mustard seeds were starting to pop she covered the frying pan with a lid to seal the flavours. She opened the kitchen door to let the smoke out and stop the sensitive alarm from going off. When the onion seeds had stopped popping she added the ginger and garlic and stirred and covered the pan as she knew that the seeds and the garlic would mature and create a new flavour. She put the dhal on the hob and turned it on before the aubergine and spices finished maturing their flavours she added a teaspoonful of ground jeera. She had stopped adding ground coriander to her sabjis as she felt that they didn't add anything to the performance. It was like having an extra walking across the final stages of *Madame Butterfly* for no apparent reason apart from the fact that they could. In fact at times she felt ground coriander positively spoilt the sabji.

She did however add it to the dhal along with the ground jeera and allowed it to boil. Chilli however was an important part of the sabji—well, salt and chilli. Dried chilli, fresh chilli, green chilli, red chilli as long as it had personality and a presence. She never ever bought the thick-skinned chilli that came from South America. They were a little conservative and somewhat shy and acted like security guard dogs with muzzles.

The smell, texture and taste of the aubergines told her that she could add the boiled potatoes which were now softer but not too soft. Together they mixed with spices to form a single flavour that would be enhanced by freshly chopped coriander and tomatoes. The coriander was the secret ingredient, the tomatoes could be left out if they were not available but they would always be welcomed.

The rice cooked in the rice cooker and the dhal boiled away in its muted mixture of cumin and coriander. She decided to prepare a *chonk* for the dhal. She didn't always do this but for some reason she wanted to go all the way. Sometimes she loved her dhal to be *saatvic* without any ginger, garlic or chilli. This was the best way to enjoy a peaceful diet that was conducive to meditation and prayer.

To a large stainless steel serving spoon which had been used to *chonk* hundreds of times, she added far too much ghee for one person but she loved ghee. She remembered watching her friend's mother making her own ghee by removing water and milk over a pot of boiling water in an open fire with patience and skill. She blamed her for her love of ghee as she had told her that it was important in Ayuverdic medicine for promoting a balance of the doshas.

For now the ghee melted and she added the last of the remaining ginger and a healthy pinch of cumin seeds. In a separate frying pan, she was frying the onions that she had cut crudely into rings. They were now caramelising and soft and she scooped them and added them to the pot of dhal which was now a uniform soup simmering gently on the free-standing cooker.

The ghee bubbled like yellow molten lava spitting out the hot cumin seeds and then gently embracing them again like the prodigal son in the bible. The pungent aroma fused with the aromatic smells of the aubergine and potato sabji. For fifteen minutes while she cooked these dishes she had cooked thousands of times she had forgotten about Andy, the 28 day hung steak, Kitley House and Imp. She had also forgotten to re-plug her phone as she had not slept after all. She switched on her phone. There was a text message from Andy.

'Where are you? Steak?'

He sent another text message.

'BTW if you don't mind can we get some vino too x.'

She didn't feel like steak, she didn't feel like driving to pick him up, it was six o'clock. The person she had rung who was at work earlier would be home. She ignored his message and without hesitation she rang the number.

'Hello,' a deep but definitely female voice answered.

'Hello, sorry erm, this is, erm, I am Andy's girlfriend, I just wondered who you were. Your number is in his phone and I saw a few of your text messages and wondered who you were.'

'Oh dear ,that's Andy for you he never mentioned he had a girlfriend, he kept that to himself.'

'So how do you know him?'

'I am his ex-girlfriend, we were together for two-and-a-half years and then on and off for another two.'

'Well he has mentioned Isabelle, Kirsty and Shelley, the girl he was with for almost ten years but he has never mentioned anyone called Imp.'

'Imp is Isabelle, that's me.'

'Oh.' She felt stupid that she had not guessed that.

'I was with him two days ago at Kitley House.'

'Oh,' the bottom of her world fell and crumbled into wafer-thin useless pieces.

'I am sorry but that's how he is; he never mentioned

202

he had a girlfriend.'

'He told me he was with Vernon.'

'No, he was with me.'

'Oh my God.'

'Where are you?'

'I live close to London,' she sensed that Isabella did not want to tell her of her exact location. 'He pressured me into coming down for his 40th and suggested Kitley House. I paid for everything.' There was a hint of regret and bitterness when Isabella said 'I paid for everything.'

Imp=Isabella not Vernon. She felt raw and uncontainable and picked up the phone to dial Andy's number.

'Buongiorno.'

'Fuck off with that buongiorno shit. Speak fucking English.'

'Whoa, whoa, whoa—what's happened to you?'

'Who is Imp?'

'Imp, that's Isabella—what's the matter? Why are you swearing? Calm down.'

'No I am not going to calm down you fucking piece of shit Andy.' By now she was sure that the old lady and her husband next door could hear her swearing and screaming.

'Where were you on your birthday?'

'Kitley House, I told you.'

'With Vernon?'

'Yes, with Vernon. I can give you his number if you like?'

'OK give me his number'

'Well I can't. It's on the phone but you can call his house and talk to his missus, he will probably be out on a job still, he works late,' he said in his usual breathless style.

'So he will confirm that you were with him on your

203

birthday?'

'He should do because I was …'

'Guess what you lying piece of giro shit. I spoke to Imp your ex and she told me you were together you lying son of a bitch.'

'How did you get her number?'

'Does it matter?'

'How did you get her number? Did you go through my phone?' It was his turn to scream while she went quiet.

'I knew you were lying; your story just did not add up about Kitley House and your rich friend and all that bollocks.'

'I don't believe it; you went through my fucking phone. I don't believe it.'

'What's worse? That I sat here worried sick about you while you were not picking up your phone. Or that I checked your phone? What's worse motherfucker?'

Before he could answer the phone she shouted in a voice that she herself did not recognise.

'I spent £150 on you and booked a restaurant while you were shagging some whore called Imp.'

'It was booked long before I met you, I am sorry.'

'You fucking asshole,' she screamed unable to believe his temerity as the tears came down her eyes, her heart ripped into two pieces.

Again.

The Chinese lady in PJ Foods was right and she was wrong: he was too good to be true.

Maya

Illusion

At the age of 37, Maya knew she had to stop searching for the truth outside herself. She had known for a while that her life in London had long run its course and had become a *Maya,* which means an illusion in Sanskrit. She could no longer stomach the endless meaningless conversations with people who were pretending to listen, but were only waiting to have their say. She would not miss the guileless architecture, the grey sky, the millions of grumpy commuting robots and their free newspapers.

She had made up her mind to go to Rishikesh in the foothills of the Himalayas but before she could make the plunge she had to say goodbye to her elderly step father. The train ride through the Dawlish coast was always a meditative experience for Maya. There were no two scenes that had ever been the same. The iron ore sheer cliffs stared over the calm silvery shimmer of the waves that crashed against the biscuit coloured beach. A lone walker with a dog stared at the waves and the distant boats. Maya remembered the days that she had gone through the coast as black thundering clouds poured out sheets of rain over frothy waves. There were days when the sun shone so brightly that the sea would be glimmering like hundreds of tiny fragments of glass dazzling satisfied sunbathers.

Maya looked at her own reflection in the mirror; it had taken her years to get used to her own face, her inner truth which was staring back at her. It was true that her hair was a dark brown and blonde and looked like a carpet of autumn leaves. Her eyes were brown at the moment but if she wanted she could have hazel or blue eyes with the most expensive contact lenses that money could buy. The bridge of her nose was no longer like a lion but more aquiline. This had made breathing unbearable in humid conditions and worse still on aeroplanes.

During the taxi ride from the station Maya fell into a deep, blue-white dreamless sleep that could have only lasted no more than three minutes as the taxi driver stopped inside the gates of Mannamead House where her elderly stepfather was resident.

Mannamead House was an old Georgian mansion the colour of strawberry pink ice lollies. All the windows were closed and most of the thick, faded curtains shut tight against the windows. The window frames were painted a dirty fuchsia-red. The small front door made of wood and glass was awkwardly placed on the side of the house and did not match the overwhelming stature of the rest of the house. The rest of the mansion had an awkwardness about it. From certain angles the house looked tilted. The oak tree in the front yard had grown so much that its branches were pushing against the roof of the house and the upper wall creating a tense conflict between the house and the foliage. The roots of the tree had forced their way through the cracks of the cement making them look like they were suffocating.

Maya rang the doorbell which was opened by a young blonde girl she had never met before. The place had not changed since she had last seen her step father a month ago, the longest she had ever been away from him. The inside of Mannamead House was packed full with octogenarian inmates.

The same smell of urine and over-cooked cabbage clung heavily to the grey air. Maya was welcomed by the same tiny old lady with mismatched socks and a pink cardigan that was not buttoned up properly. In the far right corner was old Jim shuffling down the sloping edge of the brown and white floral carpet that matched the sofas and the curtains. It was the same sound of voices of care staff trying to shove down unwanted medicine and potions to the old people sitting in the corner of the living room staring blankly. As Maya walked slowly trying to smile at the dead eyes of the old people she wondered how many of them had died since the last time she had been here.

'Hello dear,' said an over-friendly old man wearing a chequered cap and a thick moss cable knit cardigan with large brown buttons. Maya smiled back at the old man's enthusiastic greeting which he followed with a warm wave.

Maya recognised her step father's head behind the high-backed amber coloured Bergere chair with Rococo designs of peacocks and swans. Maya's footsteps slowed down as she reached closer to another living room where her stepfather sat alone staring at another TV with the sound turned down. The room was altogether more cheery and smelt less depressing. There was more sunlight that poured into three windows, the room itself led to a large modern conservatory.

'Hello,' Maya said kissing her step father on his right cheek as a frisson of surprise shot through him.

'Hello,' he looked up, his blue eyes suddenly sparkling.

'Remember me?' she asked jokingly.

'Course I do,' he said with a smile, straightening himself up.

'How are you?'

'I am fine, how are you?'

'I am fine.'

Maya was sure he had changed. It had been a while since she had last seen him, a while since she had to have an emergency operation on her nose that had stopped her from visiting. This visit was important: it was a goodbye visit, she was going away to India and sooner or later she would have to tell him. Maya was not sure whether she was going to see her mother while visiting her step father.

'I am going to India.'

'India?'

'Yes.'

'Marvellous.'

Marvellous? Was that all he could say.

'When are you going?'

For a little while their conversation seemed to make sense. He was happy for her. They laughed again as they had a cup of tea that had been offered by the staff nurse with the navy and white uniform. They walked slowly to the back of Mannamead House and sat in silence on the white plastic chairs and drank more tea.

'Have you seen mother lately?'

'Mother?'

'Your wife?'

'My wife?'

'Not for a while …' His voice trailed off and cracked and a solitary tear dropped down his left eye down to his cheek. Maya wiped his face and he grabbed her hands.

'Take me home,' he whimpered, tears flowing from both eyes. Tears flowed from both her eyes, hers were tears of guilt and anger. Guilt that she was leaving him and anger that her mother was not visiting the old man.

'When was the last time she came to see you?'

'Three months ago.'

'Are you sure?'

When Maya visited her step father she never discussed her mother. Maya never discussed her mother with anyone. Maya was not even going to visit her mother to say goodbye even though she was in the same town.

At the very moment Maya thought about her mother

she heard her voice and for a second she was not sure whether she had imagined it.

'Hello there.'

'Hello dears!'

'Aaahhh! Ahhhh,' the sound of her mother's voice laughing loudly with the care nurses in the conservatory. The middle-aged nurse and Maya's mother chatted effusively as though they were old school friends. That was her mother alright: extroverted, loud, charming, funny and engaging. She was usually the life and soul of every party. The life and soul, even if there wasn't a party.

'Maaaayaaahhh!' Her mother screeched loudly, her arms opened wide, her voice was so loud that the old man winced. Maya could not believe that her mother had finally decided to accept her new spiritual name.

'Who?' said her step father squinting up at Maya who had a perfunctory grin on her face and her arms stiffly stretching out.

'You changed your name as well as everything else and now you are going away to something else,' said Maya's step father's weak voice. Maya pretended not to hear him. Maya and her mother hugged and kissed before the senior care nurse hurriedly made a cup of tea as though her mother was a dignitary. This was the effect her mother had on people: she enveloped empty spaces, sowed invisible seeds, quickened steps and let things grow at will.

'Oh in the car I have little Stephanie.'

'Little who?'

'Little Stephanie, you know Keelah's daughter,' her mother talked animatedly.

Maya noted that her mother had not asked her how she was as usual. She would rather talk about Keelah and her daughter Stephanie. Keelah was the daughter of a neighbour that they had lived next door to when

211

Maya was a teenager. It transpired that Maya's mother had bumped into Keelah at the shops two weeks ago, a week after Keelah's sixteenth birthday. Babysitting for Keelah seemed almost as important to Maya's mother as the second coming of Jesus Christ.

'It's the only way I feel sane these days, at least now when I am with little Stephanie people think at least I too have a grandchild.'

Maya ignored her mother's usual snide comments and hoped that she would move on to another topic that did not involve the guilt trip about Maya's barrenness.

'Remember Andrew?'

'Andrew who?'

'You know Andrew, from church?'

'Yes I remember Andrew,' said Maya's step father, his eyes suddenly excited. Maya had a sneaking suspicion that he probably didn't know who Andrew was.

'Well poor thing, his American wife had a miscarriage, third one in 18 months ...' Maya looked away towards the apple tree behind her shoulder and swatted away an invisible fly. Maya's mother's conversation went from one topic to another regarding babies. Maya knew the subliminal messages behind the 'innocent' anecdotes were to remind Maya that without a child she was as good as dead.

'OOooh Maya you look so beautiful, your nose is great ...'

Maya looked at her mother and looked at her elderly stepfather with his adoring eyes glued on Maya's mother. Maya felt physically sick, picked up her handbag, kissed the old man and ran out of the old mansion house. Outside the front door was a silver blue Jaguar with a baby in the back: little Stephanie. Maya knew the man driving the Jaguar, it was Petros, her mother's new boyfriend who she kept hidden from her elderly husband sitting at the back of the old people's house.

Petros was a chubby Greek man in his sixties with a thick moustache that covered his upper lip completely. He filled the front half of the Jaguar, his tanned bald head hidden by the quilted ceiling of the car. Petros wore a light summer shirt with thin stripes that showed a sample of his thick grey chest. Petros smiled warmly and waved to Maya as she rushed out of the door slamming it shut and saying.

'Hi Petros, Bye Petros.'

'Baah-yee,' he said sounding surprised at her rush and lack of social grace.

Maya rushed out of the side entrance of Mannamead House that led to a main road. There was no bus in sight and Maya decided to run at full speed down the hill for half a mile to a bigger road with more buses.

On her way back to London, Maya tried to cry but her eyes felt tight and tired. The knot went to her chest and she felt her heart pumping low and deep. She remembered the first time she had spoken to Petros. He had called her to tell her mother had been in a car accident. Her mother had insisted that she did not want to see visitors.

Later that week after her mother had been discharged, Maya decided that she would pay her mother an unexpected visit. The visit was the most pleasant mother and daughter had had for a while, spoilt only by the bandages that covered her entire face forming a capital 'T' at the top of her forehead and over the bridge of her nose.

It was only later in the month that Maya noticed that her mother's nose had changed. It was not an accident, she had had plastic surgery. Maya forgave her for all the lies and deceit but hated her for taking away the sacred moment she had planned with the only father

213

she knew.

This was it. Goodbye.

White Onion Soup

The ride to India house was always a pain but Maya looked forward to having white onion soup at Holborn with her friend Govinda. Slough station was busy with the usual commuters going to London or Reading, Windsor or Maidenhead. Even the little villages of Datchett and Eton had a cult following of travellers that came from Australia, New Zealand and Canada. Maya had seen Shakespearean enthusiasts on cold, wet days wearing wellingtons and raincoats coming to hear their tour guides reciting a line from the *Merry Wives of Windsor* where Bardoph says 'so soon as I came beyond Eton, (cozeners) threw me off, from behind one of them, in a slough of mire'. The tour guides generally talked about the trees and the listed buildings and then the tourists would go back to the bus and ride away.

Slough was a proverbial bus stop, a thorn in the side of the regal Buckinghamshire, somewhere where everyone came but never stayed. The train station was as dreary as the rest of Slough, an honest welcome to the unapologetic drabness of the city. Behind the counter was Mr J Singh and his blue turban that was held together with an elastic cord that tightly wrapped around his pointed grey and black beard. Mr Singh had sleepy brown eyes that hid behind gold-rimmed glasses with bifocal lenses. Next to Mr Singh was Mr Sopza whom Maya guessed was a descendant of the Polish immigrants who had settled in Slough after World War II.

The train was unusually quiet for that time of the morning as it left the platform and sped through the sleepy trees of Langley and Iver. Maya dusted a bit of translucent powder on her peachy skin occasionally looking outside as she balanced her make-up against her lap. The sun was not too bright or strong and she hoped that this was exactly how it was going to be in Rishikesh. She could not stand it when it was too hot: it did not make her skin burn or get darker, it just made her skin hurt and she would have to simply sit inside or cover her face with a veil. In spite of the scant sun Maya wore dark Jackie O glasses on the train and was glad that she had applied her red Yves St Laurent lip gloss before the exodus of commuters came into the carriage at Ealing Broadway. As she rumbled through her purse she realised that she had not taken her medication since she saw her mother.

The sudden panic about her medication was disrupted by someone sitting next to her. Maya had to move her bag for the little black girl no more than 12 years old with a woman by her side who could have been her sister or could have been her mother. The daughter wore white knee-length socks which showed her bare legs, too cold for that weather. The mother or sister was a beautiful, voluptuous woman wearing a sixties headscarf and large hoop earrings. The mother and daughter struggled with bags and a suitcase which meant the little girl had to sit at an angle with her brown legs pressed against the suitcase. The little girl immediately found a pen and paper in her bag and started to write furiously in a notebook made from recycled paper the colour of weak tea. The little girl seemed uncomfortable and sat quietly all the way. Every time she wanted to say something she scratched her mother a few times on her upper arm.

'Mama, mama look,' the girl looked earnestly at her mother's eyes for approval showing her notebook.

'Lovely, lovely,' the mother acknowledged the notebook then opened her handbag to check her tickets. People-watching was one of Maya's favourite pastimes. She often found she could make up an entire drama out of strangers she encountered for just twenty minutes.

Indians, Pakistanis, Somalis, Jamaicans, Nigerians South Africans all pushed into Maya's carriage, staring into space or talking to one another. Maya stood out like a sore thumb with her white skin, blonde hair and blue eyes in the sardine-like enclave of the train. She always felt more 'stared at' in train carriages with ethnic minorities than with white people.

'Go in, go in,' a tall athletic black man pushed the rest of the carriage inwards, forwards and backwards to allow a young lady that Maya guessed would be his girlfriend to get into the carriage. The girlfriend was too pregnant, too moody and wearing too short a skirt for the weather and the size of her belly. Nobody spoke to each other, not even the couples. The little girl continued to write demonically as if her audience was the silence within.

Maya tossed a stray tendril of streaked blonde hair from her forehead as the young black boyfriend stared straight at Maya. Maya looked away and stared between the trees moving in the reflection of the mirror. She couldn't understand why all these beautiful girls insisted on being with black men. The voice of her own mother came back loud and clear: 'Don't ever date a black man. Don't ever marry a black man. Marrying a black man is going backwards. Black men are no good, they are programmed to be irresponsible.'

She remembered the time she had brought her Jamaican boyfriend home to her mum at the end of her first year at university. Rodney was a straight A student studying law and had been very close to going to Oxford when he had opted for Bristol University instead. Rodney was beautiful, with a sinewy, six-foot athletic body: he played basketball, was the president of the African-Caribbean society and was every bit the catch of the entire university. When she had brought him home her mother had not given one hint of

217

disapproval as she welcomed him. Maya was going through her phase of rebellion and did not care what her mother thought of Rodney, she loved Rodney. Maya was shocked at the way her mother changed after Rodney left.

'Didn't I tell you?'

'Tell me what?'

'About those black men. I don't want you to make the same mistake that I see stupid girls making all over. The mistake I made.' Her mother shouted until her voice crackled and became a whisper. 'No black men, Maya, I will not be there for you, I will cut you off from your inheritance.' She pointed her middle finger pulling her lips inwards in a clenched rage.

Although Maya had rebelled with Rodney for six months, after that six months she started to notice his little irresponsible ways. How he was late for more and more dates, how he flirted with girls openly, African-Caribbean girls that he knew intimidated her. In her opinion they were 'too full on', 'gauche' or 'loud'. It was as if he quietly enjoyed the power he had over her.

Since Rodney, Maya had not dated a single black man or any man for that matter and had been celibate for five years. She was contemplating being a Sannyasin living a life of detachment, simplicity and union with God. Of all her maverick ideas she knew that this would break her mother's heart. It would be worse than marrying a black man. The train seemed to be going faster and suddenly slowed down at Paddington before stopping.

Maya waited for everyone to file out and gathered her bag and noticed that the little girl's notebook had fallen on the floor underneath the seat. She opened the first page of the notebook and read the little girl's written work.

The Cultural Asylum Seeker

In the early 80s, Zimbabwe, the country of my birth had abandoned its colonial apron strings and courted its role as 'The jewel in the African crown'. At around the same time fate had me boarding a plane headed for London Heathrow to join my mother and stepfather leaving behind the euphoric new Canaan and its 'milk and honey'. Most people had envied my move to 'Great Britain'—would I see the Queen? Would I eat in fancy restaurants every day? Would I be rich beyond belief? These fantasies blinded me to the fact that the passage of time would rob me of the priceless cultural gems that made me who I was. I was the Ndebele I spoke with its clicks, the sadza I ate with my hands, the spontaneous vigour with which I expressed myself.

Most people thought Great Britain and London were one and the same thing, but I wasn't going to London but to Plymouth in Devon nowhere near London. On the train from Reading to Plymouth, I watched the daffodils nodding to the rhythm of the wind and rain by the train track. This was my first introduction to the British weather and over the next 30 years I found the weather a ubiquitous topic of conversation that I effortlessly engaged in just like Pavlov's dog. It was my para-sympathetic response to my fellows, devoid of passion, a shrewd mechanism for never really getting to know people. Well wasn't that what everyone was doing?

In Plymouth I didn't see a single black person for months on end as I walked to school, to town, to church and back home. Zimbabwe or Rhodesia (as it was called when I was growing up) had been a model colony at first; you only needed to go to Bulawayo city centre to marvel at the unapologetic indulgence in Victorian architecture and the commemoration of all things British. Most schools prided themselves on being

219

just like the British public schools. My mother did not understand this when she decided to put me in a secondary modern school. I was shocked to find that lipstick, high heels and mini-skirts were part of the uniform and swearing at the teacher would not necessarily have you caned by the headmaster. I felt isolated, tense and uncomfortable every day. On my way to school I wondered if the children laughing behind me were actually laughing at me. On the way from school I could not wait to hurry away from the school bully who often made ape sounds behind me. I never turned back to look at him; I recognised him from the shadow he cast in front of me.

As the years went on I found myself adapting to my new life. Great Britain gave me a great education, great security and even higher aspirations and values. I even got over the idea that if I wanted to get my hair plaited or relaxed I had to get a train or a coach to London or Bristol. As I reached adulthood I found myself trying to tap into my roots with erratic visits back home. It was impossible to deny that each visit eroded my sacrosanct memories of my homeland. Death, poverty and mass migration to Europe and the US saw the beginnings of a ghost culture that made my soul ache with powerlessness.

Some of those who migrated to the UK in the late 90s settled in Plymouth increasing the black population in a way that was alien to me. They brought with them colour, vibrancy and a culture that I had little in common with. I had spent most of my life in England and my core values were inherently English and somewhat in conflict with my countrymen. I lacked the poetry that Africans used when they spoke to each other; I found the humour and banter a pointless waste of time and preferred it if people got to the point. From a distance I admired their spontaneity, their ability to let go, qualities that I once possessed. To my horror I found myself unable to speak my mother tongue confidently and preferred to speak only to members of my family where I could substitute the odd word I could not remember with English.

'Where are you from?'

'Zimbabwe ...'

'Terrible how ...'

Nearly every person I met always engaged me in conversations about the Zimbabwean Tragedy; it was a topic that replaced the ubiquitous weather. Everyone had an opinion except for me. To Caucasians I was a Zimbabwean, to Zimbabweans I was a true 'coconut': dark on the outside and white on the inside. In truth I was a cultural asylum seeker not belonging to either culture, but desperate to belong to whichever one would have me – if only they could give me the PIN code.

There was no way that this was written by the daughter, more than likely it would have been the mother or the sister. Maya turned the page to find another page with an article with the heading 'Robert Mugabe is dead'. Maya tried to run after the mother and daughter but new commuters were already climbing on to the train going west, back to Slough, Windsor, Maidenhead and Reading.

Maya's Ride to Enlightenment

'Wasn't today the day Maya was going to India?"

In a hypnotic dance, Maya's mind suddenly awoke while her body lay still. The taxi was here. The car lights beamed through the white muslin curtains that draped the huge bay windows of her house drowning her minimalist living room with uninvited light.

It was a cold, heavy, unfriendly morning just like every morning.

Boom, boom, boom. The driver knocked so loudly it sounded like he was using a piece of metal rather than knuckles.

Why so loud? Why did people have to knock so loud? Did they not care? Maya felt the anger rise up from her belly to her chest unexpectedly. Maya had planned to sleep all the way to Heathrow airport; she couldn't find any of the excitement she had in the past.

Excitement about hope.

Excitement about a new life.

Excitement about shedding the past.

It was so strange how being human demands the oscillation between fear and hope. While in the back seat of the car Maya only felt fear, the fear was enough to not even allow the word 'Aum' to be uttered by her weary lips. But then Maya knew she was tired. She could not talk to the driver or his friend. Why did the driver have a friend anyway? Maya was too dazed to care, maybe he was an apprentice driver. Maya thought about talking to the apprentice driver but he seemed to stare straight ahead as if an invisible tube was connecting him to the road ahead with its rows of street lights and anonymous drivers.

'1, 2 … 1, 2 sch, sch, sch.'

What was that? The apprentice driver's two-way radio seemed to say something. It might have been a mobile phone on a loudspeaker or the two-way walkie talkies, either way Maya hated people using loudspeakers on mobiles. Maya hated noise full stop.

Noise was one of the reasons Maya was moving to Rishikesh to her beloved Ashram to experience ecstatic silence. It had taken Maya all her life to realise that her soul was not made in England. Her soul was made in the crucible of silence probably in the foothills of the Himalayas in India. In a way she had hoped her driver would be from India, usually drivers in Windsor, Slough and Datchett going to the airport were Indian. She enjoyed chatting to them in the little Hindi she had picked up, the odd word or two in Urdu to the Pakistani drivers. No matter what time of day it was they were always in awe of someone of a different colour and culture knowing their language.

'Where did you learn to speak Hindi?

'Delhi, Rajasthan, Goa, Bombay sorry Mumbai ...' Maya always enjoyed listing all the places she had visited over the years.

Maya was only two hours away from leaving England for good. England where everyone had everything, even the poor have everything: cars, designer clothes and free education. The poor in England can afford holidays, but the poor and the rich have no joy, no love and no spontaneity. In England you rarely say what you mean and hiding your real self is an important part of any given day.

England and the endless talk of the weather, endless preparation for tomorrow, roast dinners, binge-drinking, celebrity madness was not for Maya. She was annoyed that she had taken so long to do something about it.

Maya decided to recite her mantra to Lord Shiva and dissolve the anger and ego that was starting to overwhelm her along with the tiredness.

Om Nama Shivaya.
Om Nama Shivaya.
Om Name Shivaya.

One bead, two beads. Maya's fingers counted her Mala using her right hand and thumb, remembering not to use her index finger, the 'I' of the ego. Counting was not easy with the heavy silver bangles that Maya wished she hadn't worn now. But, beauty was always important and external beauty was a celebration of internal beauty of God the infinite, who always made beautiful and harmonious things. Maya was willing and ready to propound her philosophy on external beauty which she knew was going to cause a level of upset with the swamis in the Ashram but she would cross that bridge when she came to it.

Maya vehemently disagreed with those who felt that being a spiritual being meant dressing up like you didn't care about yourself. Although there was a point during the low spots in her life when Maya had felt ugly, she now felt beautiful. She felt philosophical about her 'ugly' days as she called them. They helped her to appreciate the science and art of beauty.

She knew she was the frequent source of envy for many women. If it wasn't the baby blue eyes they asked about it would be

'Oh I love your high cheekbones',

'Oh your Angelina Jolie lips are stunning'

'Do you have Italian blood?' and

'I love your almond eyes.'

These were daily conversations from the pointlessly sycophantic and shallow women that Maya wanted to run away from. The compliments were always followed by giggles and bitchy snide remarks that Maya found tiring and pointless. The 45-minute journey to the airport seemed to take an age. Maya had the consolation of watching the sun rise as the darkness gave way to the palpable beauty of the morning sky on the outskirts of London. The backseat of the car was cold and the driver and his apprentice seemed to grow further and further away from Maya; they seemed to whisper something to themselves and if Maya could be bothered to be paranoid she would have thought they were talking about her. Maya closed her eyes and enjoyed the silence that came with chanting and ignored the two men.

Waiting

The car came to a sudden stop.

Boom, boom, boom. The apprentice driver was knocking on the glass window, just like he had knocked on Maya's door.

Maya's heart jumped. The heavy bangles on her wrist hurting again, Maya was wishing she had not worn the heavy silver bangles. Heart jumping and confused her legs felt numb, her sleepy eyes blurry. Her head felt drugged and heavy.

Damn those bangles. They would no doubt beep again at security as would her belt. She wished she had had the common sense to not have worn them. They were beautiful square bangles that jangled noisily and reminded her of the first time she visited Rajasthan and its vast exotic colours and unashamed gaudiness.

The driver and his apprentice looked identical in the bright light. They wore the same uniforms which made them look like they were grown up identical twins. She wondered why taxi drivers wore uniforms these days. It was just a means of marginalising rogue Polish and Bangladeshi taxi drivers. Everybody knew that.

The apprentice driver was not very friendly Maya thought but at the moment Maya didn't care and felt slightly sorry for him. Sorry that he probably didn't enjoy his job, he probably would spend his life lying and hiding from his true self.

The car doors opened as if by magic. The driver was now to her left and the apprentice to her right. They looked like twins again except that Maya noticed that the driver had a hook nose and blue eyes and the apprentice had brown eyes and a longer face. Maya was annoyed at herself for being so judgemental at these two men who were being kind enough to escort her further than duty called.

That's why Maya wanted to escape from England: she inevitably found herself more judgemental and more ill at ease. Maybe the apprentice was happy with his life, his suburban home and kids … why not? Maya wanted to move to India to train her mind to not be a slave to compulsive thinking. Thinking that oozed like pus from a broken scab, leaving behind pain and throbbing and waiting.

Maya was waiting, waiting for the plane to Delhi Flight No DH 4705 via Dubai.

'Name?' the woman behind the glass said loudly.

What the heck? Maya thought to herself. *Why was everyone so rude, so gauche today?* Maya wondered if she had imagined the butch flight attendant-cum-air steward's distinctly unpleasant manner. Maybe God was preparing Maya for the journey ahead. Maya gave her name, address, etc., etc. The flight attendant seemed to ask numerous questions. After 9/11 flying was just like going to prison.

The woman behind the desk was tall and seemed almost artificially elevated. She had greeny-grey eyes that peered over the rimless glasses that gave the illusion that she was not wearing glasses. She was in her mid-thirties but heavy with large breasts and a frame that made her look older than she probably was. Just like the driver and the apprentice, she looked unhappy and didn't mind if you knew.

After ten minutes of scribbling and writing and answering questions Maya found herself sitting down facing the woman waiting on a bench that felt unnecessarily hard making her lower thighs numb.

Airports had always fascinated Maya ever since she boarded her first plane to her first trip abroad. They made waiting a sweet melodious poem with undulating stanzas full of song and fantasy. The airport was full of tall, elegant women with hair extensions and Chinchilla fur coats. They wore ridiculously high heels and left behind the whiff of expensive scent. Children looked around in amazement at people, more people, suitcases, neon lights, announcements, changing notice boards, trolleys and endless queues.

At the far end of the waiting room was a family of Arabs: women in black Burkhas following slowly behind a fat man wearing a doppa and an afro beard, hands behind his back without a care in the world. Maya suddenly noticed that there were so many people with their hands behind their backs. Maya couldn't help but notice how much the people today lacked flamboyance and drama. Maybe it was because Maya was tired. Another strange thing she noticed was that many people seemed to have tattoos, something that Maya was not fond of.

'Hypocrite,' Maya said to herself. She was able to love the Mendhis in India but somehow disliked the Celtic art she was seeing on ankles, calves, some necks and fingers. Sitting next to her was a woman whose age she could not tell, only her hands gave her away. She was black with rouge noire nail polish, just like the one Maya had in her cupboard. The woman was obviously an intellectual as she had *The Times* folded neatly between Maya and her with one headline.

'Robert Mugabe Dead.'

'Can I read your paper please?' Maya suddenly found the courage to ask the complete stranger next to her.

'Oh yeah, yeah of course,' she said with a beaming, round face with pure pearl white teeth.

'Oh thank you so much,' Maya said, immediately hating adding 'so much' to the end of her sentence. Why was everyone saying 'Thank you so much', it sounded so American and so fake.

Woman Murdered By Jealous Rival

A woman thought to be in her early 50s has been murdered in country alley on her way home from her local pub in Datchett. The woman was found mutilated during the early hours of Monday August 27th. The woman was an administrative assistant ...

Oh my God, Datchett, that is my village what is it doing in a national paper, Maya thought to herself. Who could Maya phone to find out about the situation? What school was this murdered woman an administrative assistant in? Could it be St George's? Maya knew it well, or could it be Dedworth Middle School, the newer school.

Maya had lived in Datchett for the past few months and nothing ever happened there. Datchett was a tiny village, an insignificant leaf in between a rose and a thorn, Windsor and Slough. It was a sleepy little village with a single high street with a pharmacy, a rectory and the Royal Stag pub. It took just three minutes to walk the length of the empty high street. Datchett always felt like an afterthought to Maya, somewhere where your eye would blink before you turned a corner to visit Windsor Castle.

Someone somewhere would know. Maybe Laura her best friend, Mrs Phillips her lesbian neighbour who knew everyone's business. Of course someone would know, why didn't she know? Why was she at the airport getting ready to go somewhere?

It wasn't long before Maya was filled in by the flight attendant of all people. The woman who had been killed was a well-known local woman. The woman had failed to come home after a raucous party at the annual bank holiday hog roast. The woman had a 17-year-old daughter Naomi who had not reported her mother missing as her mother was a well-known party animal

229

who frequently stayed at friends' houses. Datchett was a close-knit community where everyone knew everyone and their business. People stayed in each other's homes often, this was one thing Maya loved about village life.

Who would kill her? How was she killed? Maya thought to herself. It was no secret that the woman had been involved in a love triangle, something that she talked about all the time to her friends. Her on again, off again boyfriend was two-timing her again with a younger woman. The dead woman would tell anyone who would listen when she was drunk.

'The bitch, slapped me when I saw her.'

'The mad cow, she deliberately drove into a tree?'

'She called my boss and told him I was with him and that I was not sick.'

'She emailed my whole family.'

'She torched his entire wardrobe.'

The stories of the woman and her love triangle were a Friday, Saturday and Sunday entertainment spot for all the villagers and now she was dead Maya could not believe her ears; this was the last thing she wanted to hear before she departed to go to India.

-Becki-
The Weeping Mulberry Bush

Baron was dead, Otheliya had left for good. Annie had lost her eye and was in Mater Dei hospital getting a glass eye. Ruthie was deaf and now went to King George the VI School. Next week Ruthie and her family would move away to Salisbury. Father Uncle Henry had finally left for Australia for good. Becki was glad he was gone.

Things would never be the same without Annie and Ruthie: they made the gang what it was. Becki knew that if she did not approach Yvonne and Barbara they would not approach her. Angie was enjoying reading her comic books from the Comic Exchange store and bleaching her hair and felt too grown up to be playing rounders.

After Titus had suddenly left, Becki had to do some of the gardening that Titus did after she came back from school. Mother and Uncle did not want to pay more than the $10 a month for Titus or to hire another house girl. Becki hated watering the lawn and the roses; she hated sweeping the dried leaves from the floor with Titus's broom.

It was almost five thirty and Uncle Trenholm would be coming home to have his cup of tea, scones and jam before reading letters from England. Becki cooked curried beef with vegetables and pap for herself and her mother.

After the news was finished Uncle finally put down the last letter from his daughter in South Africa and rolled his newspaper and decided he was going to bed. After removing his false teeth and putting them in the glass, Becki and mother could hear him snoring softly at first but they both knew it would get louder and louder with time.

The green curtains were shut tight, kitchen door shut and locked, the outside light switched off. The dishes were washed and put away and saucepan scrubbed of the burnt remnants of the mealie porridge. The little bit of leftovers was put in the fridge and all the work surfaces were cleaned and the cupboards wiped. Becki was proud of herself for doing the garden, cooking and washing up. She was also very proud of herself for putting away the last pot just as the weatherman was talking; this meant she could enjoy an hour of television before going to bed.

The New Avengers were on TV starring:

Patrick McNee as John Steed.

Gareth Hunt as Mike Gambit.

Joanna Lumley as Purdey.

Becki loved *The New Avengers* especially Purdey and her hairstyle, which most of the white girls were trying to copy in Bulawayo but never quite got right.

Purdey was running around in an empty Lunar Park with giant fairground slides and a big wheel that reminded Becki of the Trade Fair. Becki usually watched *The New Avengers* by herself if Titus or Otheliya were not there. Becki's mother seemed distracted; usually she would be wearing her long quilted night gown and slippers by now.

'Bekezela,' her mother said with her hand on her cheek and elbow on the olive green rexin sofa.

'Did Henry ever touch you?'

'No Ma.'

There was silence as Becki's heart missed a beat and then commenced to beat faster and faster.

'Bekezela, you must tell me the truth.'

'Yes Ma, I am telling you the truth, really.'

Becki hated it when her mother called her by her African name as it always meant trouble.

232

'Are you scared I will beat you?'

'No.'

Becki shifted her legs to a new position on the sofa trying to concentrate hard on *The New Avengers*.

'Becki I will not hurt you or harm you, I just want to know if Henry ever put his thing in you.'

Strong grip, lavender, brown snakes, vomit, fast car. Becki's heart beat faster as she remembered the day Father Uncle Henry had stroked her the first time and her mind went blank. Becki looked down at her knees and a knot tightened in her tummy. *The New Avengers* stopped talking. The wind outside hissed. Loudly.

'Tell me the truth.' Becki's mother softened, moving forward to face her daughter.

'No he didn't.' Becki found courage from somewhere and hoped this time she would be able to convince her mother and the subject would be dropped. The knot in her stomach melted into hope that rose into the middle of her chest for a moment.

'Becki if he has I need to know, I will not hit you, it's him that I will go after.' Becki's mother moved from the three-seater chair to the one where Becki sat and hugged her daughter. 'I love you, you are my daughter.' Becki felt a wave of relief as she experienced the warmth from her mother's hands.

It smells just like Mrs Sibanda's perfume ... the knot in Becki's stomach loosened and she remembered clearly the mother's love that she had forgotten. Knowing that if she told her mother the truth she would have bad words with Henry and hopefully he would never come back.

I do not want that Henry or Father Henry or Father Uncle Henry whatever his name was back here. I hate his big nose; I hate his glasses that changed colour when he came into the house. The knot in Becki's stomach turned to anger, an anger that felt safe

233

knowing that she was cocooned by her mother's love.

'Yes Ma, he did.'

'You were lying to me?'

'Yes.'

'Where did he touch you?'

Becki looked down.

'Where?' Becki's mother's voice was more steely and menacing and Becki quickly pointed to where Father Uncle Henry had touched her.

'Where else?'

'Here,' Becki said pointing to her chest.

'You are a liar aren't you? How many times did I have to ask you before you answered?'

Becki's mother stood up and removed her slipper with one straight movement.

'Give me your hand,' her mother said.

Becki knew what this meant and put out her left hand.

Slap. Left hand.

Becki left her left hand out. Slap, slap until it was too hot and painful and then brought out her right hand. Slap, slap with the purple slipper from her left foot.

Faster and faster her mother hit her with her slipper, hot tears streamed down Becki's face. The pain from both hands was the same and her mother was hitting her so fast that there was no time to recover. Suddenly her mother stopped. Relief, it was over. Becki wiped the tears from her eyes, feeling betrayed by her mother.

Did she not say that if I tell the truth she would not hurt me but she would hurt Father Uncle Henry? Becki thought to herself.

'Come … here.' Becki's mother suddenly grabbed her by her neck. 'Come here,' her mother hissed. Becki was confused about where they were going. Kitchen light on, outside light on, backdoor kitchen open and Becki could feel the biting wind coming towards her.

234

Becki's mother pushed Becki forward by her neck towards the tortoise pen and then suddenly let go as she picked one long mulberry bush stick.

Two mulberry sticks, three, four, five and six and she was pulled back into the living room. Right hand slap with the mulberry bush, this time fast. The pain of the mulberry bush stick was more intense than the flat shoe. The pain felt like a razor slicing through her right hand. When the right hand was tired, Becki changed to her left hand while her right hand throbbed violently. A flood of hot, salty tears came down from Becki's eyes by the time the first mulberry stick was broken and both her right hand and left hand had been hit.

Becki hid both her hands behind her back, enough was enough.

'Give me your hands!' Her mother's face was crazed as she rolled her lips inward in fury. Her mother's face reminded Becki of the day her mother had fought with Rhoda and her daughter. Becki showed her mother the back of her hands, her mother wasted no time in using as much force as possible from the mulberry bush to the back of Becki's hands.

Whack.

Whack.

Whack

The mulberry bush sticks left puffy visible lines on her arms that stung like electricity and vinegar. Some of the lines left fine tracks of blood as the mulberry stick broke and Becki knew that there were five sticks left.

Becki's hands were boiling and felt like someone had banged them with her hammer. Becki thought to herself that if she hid her arms mother would stop.

'*Buya lapha inja yo thuvi le!*' (Come here you filthy dog!) her mother screamed in Ndebele. Becki knew that when mother said anything in Ndebele their mother tongue she meant business.

Becki's mother's scream made Becki scream louder too, tears and snot mixing as Becki wiped her tears and eyes at the same time. With twice as much force her mother struck her with the third stick on the back of her neck and back and around her shoulders and Becki wailed just like Otheliya had wailed.

If I scream louder maybe the neighbours will wake up, maybe Mr Shatapu's dogs will wake up and he will call the police. Becki thought to herself but instead screamed so loud, that her pain drowned the sound from her wide open mouth. Her hands covered her face which was covered in blood, tears and snot.

After the fourth and fifth sticks had finished, Becki felt pain all over her body not just her hands. The only parts of her body that her mother had not hit were the top of her feet and the soles of her feet. Becki's eyes, legs and arms were swollen as her mother had forced her to take off her blue jersey which did not make any difference to the pain that Becki felt.

Becki was still wailing when she glanced over at the television. *The New Avengers* had finished, mother had been hitting her with the sticks of the mulberry bush for one hour non-stop.

'*Hamba phandle,*' (Go outside,) Becki's mother barked at her daughter who was now shivering with pain and crying uncontrollably, her convulsions making her hiccup.

Why does she want me to stand outside to stand by the weeping mulberry bush again?

'*Thatha inswazi!*' (Get the sticks!)

With her cold, wet, bleeding hands Becki started to cut down the remaining branches of the bush. For a second Becki hated that mulberry bush that never seemed to bare any fruit and wondered why it was ever called a 'mulberry bush'.

Becki's mother made Becki carefully remove all the extra leaves from each branch and lay them on the *stoep*. Becki worked slowly knowing that she was picking the very branches that her mother would be hitting her with.

They walked back into the house, Mother locked the door behind them switching off the outside light, then switching off the kitchen light. Becki wiped her nose and picked up her blue jersey hoping that it would protect her from bleeding and swelling.

'*Khupha, Khupha!*' (Take it off, Take it off!) Becki's mother pulled the sleeve of her blue jersey spinning her in one motion until she had pulled off the other sleeve and Becki's arms were exposed again.

'*Khupha yonke into!*' (Take off everything!) Becki wished she hadn't tried to put on her blue jersey, maybe her mother would not be asking her to take everything off. Becki took off her red dress and her yellow panties and let them fall to her feet. Her mother used all the force in her body to hit her only daughter with the mulberry branches.

I wish I was with Baron. Dead.

Before she knew it the tears from her eyes had rolled down her torso as the rhythm of the mulberry bush branch flowed from her mother's anger.

'*Puma, puma!*' (Get out, out!) It was only when Becki saw a black stain at her feet that she realised that she had wet her mother's carpet. Becki ran out of the living room for fear that her mother would hit her even more. Becki sat on one of the yellow chairs in the kitchen.

'Sit down there you dog, don't sit on my chairs,' her mother spat out the venomous words.

Becki sat down on one of the cold black and white tiles next to the stove as far away from mother as she could go without leaving the kitchen. The weeping

237

mulberry bush was now bare, without fruit, branches or leaves. *The World of Sport* had started and finished and the last news bulletin was on the television again.

Becki's mother had gone to the bedroom and Becki could hear the Rhodesian National Anthem coming from the television.

Rise, O voices of Rhodesia.
God may we thy bounty share
Give us strength to face all danger and,
Where challenge is, to dare.
Guide us, Lord, to wise decision,
Ever of thy grace aware.
Oh, let our hearts beat bravely always,
for this land within thy care.
Rise, O voices of Rhodesia,
bringing her your proud acclaim,
Grandly echoing through the mountains,
Rolling over far-flung plain.
Roaring in the mighty rivers, joining in
One grand refrain,
Ascending to the sunlit heavens.

The music to the Rhodesian National Anthem was sung to Beethoven's 5th Symphony. Becki imagined the picture of the Victoria Falls, the singing choir, the statue of Cecil John Rhodes, the giraffes and the elephants: that was what you always saw when the National Anthem came on. The sun was rising outside.

-Kieran-
Neptune Square Venus=Pond scum

'Neptune is a beautiful planet made from the same vibrations made by violins and cellos. It is the planet of the salty, sweet tears of compassion that run into the sea making Neptune the God of the sea.'

Kieran listened intently as his Grandfather talked fondly about Neptune, watching his eyes blaze from gold to copper to an azure blue like the blue oceans of the clouds of Neptune itself. Kieran didn't always understand what Grandpa was talking about. He talked in riddles about planets, water, life, death and joy. When he spoke of his son he spoke with the greatest passion and love. Kieran was only interested in what happened to his mother and father and when he would be able to go back home. Grandpa had mentioned someone else, a sister. Had they been separated and sent to different places? Kieran felt fortunate that he was with Grandpa, certain that he would go home soon.

'What happened to Ma?' Kieran whispered, scared to disturb Grandpa from his solipsistic thoughts, a film of tears in his eyes. Kieran felt selfish for taking him out of this meditative moment.

'When Ma met your Pa, she met her truth. Pa was born to be like Orpheus.'

'Orpheus?' Kieran's face was puzzled.

'A poet so beautiful himself, his singing so sweet it made the trees weep with joy.'

'Pa was like that?' Kieran tried to take his Grandfather out of his trance-like meditation to hear more of his beloved mysterious father.

'Oh yes.' Grandfather looked straight at Kieran his eyes now a blue black colour he had never seen before.
'Orpheus was beautiful like your dad and had the same

239

effect on many women including your mother,' Grandpa continued as if he was talking to the cosmos again, the film of tears becoming stronger until a tear dropped from his right eye slowly making its way to his cheeks then disappearing into his mouth.

'What happened to mother that day?' Kieran interrupted Grandpa's thoughts determined to get more out of his Grandfather.

**

She got up the next day tired from crying and sobbing, the white of her eyes a red, yellowy grey colour, her cheeks sunken. For a few days she forgot him: the liar, the thief, the cheat. In her heart he was Diablo himself. Didn't God say the Devil only had only one mission to steal, kill and destroy? He had stolen her heart, killed her love and destroyed her spirit. How could the truth turn into a sudden lie? She could not work again for days, she tried to forget him, deleted his emails and any memory of him. She would give the lovely shirt to someone that needed it, maybe give it to Oxfam. The scent she would keep, but she knew that she was fooling herself because the notes of sandalwood automatically evoked memories of him.

At home the phone rang as soon as she put the key into her front door. She ran to her living room unconsciously hoping that it was him.

'Hello.'

'Har-low,' it was her mother, dragging her hello as she usually did.

'Hi mum.'

'How are you my darling?'

'I am ok, thank you.'

'I have cooked a nice chicken curry just like the way you cook yours. Can you come and tell me if it's any good.'

'Now?'

'Now of course. I am going to go to work by six so come now. Just get in your car then you don't have to cook.'

Not cooking tempted her, but she just wanted to go to her room and smoke cigarettes and not think.

'Oh mum I am tired, too tired really.'

'You are always tired. Helen is coming with her daughter Rowena. Guess what?'

'What?'

'Rowena is pregnant again. Can you believe it?'

'Really?' It seemed to her that everyone was pregnant. Every time her mother rang her it was to tell her that someone was pregnant.

'Really?'

'Yes, when are you going to make me a grandchild, I am so glad that your new boyfriend wants to have children, hold on to him don't let him go. Don't do what you did with Giles and all the others. Giles was a good man. You could be having your third or fourth child with him by now you know. He was a good man, tall ...' Her mother trailed off into the usual monologue. Something that happened on a daily basis.

'Mum, it will happen by the Grace of God.'

'God only helps those who help themselves. When I was half your age I already had a baby and was working. I was looking after my baby by myself.'

'I want my child to have a father.'

'You didn't have a father, not really, but look how you turned out. Just have a baby with him, what is his name? I can't remember. The thing is once you have a baby you will have that bond together forever. He can have countless ...'

'Mum we broke up?

'What? Already? What's wrong now?'

241

'He cheated on me?'

'So what? Men are all dogs, they all cheat. You should have called me and talked to me first, who broke it up? I bet it was you. Was it you?'

'Yes Ma, he was cheating on me for God sake.'

'So what? Like I say, just have a baby with him and all the others can come and go but you, you he will never forget because you have a baby for him.'

'That's crazy plus that's not me, I prefer to be honest.'

'Honest, my child, maybe you read and believe the bible too much. Nobody is honest. Listen when you go to church and you see the priest talking and you think he is honest and he is a man of God. My child nobody is honest. Don't tell him that you want a baby, I bet you told him you want a baby.'

'I just wanted to be honest and yes I told him.'

'What you don't know is that you scared him off when you said that.'

'Mum, he said he wanted a baby too with me, he wasn't scared off.'

'Then why do you think he went with another woman?' She felt a mixture of anger and tiredness. Her mother had this effect on her, a unique ability to make her feel guilty and angry at the same time.

'So anyway come over and we will talk about it.' Her mother sensed that she might have upset her daughter.

'Mum I am tired now, I didn't sleep last night,' she lied.

'Does that mean you are not coming?'

'No, I will come tomorrow,' she lied again knowing too well that the last thing she wanted to talk about would be Andy to her mother.

She hung up the phone to feel a deeper anger that turned purple and curdled like old blood, her heart slowing down and her palms sweating. How dare he play with her emotions and dreams? *Tread softly for you tread on my dreams* she had told him but he had not listened. She felt played, used, useless and naïve. Most of all she felt she had let down her mother who wanted grandchildren more than anything else. At times it felt as though that was all she was living for. She felt sad that she had been a disappointment to her mother.

Without thinking she picked up the phone to call Andy's mother to tell her exactly what her son had done. Surely she would berate him and tell him that what he had done was cruel.

'Hello.'

'Hello.' It was a man's voice. Andy had told her that his mother had remarried after her husband had died.

'Hello, is that Mrs Matthew's house?'

'Yes,' the man suspiciously answered in a deep baritone voice and she immediately regretted not thinking through what she was about to do.

'Is she there?'

'No, she is not here just now, who is calling?'

'It's a friend of Andy's.'

'Andy? What's wrong is he ok? Is he in trouble?'

'No, no. I am sorry he is not in trouble.'

'Whom shall I say called?'

'Oh don't worry, I will call again. Sorry OK bye. Thanks. Bye.' She felt shame hanging over her like a beige cloud lined with grey tones. She put her handbag down which was still hanging on her shoulder. What a stupid thing to do, what did she think she was going to achieve? She lit a cigarette, which made her dizzy and hollow making the beige cloud darker and heavier with little droplets of water that merged with the tears that swam like a giant flood from her eyes.

After three puffs she sat down, regretting lighting

the cigarette, walked to the kitchen to pick up a mug of coffee she had used that morning to stub out the half smoked cigarette. She watched the cigarette curl up soaked by the dark liquid until it spat out its insides and the tobacco floated like dirty debris after a bad storm. The phone rang. She hoped it wasn't her mother with another lecture about babies and men.

'Did you just phone my mother?' This time it was Andy, his voice angry. She had never heard him sound angry and it scared her.

'I did, she needed to know what pond scum she gave birth to.'

'I should never have given you her number. No wait, where did you get her number?'

She didn't answer but he filled the silence.

'Whatever you do don't you ever ring my mother otherwise I will kill you and that is not a joke. I am not joking, my mother has been through enough.'

'What about me? What about what you did to me?'

'Listen I don't care but just don't involve my family. What I did was bad I said I am sorry OK?'

'No, you never said sorry,' she heard herself shouting over him to make herself feel better.

'Yes I did, I sent you that email.'

She remembered the emails.

Andy says:>>*I am sorry, for what it's worth it didn't mean anything. She had planned this long before I met you. I miss you a lot x*

At the time she was so angry and told him exactly what she thought in another email.

>>*For what it's worth you are a liar. You have broken my heart and let me tell you a thing or two that you probably do not know about yourself.*

1. You are selfish, self-absorbed and only care about you and nobody else.

2. You lie all the time, in fact you don't know the difference between the truth and lies.

3. You have no remorse or guilt about hurting and taking from others. You didn't care that I had spent all that money and effort on your birthday while you were sleeping with whatsitsface did you?

4. You have delusions of grandeur and live largely in a fantasy world. The way you talk about photography is as if you have already made it. The Times? Don't make me laugh. Your whole world is a fantasy.

5. You are arrogant and vain and think that you are God's gift to women. Let me tell you all the pictures you showed me of yourself. Well you are a shadow of that man and nowhere near as good-looking as you think.

6. Most of all you are a hurt little boy that needs help to deal with unresolved childhood issues.

She hadn't signed it off but remembered finding a website after keying 'Cheating boyfriend' into Google and finding out all about the Narcissistic Personality Disorder. She was sure Andy had this disorder especially after he replied to her cutting missive by saying.

I think you are right about me needing to deal with issues in my childhood. I don't think you are right about me not feeling guilty: you bought me that scent because you liked it and the shirt was your taste. That is trying to change someone in my opinion.

His last email had fuelled her anger and she decided to have the last word by saying.

>>There you go, proving my point, it's not your fault you are turning it around and making it mine. Only you would say a gift bought with love was me

245

trying to change you. I bought that shirt because I thought the blue would go perfectly with your eyes.

Andy was still at the end of the phone as she thought of their emails. He had said sorry and that had created a hole filled with guilt. Suddenly she missed him and both of them fell silent.

'I am all alone,' he said in a humble voice.

'What?'

'Why don't you come over. I want to fuck you on the leather couch while nobody is here, you know you want to.'

She couldn't believe how he could change his tone so quickly. She couldn't believe how her heart had melted from a hardened anger to a sudden mushy desire.

'No I am not coming to your sister's house, are you crazy?'

'She doesn't come in till six?'

'What about your brother-in-law?'

'He doesn't come in till eight, he works late. She reckons he is having an affair anyway. Come over,' he insisted.

'No you come over.'

'Come and get me.'

'Get a taxi.'

'It will cost £10; my giro doesn't come in for another week.'

'We will split it in half then?'

'OK, have you got any fags?'

'Yeah I have two packets my friend sold me some duty-free ones.'

'OK then.'

**

They slept on her bed in the white cotton linen that he

loved. Andy always told her how much he loved Egyptian cotton. By his side was a large glass of red wine that he sipped as he stared into space and she looked at his mesmerising blue eyes. Before midnight she knew she was going to ask about the other woman and chose her moment carefully.

'So why do they call Isabella Imp?' she tried to sound casual as if it didn't bother her.

'She told me that when she was a child her little sister couldn't pronounce "Is" which is what everyone called her and she pronounced it Imp,' he said very casually flicking his ash into their mutual ashtray. She wished he would say more on the subject of Imp but he didn't volunteer any information and a pregnant silence fell between them. She was lost for words and almost asked the same question again.

'Is she pretty?'

'Not really, she is 52. She has taken so many drugs and smokes so many fags that she is quite haggard and ravished.' She was jubilantly pleased that this woman was neither beautiful nor young. In her imagination she had seen a beautiful, long-legged, blonde goddess. After all he was handsome enough to bag any woman that he wanted.

'52, 12 years older than you, that's mad!' she said all the jealousy dissipating making her feel slightly drunk although she had not had a drop of alcohol.

'I mean she has a fabulous body and great tits. If you covered her head up she could easily pass for a 25 year old.' She didn't like to hear how great her body was.

'So she has great tits, is that why you fell in love with her?'

'No.'

Did you love her more than most out of all your girlfriends.'

'I loved all my girlfriends; they each have a special place in my heart.'

'Does she have the most special place in your heart?' she asked exaggerating the 'most special' to make it sound not as unimportant as what she wanted it to be.

'No, what is this? Do you hear me asking you about your boyfriends? Forget it, we are here together now.'

In the morning she felt comfortable and happy to wake up next to Andy, next to her truth. When the time was right she would tell her mother that they were back together again. Andy made sure his phone was next to him when he slept. When she woke up at night she was tempted to sneak it away as he snored but she daren't get caught. She decided to leave him in the house as there was no rush to go anywhere. All he had to do was to go home to help his sister with her chores.

At 11am Andy had sent her an email after getting the bus back home to Plymstock from Exeter St. His email was simply headed 'News' and she wondered what that had meant.

>>News

Two pieces of news, one good and one bad. My sister wants me to move out in two weeks and my best friend Rafa is having a boys' weekend in London. So good news, bad news x

His emails were always short and to the point and somewhat dull compared to the excitement her heart felt when she saw his name in her inbox. As soon as she heard that his sister had kicked him out she knew that this was God's way of making it happen between them. She would take her mother's advice and ignore the other woman.

By mid-afternoon they had driven to his sister's house and collected all three of his suitcases, a bin liner of CDs, hangers and bed linen. It seemed to happen in the blink of an eyelid.

**

'Wow Grandpa, just like that?' Kieran said.

'Well, from the first time they met they both had a mutual feeling that they had met before.'

'Wow. How?'

'This was because her ascendant in Leo mutually aspected his Sun in Gemini and his Ascendant was Sagittarius,' Grandpa said, putting his hands together to form a steeple.

-Becki-
Overnight

The day after the all-night beating with the mulberry bush, Becki never felt the same again. Her body was scarred; she was covered in congealed blue and black blood. She washed herself in the cold shower in the boys' *Khaya* where mother said she would now sleep. Mother had given up beating her at the point where fresh wounds were starting to swell while others were starting to reveal raw white sinew. At that point Becki felt that something in her had mutated. Like her soul had changed into a formless, shapeless object with no power, no direction, no knowledge, no joy, no connection to the source. Becki slept on the hard floor and dreamt of running in a forest made of thick thorny bushes while being chased by a mile long, fat, black cobra.

'*Vukha, Vukha!*' (Wake up, Wake up!) Becki's mother had woken her up by throwing clothes on her. Her mother told her to get dressed; they were going to the police station. It was the same station where she had sat with her mother and her aunty after the fight. The wait was long, silent and heavy. Becki's mother barely spoke to Becki on the way to the police station. By lunchtime mother stood up without saying a word and went away for what seemed like hours. For a while the waiting room was completely deserted apart from the clerk who kept writing in a book. Becki's stomach rumbled with hunger, her throat was parched.

When mother finally returned they were asked to go into an 'interview room' by a white policeman who kept looking at Becki over his spectacles. Becki's mind wandered to Uncle Trenholm and wondered what mother would have told him about why Becki was not going to school. For a moment her mind drifted to the daily journey through North End and the bridge past Paddonhurst, through the Jacaranda tunnel into Main Street and Third Avenue. The smell of fresh, hot chips with mango pickle entered her mind. That was followed by the dream of thorny bushes and the pain of the weeping mulberry bush.

'Where is he now do you know?' said the policeman to Becki's mother.

'Australia.'

'Do you have his address?'

'Yes, but at home.'

'Mrs Trenholm, you know there is nothing we can do now that he is out of the country, you know that?' Becki's mother sighed, pulling out a tissue that was wedged under the strap of her gold watch.

'Is he likely to come back?' the policeman asked, removing his glasses, his eyebrows furrowing with sympathy towards Becki and her mother.

'I don't know. I can ask the church, he is also a priest.'

'A priest, aah you joking man. A priest, that's disgusting for sure.'

Becki kept staring at her feet looking up only once or twice when her mother wanted her to elaborate to the policeman.

After the statement they went back to the waiting room which now had a few more people. Before they sat down again a pretty, slender, young coloured woman asked Becki and her mother to follow her behind a white door. Becki's stomach was knotted by a combination of hunger and the fear she had of her mother. The door opened into a dark, cold and narrow corridor. At the end of the corridor was a little light that was borrowed from the tiny window at the far end. The floor was the shiniest floor that she had seen in her life.

The last door had a little notice with red letters that said 'Dr Patel'.

'Knock, Knock, Dr Patel,' said the young coloured girl in a soft, cotton wool voice as she opened the door.

'Come in, sit down,' said the Indian doctor. Dr Patel was a slim man with dark skin and a pink lower lip. He probably originated somewhere in South India somewhere like Gujarat. He had bulging but peaceful eyes that sat comfortably over dark crescent-shaped circles. The doctor had a grey and orange picture of Lord Shiva dancing next to a picture of Vishnu. On his table next to a forensically neat pile of papers was a shiny copper statue of Ganesh. Becki stared at Ganesh's trunk for a few seconds. The doctor serenely motioned Becki and her mother to sit down in the small freshly painted cornflower blue room with the white door. Opposite the white door was a small window that was framed by cheap cotton curtains with small pink and cream flowers. Outside Becki could see that the afternoon sun was awake, vitalised and sending potent rays that tickled the back of Becki's back and neck leaving tiny beads of sweat on her skin.

Doctor Patel spoke in the same soft, cotton wool soft voice as his secretary and asked Becki's mother questions as he filled a form. A few minutes later Dr Patel stood up and shut the window and curtains making the room almost as dark as the corridor. He made Becki take off her panties and lie on the dark blue leather bed that hugged the wall adjacent to the mirror. He put on plastic gloves, switched on a light whose heat Becki could feel on her knees. Becki didn't like the feel of his hands on her private parts just like she hated Uncle Father Henry that day he had pulled down her panties and touched her. Dr Patel wrote something down and Becki could see her mother staring at the pink and cream flowery curtains.

The doctor came back and this time he had a big silver tube in his hand. He pushed Becki's knees apart without saying a word and fear welled in her stomach.

Slowly, slowly, slowly.

Pain, pain, pain.

Stinging tears. Hot tears. More tears.

It felt worse than when Father Uncle Henry had tried to put his thingy inside her private parts. Becki hated what the doctor was doing, it hurt too much, she wiped away a tear.

'*Unga-kha-le,*' (Don't cry,) the doctor said as he tried to speak Ndebele to Becki. At 4pm they left the interrogation and examination room and went past the waiting room which was now packed with people who seemed to know what had happened. They all looked as though they had been listening through the walls. Becki felt naked again and felt that everyone could see her dirty little breasts that she shouldn't have at eleven, her dirty, filthy hair in her private parts. She saw each person holding their jaws and hiding their eyes away from the dirty, filthy little girl that she had become overnight.

It was not just Becki's soul that had changed overnight but her body. Overnight she could not fit into her olive trousers that she liked to wear with her red stripy boob tube. She tried on the brand new sky blue bell-bottoms but they were tight, her bottom stuck out in a vulgar, filthy dirty way making it impossible for her to close the zipper. Her flat stomach was visible and fat like a balloon full of water. As well as her body, her face had become, shiny, oily and sweaty with thick pimples glistening with pus. That had all happened overnight.

As her dresses became tighter, her mother refused to replace them with the same enthusiasm that she had in the past. After the visit to the police station, she didn't

253

replace the nanny or Titus the garden boy. Titus had got a better paying job in a factory near Becki's Grandmother. There were hardly any braais, Becki hardly played with the other girls. There were hardly any words spoken between Becki and her mother.

Becki washed dishes, washed all the dirty clothes, cooked the family meal, mowed the lawn, and ironed just like Otheliya and Titus had done. Sometimes Becki would catch moments of joy when she was watering the garden and it would feel just like it did before. As her heart danced in delusion she would suddenly feel the heavy silent look that mother would give her now and again.

'My God you are ugly,' her mother would say in a sharp, menacing voice that cut Becki's delusional heart into a million tiny pieces. The first time she heard her mother say that it hurt more than the beating by the mulberry bushes. When she said it every day, all day Becki wished she would beat her again instead.

Becki was not allowed to sit on the sofas and had to sit on the floor when she ate the food she had prepared. Every day mother had new and different ways to remind her that overnight she had changed from the second most beautiful girl in the class to an ugly, filthy disgusting monster.

'When you sleep with a man you get pregnant, you will be the youngest girl pregnant at 11.' You don't know this but Henry had gonorrhoea—do you know what that is?

'He was such a filthy dirty pig he also had syphilis.'

'Becki you are rotten, you smell rotten and look rotten.'

'Becki what does it feel like to be ugly?'

'Becki you are ugly on the inside and out.'

Overnight, Becki lost the desire to play with her friends. Her stomach collapsed inside when she realised that she could be pregnant. Her mother had told her to drink two big glasses of hot water with Epsom salts, which she told her would flush out the baby when she went to the toilet.

Eventually mother had begun to go out with her many friends again and when she went away Becki looked up the meaning of 'gonorrhoea' in Uncle Trenholm's old encyclopaedia and felt sick. The description under syphilis talked about 'pain' and a 'slow death' which showed pink-reddish coloured pictures of people's jaw lines showing just a lip with sores and sores under the soles of feet and hands. The fear moved from her stomach to the middle of her chest and took on the shape and form that transcended tears and words.

-Kieran-
The Burnt Moth and the Unlit Flame

Andy was on his way to his friend's 40th birthday. Kieran's mother wished she was going to Fulham to celebrate his birthday with his friends. She wasn't sure she was ready to meet his friends especially if they lived in Fulham. She had known that life and those types of people before and they always made her uncomfortable. Instead she opted to visit Michael, an old friend of hers. Michael lived in Oxford and was doing his final year of research. It seemed that Michael worshipped everything about Oxford and was likely to die of old age in Oxford.

Getting to Oxford was a disaster: the traffic was at a standstill because of thunderstorms and floods. She arrived at Michael's flat in the centre of Oxford close to Jesus College where Michael cooked an amazing pasta bake to warm her up. The best she had ever had. When she told Michael this he could not hide his pride and gave credit to the cookery course he had attended in Assisi while he was doing his research on St Francis. They talked about everything and anything but her mind kept wandering back to Andy. She was so much in love with him, flaws and all. St Francis was Michael's new obsession.

'Oh right, its eb-so-lit-utely fantastic,' he continued. She couldn't help but think how affected his new posh voice sounded.

'Oh right,' she said again starting to sound like a parrot. She wasn't sure if she was just listening to Michael out of politeness and adding the odd sound to make it sound like she was listening.

'Even then you know we have had a great deal of

support from Harvard of all places, and the British Academy so it's all good, all good.'

'So what are we doing tomorrow?' She decided to change the subject; she couldn't listen to another word about Byzantine programmes, she just didn't see the point of wasting all that money on something that could be left to the history books.

'I don't mind, it's up to you, we can go to an art exhibition, visit the college again, see a film, anything you want.' She felt weary after the six-hour drive and decided that she would call it a day after smoking a cigarette in his backyard. The break from Michael and his stories meant that she could phone Andy and see how he was. She knew he would be up even though it was late.

'Hi.'

'Buongiorno'

'How was your journey?'

'I am still on the fucking train, can you believe it?'

'Yeah my journey was pretty awful too, just arrived only two hours ago and now about to go to bed.'

'Yeah I have only just arrived in Reading. It might be quicker for me to get off and go to a friend's house who lives nearby because the journey is just fucking terrible. They are not even giving an ETA for Paddington.

'Really?'

'Yeah, just a bit of rain and the whole country stands still. If there is no tube from Paddington to Fulham then I am stuck there all night.'

'Wouldn't Rafa come and pick you up?'

'I don't want to bother him, anyway it's Friday and he sounded pretty fucked when I called him.'

'So what are you doing for fags? Are you not dying for a fag?'

'Well the train has been stopping for ages, for

example it stopped for 30 minutes at, er, I don't know some fucking hellhole in the sticks and I had 30 minutes to …'

Suddenly the signal was lost, she tried him again and the phone went straight to voicemail. She lit another cigarette and looked up at the dark cloudless sky. She dragged on her cigarette, heard Michael moving around in his room and decided to phone again. The phone went to voicemail and she decided that she would try again after she had finished her cigarette. She enjoyed feeling drowsy and listless when she smoked at night. She often chain smoked at night one after the other without thinking about it. Smoking helped her to think about things that she had shoved into the back of her mind. It made all the gaps between her thoughts one linear thought that would make no sense if she voiced it, but nicotine made it palatable and coherent.

This time Andy picked up the phone, this time she could hear the imposing sound of a train in full speed with a loud voice over the tannoy which she could not make out.

'Sorry must have lost signal there.'

'I thought as much, are you nearly in Reading?'

'Yeah in fact that's what I think she is announcing. So sleep well my angel I hope you have a great day tomorrow.'

'I hope you have a great time tomorrow, I hope the boys' party is good.'

'It will be boring without you. I've told everyone about you, you know they all want to meet you.'

She couldn't believe that he had told all his friends about her, it made her sleep well and dream dreams in blue, orange and yellow.

**

258

In the morning breakfast was a strong, fresh Italian coffee with hot milk, oat bread and salmon and dill omelettes. She was not really a breakfast person but utterly loved it when other people cooked it for her. There had been more floods the night before; the papers were calling them 'Destructive Floods'. The floods had been particularly destructive in Yorkshire, Gloucestershire, Worcestershire, the Midlands and Oxfordshire. The rainfall had been the highest since 'records began' said the small antiquated radio that went with Michael's post-Second World War furniture.

There had been rescue efforts involving the military and the police and there had been reports of deaths and houses simply collapsing and cars being washed away.

'I am not sure what to do, whether to put sandbags out or not?' Michael said sounding more hungover than she had expected.

'Have you got any bags?'

'Yeah, I have four I think. I will have a look in a moment.'

Meteorologists are stating that the current floods are related to active frontal system moving across England. There is speculation that the floods could be related to this year's appearance of La Niña in the Pacific and the jet stream being further south than normal.

The extended weather forecast seemed to go on throughout their breakfast and they decided it was best to wander out into the colleges and get some fresh air.

Outside it was cold and fresh and did not feel like August as the sun was covered by a blanket of gun-metal grey menacing clouds. There was a sharp breeze that made the leaves on the trees shiver as they walked through Market Street turning left into Turl Street.

In spite of the cold and wet weather Broad Street

was full of students cycling purposefully through Oxford. There were brown and white scarves for New College, brown and black for Corpus Christi, blue and white for Trinity. She knew all the colours by now.

Everywhere you looked were bicycles either being ridden, chained up or being pulled along. Throughout his three years as an undergraduate, she had visited Michael at least once a year. To her, visiting Oxford was like going on a holiday abroad. It had been said by some that Oxford was more beautiful than Tuscany.

The two of them walked down in comfortable silence towards Baliol College immersed in the type of silence that can only exist between two people who know each other very well, each one comfortable in their own individual thoughts. Baliol College is one of the oldest colleges at Oxford and occupies most of Broad Street in Oxford. They had decided to visit Baliol because Michael had told her that Baliol had a pair of new tortoises that had been donated to replace Rosa Luxemburg, Baliol's tortoise which had been stolen in 2004. Michael knew that she had an almost spiritual affinity with tortoises and maybe seeing the tortoises would make her day.

They reached the front of the college with its Victorian architecture and a façade that looked like it had been dusted with layers of fine brown sugar. Her mobile phone rang and she hoped it was Andy and it was.

'Hey.'

'Hey.'

'How's the party?'

'Well it's just starting out, it's a bit cold but we are at a pub between Battersea and Fulham, I don't know these places.'

'What's the road?' she asked.

'Don't know, let me ask?' Andy shouted back.

There was a lot of noise, shouting and laughter in the background.

'Rafa, Rafa, what's this road?' Andy screeched even louder.

'Not sure mate, not sure, it's Battersea though.' Rafa shouted back his voice drowned out by traffic.

'I know it's Battersea, but what is the road?' Andy said and she had a gaggle of girls laughing in the background.

'Baby, don't worry it doesn't matter, are you having fun?' Andy's voice was much clearer now and she was sure he had moved away from the party.

'Yeah loads of fun, we are with some of our old friends from school, Ali and his wife Rowena' said Andy sounding like he was putting a cigarette in his mouth.

'Ali, isn't that a girl's name?' she said trying not to sound jealous.

'No, no Ali is a boy do you want to say hi to him?'

'No, no, no ... baby? ... I don't know, is Ali short for Alistair?' She tried to coax him away from making her talk to a complete stranger.

'That's right,' he said in a faux American accent raising his voice in an exaggerated way.

'I thought you said there were no girls, it's a boys-only party.'

'Well that's what Rafa said to me but there are tons of girls. Rafa, Rafa! RAFA,' he shouted Rafa's name and the background noise increased exponentially making her pull her phone away from her ear. 'Look baby, I better go now, but call you later or maybe you call me, it's a bit noisy and crazy at the moment.'

They put the phone down and she was glad they had arrived at Baliol College, which although the closest to Andy's Jesus College she had never visited before.

'Is that your new man?' Michael said as they

walked past a tall Swedish looking student wearing a black, white and purple scarf. Michael had a penchant for Aryan looking men and the two of them exchanged a brief but intense look.

'I don't know if I would call him my man, *per se,*' she said noticing the fleeting glance between the two men. 'No more than I would say that man who just walked past is *your man*.' They laughed hysterically at the fact she had noticed his surreptitious glance at the handsome stranger when he thought she wasn't looking.

'Oh, oh, oh, do you remember that time I came to see you in Assisi and we went on that meditation trail in er, where is it again, Greccio was it called?' she said changing the subject to Andy again.

'Yeah, Greccio.'

'Do you remember when I said I had that vision?'

'Not really, continue.'

'God Michael, do you ever even listen to anything I say?' she said whacking him hard on his upper arm.

'Ahhh, I do, I do.'

'Well I had a vision and I remember telling you. I say it's a vision but basically I had my eyes closed but wasn't properly meditating because my thoughts were all over the place. So at first it was like an image of St Francis came into my mind but he was sort of in a modern kitchen. With him was the nun that was with him all the time, her name was Ciara. She was quite fat and chubby. At the time I think I was quite fat, but as I carried on seeing these images. I sort of crossed from a stage where I was neither awake nor asleep but conscious. St Francis became a man and this man became exactly like Andy the guy I am seeing now. Although I had never seen him before this vision. I could not tell you for example what his physical attributes were. All I know is that my soul knew him through and through.'

'Really you didn't tell me all this, you must be mistaking me for someone else.'

'I told you as soon as we got back from Greccio.'

'So do you think this guy is the guy in your vision?'

'Yeah because when I first saw his picture I recognised his soul in the same way. On top of that, get this. When I carried on in this weird state the image became that of a child or two children, a girl and a boy. The girl was older, naughty, mischievous carefree and had taken after him. The boy was a little bit more reserved and was very keen to protect me as his mother.'

'Ahhh how sweet. Oh my God, if I didn't know you any better I would think you were mad.'

'So anyway I believe he is destined to be the father of my children.'

Michael didn't respond as she wanted him to as they walked past a lugubrious looking man in his late sixties. The man looked like he could be Mediterranean, Arabic or even possibly from the sub-continent. When he spoke he sounded distinctly cockney and painfully unfriendly.

'Excuse me, can we go into the gardens?'

'I am sorry, tours start at 1pm.' The man did not want to engage in any further conversation which spurred Michael to ask him even more questions which made her pull her lips together under her teeth to hide a smile.

'Oh right, right I am from Jesus and I have just brought my friend here, who is really into tortoises,' Michael said pointing at his scarf with his left hand and at his friend who was now trying to find things to look at behind her so the man would not see her.

'Well, well, the tortoise race is normally held at Corpus you see,' the man seemed to come alive. 'It's already happened already you see, happens every May you see.'

'Can we see the tortoise?'

'Well Rosa was the longest one we had,' the man was determined to tell Michael what he wanted to tell him in his time. Michael decided to not push his luck and let him tell his story. When he had finished Michael asked the question.

'Can we see the tortoise?'

'Oh there is no tortoise here.'

They walked out of Baliol with her giggling insanely as they walked past groups of French tourists wandering into St Giles Street to sit down and have coffee.

'So what's your fetish with tortoises anyway? Were you a tortoise in your last life? Were you made to read Roald Dahl books? What?'

'Shhh, never mind, so anyway I was telling you about Andy.'

'Oh God,' said Michael pretending to faint and wipe his brow in a camp exaggerated manner which made her laugh even more and put her arm around his.

They sat down and ordered an espresso and a latte, since it was almost lunchtime. She ordered her favourite panino of chorizo, sweet potato and chilli jam and he ordered a bacon sandwich that would cure his hangover.

'Yeah, so we stopped talking just before your "big but" before we went in there. Sorry about the tortoises.'

They both laughed.

'No worries.'

'It's my fault. I should know more about these things but tortoises seem to be at the bottom of my list somehow.' She thought how much she hated how chaotic and sporadic conversations were with him when he was hungover. She decided she would not tell her best friend that she was crazy in love with Andy but felt he was one of these inveterate liars that would turn her life upside down.

-Becki-
The Spectator

The morning breeze gently shook the white curtains in Becki's room waking her up with the dull ache that she was now used to. It was an ache that could not be cured by aspirin or medicine: it was hers and only she knew of it. Everything was the same and everything was different. The sun rose each morning and set at night, the wind blew, the dogs barked. The garden gnome was the same with his optimistic smile, rosy cheeks, red hat and blue trousers. The paint on his trousers was now weathered and chipped showing his vulnerable cement-coloured self.

She had accepted that she was ugly and fat. Becki put her small hands through her hair. At least something had changed. The day before yesterday her mother had 'tried' new hair straighteners on her hair that was fresh from America.

'It will make you beautiful,' she said putting the tub of cream that smelt like a mixture of old sewage, boiling cabbage and burning rubber. More than anything, Becki wanted to be beautiful like she was when she was in Grade 1. Even if the smell and fumes stung her nostrils. Her neck hurt from bending over the bath while her mother smothered it with her gloved hands. By the time her mother was finished Becki's hair was indeed straighter, shinier and blacker than her dolls. She had not played with her dolls since the day of the beating. She could pass for a dark coloured now although her hair looked more like a newly born Indian baby.

'Now that your hair is so nice you must mind that skin,' said her mother to a confused Becki as she went to her bedroom. In her hand was a tube of 'Ambi'.

'Every day in the morning after you wash make sure you use this, it will make your skin light like mine,' said her mother admiring her own reflection. *How beautiful, smooth and pretty she was,* Becki thought to herself. *Maybe this is going to make me light-skinned and beautiful like my mother.* Becki felt the knot of fear that she lived with slowly loosening and wondered if she could be friends with her mother again. She regretted the moments she had hated her mother, her evil mother who she wished was dead every day.

She hated herself for thinking the mother she loved was irascible and evil. Her mother wasn't evil, evil was a choice, something that was separate. Evil was the fire that is used to make a beautiful clay pot; evil is the pressure that distinguishes boring carbon from glistening diamonds.

At McKeurtan School everyone commented on Becki's new hair. She felt proud and wished those bullies who had called her a *Kaffir* would see her now. After school Becki bounced out of the school gates and shared a quarter of a Cadbury's Flake, a red supercool and her favourite tomato flavoured crisps with Caroline. It was Caroline's turn to bring the money for them to share. Tonight Becki would have to go into her mother's handbag and take 25 cents when she was having a bath or watching the news with Uncle Trenholm. Her mother never noticed.

With her new-found confidence Becki thought she would muster the courage to ask her mother to buy her a new dress or maybe some bell-bottoms that fit her. When she got home her mother's car was parked in the driveway. Parked under the weeping willow was a beige car that Becki did not recognise. In front of the double doors on the white garden table were two empty glasses of Castle beer with dried froth and less than a suckable mouthful of beer at the bottom. Becki knew that this was yet another uncle who came when Uncle Trenholm went to work.

After the clandestine jouissance Becki always knew that her mother would be in a good mood and maybe this would be a perfect time to ask her for a new dress and maybe even a pair of bell-bottoms.

'*Mama ngicela lingi thengele o bell-bottom?*' (Mum can you buy me a pair of bell-bottoms please?) Becki spoke fast and confidently to her mother in her native Ndebele.

'*Uthini?*' (What did you say?) Her mother whipped her head from the fridge where she was pulling out a bottle of beer.

'*Ohhhh Ufuna izigdoko?*' (Do you want clothes?) Her mother told her to remove her school uniform in a voice that sounded kind. The way her mother used to be all the time. Becki smiled to herself and wondered what her fear was all about. Becki quickly took off her school uniform and put on one of the only two dresses that fit her now. A red polyester dress with big flowers and floppy sleeves and a bow that tied in the middle. The dress had been made by a tailor friend of Aunty Mrs Conceicão near Bulawayo post office.

While she was tying her bow and looking at her face in the mirror, which didn't look as ugly as usual thanks to her new hair, her mother entered her bedroom. She was wearing a two-tone peach see-through night gown. The dining room was dark because the curtains were drawn and the door to the bedroom was closed; the only light came from Becki's bedroom.

'Come here,' Becki's mother said and brought her in front of the mirror and stood behind her and looked at her, her eyes not betraying her emotions. 'Try this,' her mother handed her lipstick and Becki's heart beat faster. She took it without questioning why her mother wanted her to wear lipstick. Becki put on a faint layer of the lipstick that matched her red dress. When she was finished her mother handed her a trio eye shadow that had little circles of petrol blue, electric blue and shimmery silver colours. The electric blue had been worn down to reveal the silver container. Becki hesitated staring at the eye shadows. Her mother grabbed the eye shadow a little too roughly and applied it to her daughter's eye making the iris of her eye jump suddenly to the bottom of her eyeballs.

Becki opened her eyes and said nothing as her mother picked up her black eyeliner to darken her eyebrows. Before she knew anything her makeover was over. It was only the smile on her mother's face that told her that her mother was pleased with her own efforts.

'Come here,' her mother dragged her away suddenly and quickly through the bathroom door into her own bedroom. She must have wanted her daughter to see herself in her larger mirror. Inside her mother's bedroom sat a white man who was smoking a cigarette and lying back against the red leather and wood headboard. He seemed surprised to see Becki and her mother walk in.

'Hey Len, here is someone who wants some money.'

'What?'

'This one, she wants to make money,' her mother said putting her hands on her hips and looking at Becki up and down.

'She's *lekker*, no?'

'How old she?' the man asked stubbing out his cigarette.

'Nice make-up, pretty' her mother ignored his question and gestured to her face.

'Is that a child or an adult?'

'She needs money for dresses, can you help her?

'Is this a joke man, she is a child. Or not?' The man sat up and pointed to Becki's white socks that she had forgotten to take off. Becki's mother pushed her out of her room and shut the door behind Becki who could not believe what had happened. When Uncle Len left her mother came into her bedroom and said.

'My God you are an ugly bitch, not even that man wanted you.'

'You use Ambi now to make your skin light so I don't know why you can't be pretty. Your hair is nice and straight, not *amaqwayibana*. Here, your nose, see, do this,' Becki's mother stood in front of the mirror and pressed down her nose with her thumb and index finger. 'Everyday press your nose down a 100 times then your nose will not be ugly like that. Since you are a woman and can sleep with Henry then you can earn your money. I am not buying you any clothes.'

Her mother started to walk to the door and then walked back to Becki's reflection that was frozen.

'That's what bitches and prostitutes do. You are a bitch and bitches earn money from their men.'

When 4:30 came, Becki made fresh tea in a silver tray and doilies for Uncle Trenholm. There were fresh crumbly scones with butter and jam that Uncle would munch on while reading *The Bulawayo Chronicle* as usual.

-Kieran-
August Floods

The evening was spent eating and drinking some more before they went to a choral recital by the university's choral society at New College. After the recital she was ready to sleep in the joyous state of knowing that she was going to see Andy tonight. She recalled with horror a conversation they had had last night where he sounded very drunk and possibly had taken drugs. He mentioned some story that she did not believe about the many women that were trying to sleep with him. He had sounded as though he was trying to make her jealous.

Before she had set off to go back south they had had a conversation that lasted about twenty minutes because first he had insisted she drive to Fulham to pick her up. Then he had said he was happy to get off at Reading and she could come and pick him up. She was worried that the journey would take too long because of the floods. Eventually they agreed that he would use his return ticket to come back home and they would meet at her place around 5pm when his train was due in. She agreed to pick him up from the station.

She finally left Michael's house around 2pm after she had devoured his delicious world-famous Sunday roast which was crowned by his 'funky' gravy. Michael's roast was learnt from his travels in Louisiana where he had learnt to cook soul food and his stay in Italy. A sumptuous eclectic mixture of roasted sweet potatoes, green beans in cream, marinated chicken in Louisiana spices, corn on the cob, cornbread and funky gravy. The gravy was mixed with crushed garlic, olives and fresh rosemary.

As she drove away she could see that Michael was

hungover and probably could not recall the drunken conversation they had had last night again. She worried for Michael because his memory seemed to worsen and his hangovers seemed more intense. Overall Michael seemed to drink more and more and lose control more often. He had been fine last night but as it seemed to be these days, the conversation had gone to Andy again. Andy. That is all she seemed to talk about these days and she was starting to get on her own nerves at times. With Michael she knew she could be completely herself, he knew all her flaws.

'So you want to have a baby? A real baby, a live baby?' Michael said with a cigarette clutched between his lips. Michael only ever smoked after he had reached a certain threshold of alcohol.

'Yes, Mikey, a real baby, ngwa, ngwa,' she said mocking the sound of a crying baby.

'But you've only just met him.'

'So?'

'So you don't know him,' he said in a low, sincere voice.

'Did you even hear what I said to you about that time we were in Greccio?'

'Greccio,' he repeated the word as if he had never heard it before and didn't confirm either way dragging some nicotine into his lungs. 'Why don't you have a baby with me?' He ignored the Greccio question and tapped his cigarette against the rim of the ashtray and sipped some more of his wine.

'It would fuck things up between us.'

'No it won't.' He looked at her straight in the eye with the same deep sincerity that he had at a certain point when he was drinking. The look usually meant he was either about to go to sleep or get a second wind and do something crazy. When they were in a home environment it was usually the former. At a nightclub in a foreign country it meant Michael would either take his clothes off, simulate sex with any object living or dead, water-features, people, trees, anything. It usually also meant that she would be going back home by herself as he went with his latest find.

'It's OK, let's drop it.' They had had these conversations before as Michael had always said he wanted a baby. She knew that he had forgotten the Oluz Denis incident where he slept with someone that had given him an HIV scare. She didn't tell Michael but his HIV scare had made her think twice about having a baby with him. What if he inadvertently passed on the virus to her? What if he had the virus and they had a baby together and all she would do would be to worry about his well-being throughout the child's formative years.

From the look in his eyes, Michael did not notice what she was thinking this time. As she meandered through the windy roads, framed by a flat quilt of yellow, brown and green fields her thoughts undulated between her best friend Michael and her soulmate Andy

As soon as she got home she dropped her bag through her front door and rang Andy to see if he had got on the train.

'Where are you?' she said before saying hello. His voice sounded heavy. They had spoken at 11am while Michael was preparing their Sunday roast and he told her how he had slept at 7am and was going to bed.

'I am on the train,' he mumbled as though he hadn't moved a single muscle around his jaws.

'I know you are on the train but is it on time? Where are you roughly so I know when to pick you up?'

'Errrrr I don't know, it all looks the same.'

'Are you tired?'

'No.' He sounded as though his mouth had closed

again.

'OK can you let me know when you get to the next station roughly where you are?' She decided not to be annoyed; he was probably tired after partying all night long. After all he was 40 and not 14.

'OK.'

'Bye.'

'Bye.'

She took off her trainers, unpacked her clothes, put her clothes in the washing machine, mopped the kitchen floor and read the bits of *The Sunday Times* that interested her. She flipped through the culture and style section before she realised that it was six o'clock and Andy had not rung.

She rang him and his phone went straight to voicemail. Five minutes later she rang again. She watched a few programmes on Channel 4, another cookery competition on More4 and then rang him again. She decided to ring First Great Western to find out if there had been any delays with any trains coming from London. There were no problems.

At 9pm she decided to ring his sister to find out if she had heard from him. She sounded as though she was nursing a hangover herself and did not want to engage in any intense conversations.

'All I know is that he was going to London and could be away for as long as the whole week.'

'Really?'

'Actually not sure when he said he was coming, he left in such a hurry, didn't really speak to him.'

His sister did not seem very helpful and she really didn't want to press too much. Eventually she fell asleep deciding that Andy had probably decided to stay in London after all. She watched *Fight Club* and fell asleep at midnight.

In the morning Andy was the first thing on her mind

when she woke up quite late because of a sleepless night. She decided to send him a text message, annoyed with herself for not sending one in the first place.

>>*Please let me know if you are ok xxx*

She arrived at work and went to the canteen to order a large latte and an almond croissant as she did almost every day. The lattes that they sold at her work were the world's best kept secrets and were cheaper and tasted a hundred times better than branded coffee. The coffee was from Sorrento and had a smooth, aromatic flavour without any of the harsh, gritty, bitter aftertastes of many of the Latin American or even South East Asian beans.

By the time she settled down and checked her computer for an email from Andy she had woken up and firmly focused. There was no email or text message from Andy. Just before lunch she picked up her floral notebook where she had written key numbers from his mobile phone. His mother, his sister, Rafa and Imp.

Without thinking she dialled Imp's home number and to her surprise Andy answered sounding a little less tired than he did the afternoon before. She hung up without saying anything. That night she cried herself to sleep. She couldn't believe that he was back with her. It broke her heart, reminding her of her bad luck with men, confirming her deep fear that she was unlovable.

-Maya-
The Swami, the Surgeon and the Shrink

The Swami

'Can you state your full name?' said Lord Justice Gilbert, his piercing black eyes looking over his glasses.

'Swami Dayananda.'

'Is that the name your parents gave you at birth? Are you a Hindu or maybe Indian?'

'No, my name is Alexander George.' The swami responded, his face deliberately serene, his matt shaven head blending with the browny-orange robe that draped over his shoulders.

'How do you spell that Alexander?'

'Your Honour, the witness is not on trial and this line of questioning is irrelevant,' said QC Harris.

'Overruled,' said Judge Pierson, looking uncomfortable and bored.

'Alright, Mr George. is your second name spelt D-J-O-R-D-J-E in your native Croatia?'

'It's spelt like that in Croatia, but of course, here it's George, its po-tay-toe and po-tah-toe,' the Swami said betraying layers of his indigenous accent as he spoke. The people in the gallery laughed out loud, much to the amusement of the swami who was visibly pleased to have an audience even though he had not deliberately planned to. Lord Justice Gilbert ignored the sniggering in the gallery and looked straight at the swami.

'Well ... George, how long have you known the defendant?' Lord Justice said emphasising the swami's Western name eliciting a suppressed smile from some of the observers.

'I have only known her for about eight months.'

'How would you describe her state of mind?'

'Well she was quite unhappy when she came to the centre. She was drinking too much, sometimes she used bad drugs and she was looking for peace of mind.'

'You say bad drugs ... are there good drugs?'

'Yes, penicillin for example, good drug,' the swami said shrugging his shoulder, smiling playfully and visibly annoying Lord Justice Gilbert and making the gallery snigger again.

'How did you help her find peace of mind?'

'Well, so many people come to the centre who are looking for peace of mind; she was not unique in that way ...' The swami continued, his face softening as he smiled to show pure white even teeth.

'Mr George if you can just answer the question I asked you that would be fine. What was her state of mind?'

'Objection your honour, the witness is not a qualified psychiatrist,' said Lord QC Harris looking frustrated and impatient.

'Your honour I am simply trying to establish the defendant's character as identified by someone who helped them through their trials.'

'Sustained.'

'I repeat, what did you do to help the defendant with her problems?'

'At first I recommended that she attend some courses on how to develop willpower to help her to stop drinking, then she did a course on yoga, then she did weekly meditation discourses. She was very interested in the Upanishads and Sanskrit and studied ... after a while she wanted to be a *sadhu*, but ...'

'Did that help?' Lord Justice Gilbert interrupted.

'It did for a while and she joined the centre to attend *satsang*?'

'What is *satsang*?'

'*Satsang* is a Hindu devotional celebration that is done in a group and is a joyful thing with singing, reading, playing instruments that kind of thing.'

'Is it true that she then joined your commune?' Lord Justice Gilbert asked the next question as though he had only half-listened to the swami's answer.

'It was not a commune.'

'Is it generally considered a cult?'

'Objection your honour, the witness is being badgered and quite frankly this is pointless hostility. Mr George is not on trial.'

'Sustained.'

'No further questions your honour.'

The Surgeon

'What was the state in which you last saw her?' Lord Justice Gilbert asked Dr Newman.

'The accident was near-fatal for her; she had a severe posterior epistaxis.'

'Can you explain that to us?'

'The patient had had a rhinoplasty in Turkey, which had got infected. The bleeding from her nasal cavity had affected the old surgical wounds. Over the years we had worked to correct the bad work and then to give her what she had wanted in the first place. The trauma from the impact of the collision would have resulted in the internal bleeding and mucus.'

'As her surgeon, she asked for you to come and fix her?'

'Yes.'

'How did you manage to stop her from bleeding or dying as it were?'

'Well when I arrived, half an hour after the patient called for me it was lucky I was in the area. Her blood was not clotting and I had advised her to sit upright.

This was to stop blood from going into the lungs and such things. This would have certainly killed her. We had to use some petroleum jelly to actually stop the bleeding. I have done this before many times. I was careful to make sure that not too much petroleum jelly is given as this can also cause lipoid pneumonia which can also be fatal so it's a very, very delicate process.'

'So all she needed was a little Vaseline?'

'Not exactly. It was a very serious impact that required an ostiomeatal complex sinus cryosurgical procedure.'

'Could you explain this to the court, Dr Newman?'

Dr Newman was a slight, unassuming man with very little hair that parted to reveal sandy, straw-coloured skin. He wore an old-fashioned black suit and a muted tie, with brown brogues. Dr Newman stood in front of a giant image of the cross-section of a face showing red sinew, a paranasal cavity and an oversized protruding blue eye that was attached to blue and red vessels.

'This is a cryosurgical probe which must be cooled down to very, very low temperatures using helium or hydrogen,' Mr Newman said holding up the grey and white probe and its ancillary attachments.

'Was this a new thing?'

'No, it was not a new thing, the patient had several visits which ... erm, more or less I established had been caused by her excessive use of alcohol which caused obvious vasodilation of the capillaries and of course I think narcotics may also have been involved.'

'What narcotics?'

'Well she never said, maybe cocaine, more than likely cocaine. She only admitted to drinking heavily but that would not be as detrimental as taking cocaine after various rhinoplasty procedures.' Lord Justice hurried Dr Newman, the inflexion in his voice giving away that he was about to reveal something important.

'Dr Newman ... you say procedures, could you clarify?'

'She had the first procedure to elongate the septum, but was not happy with the diameter of her nostrils and had that corrected by using cartilage from her hips, then she had the bridge narrowed slightly. She had some discolouration at the tip of the nose. After that she had a further elongation.'

'Dr Newman ... could you reveal to the court the exact number of procedures you conducted?' Lord Justice repeated the same up and down inflexion questioning style.

'In total maybe nine under complete anaesthesia.'

'Nine procedures?' Lord Justice Gilbert removed his glasses and furrowed his brows to show that he found Dr Newman's answer incredible. 'Is that unusual Dr Newman?'

'A little.'

'Why do you say that?'

'Because I believe she was trying to deal with deeper phsycolo ...'

'Objection your honour, the witness is a surgeon not a psychiatrist.'

'Overruled. You may answer the question.'

'I have worked with numerous people who had nothing physically wrong with them but insisted on drastic surgery to change something in them.'

'What do you think your patient was trying to change?'

The Shrink

Dr Leighton-Boyce stood at exactly 5 feet 2 in heels. She was neatly dressed in a blue trouser suit with a light powder-blue shirt. Her hair was silky straight, shoulder length with a few highlights. She had a no-nonsense gaze that could melt a king. She walked to the stand with a determined gait and defiantly answered the prosecutor's questions. The questions were few and gave the impression that the prosecuting team felt she was not adding anything more to the theory that the defendant had murdered her love rival in a jealous rage. It was QC Harris's turn to question the psychiatrist.

'Dr Leighton-Boyce, when you met the defendant after she was arrested, where did she think she was?'

'She thought she was at an airport going to India, she thought the female officer was a flight attendant.'

'And the arresting officers?'

'She thought they were taxi drivers taking her to the airport. She tried to pay them but said she was struggling with the very heavy bangles which she had not realised were handcuffs.'

'Dr Leighton-Boyce, do you know if she was or is taking any medication?'

'I believe she had been taking a combination of anti-psychotics and possibly anti-depressants which may have rendered her insane.'

'What was the reason for this?'

'It is my belief that the defendant was suffering from a severe case of dissociative disorder, which was triggered by a recent relationship and loss of a baby.' Dr Leighton-Boyce went on to explain in detail how patients created new realities in order to cope with childhood trauma.

'Explain to the court what you mean by "new realities".'

'For example, when I asked the defendant what her name is she said "Maya", a name she had adopted in order to be a nun in India. This meant she could forget who she really was ...'

'Dr Leighton-Boyce, tell us who she really was ...'

'She was born Bekezela in Rhodesia in Africa, her name was changed to Becki to Anglicise it. This was the first psychological conflict she experienced.'

'Surely that could not lead to such a heinous crime Dr Leighton-Boyce?'

'Not in itself no, but she experienced prolonged and profound emotional and physical abuse that led her to want to erase who she was.'

'Are you referring to the plastic surgery?'

'Yes sir, I am talking about the plastic surgery. Maya or Becki subjected herself to extensive plastic surgery so she did not have to face herself. Apart from the well-known and well-documented Michael Jackson case she is one of the very few known black people who has tried to change their skin colour and ultimately their race to such an extent.'

'Why did she do this?'

'To please her abuser, who told her she was worthless.' Dr Leighton-Boyce continued to talk freely on the stand for another five minutes explaining Becki's recent visit to her hometown in Bulawayo. 'Becki or Maya had experienced trauma after trauma in her life: she had witnessed her own family being killed by the regime's terrorists. A whole village burnt down, raped and pillaged. When she herself returned to Zimbabwe she was raped and ridiculed for the way she looked. This all led to this situation in my opinion.'

'Doctor you mentioned something about her losing a baby, can you elaborate please?' QC Harris was now seated and the whole court was transfixed by what the doctor had to say.

'According to the notes that I had and conversations with the patient, I am led to understand that she was either pregnant or was planning to get pregnant.'

'Tell us about Kieran, doctor.'

'Kieran is the name she would have given her child

had he been born. She talks about Kieran as if he exists. At present she believes he is waiting to come home: he is with his Grandfather, who happens to be Andy's deceased father.'

The Rain that Washes Away the Chaff

When dark clouds gathered in the early evening it brought a solitary hope to Matebeland after months of tyrannical heat and drought that had wiped out the beauty of life in the fields. The atmosphere was heavy, dark and brooding and the clouds became more aggressive, completely dominating the docile sky. The sun was pushed out into a small strip near the edge of the horizon, its rays subdued, its magnificence a mere illusion. The dams were choking with mud and the dust was biting when the wind blew over the edge of the Kalahari desert.

The children at 203 New Luveve picked up scattered twigs and dried branches from nearby *Gwabalanda* woods to light a fire to make *imbawula* and tell stories when it got dark. Aunty Hetta had cooked the evening meal when the rain fell on to her blood-red veranda forming perfect pools of water. The Ncema dam would be filling up with water to quench the thirst of the parched fields. The sound of jubilation could be heard as Ndebeles everywhere celebrated the rain.

The Umzingwane and Insiza rivers would be overflowing to the great grey-green greasy Limpopo river in Rudyard Kipling's books. MaNkomo and her remaining grandchildren sat in the dining room. The dining room walls were a deep dirty green, which was made to look duller and more sombre by the humidity of the unexpected rain outside. A subdued 30 watt light bulb was covered by a dark brown conical lampshade reluctantly giving out muted light, which made the brown and yellow sofas seem like dark shadows. The dusty gramophone in the corner of the room's low muted bass tones were turned down low so that you could only hear it if you were in that room. Uncle

Gabriel still loved the news and would sit and listen with his mother while Aunty Hetta and her younger sister Anna had gone into the spare bedroom next to the kitchen to gossip, giggle and clap hands every few minutes.

As soon as the eight o'clock news came on the radio the young children knew they had to hush and not utter a single word. A quiet, gentle knock at the door came as soon as the news finished. Everyone in the living room missed it until it repeated a little louder.

'*Qoki,*' (Knock knock,) said the gentle, humble voice of a stranger wearing grey trousers and a matching grey jacket with a brown-red polo neck. The man was soaking wet and started to respectfully kneel on the front door mat which was wet from the rain water. When he took off his hat the old man continued to look at his feet until Grandmother MaNkomo told him to come in and not to get himself wet.

The children stopped talking to look at the man who had moved an inch away from the door but was still looking at the floor. As soon as the news finished the children would fight and shout and one of them would tell the Ndebele fairy tale of 'The Hare and the Elephant.'

'*Ngenani, ngenani,*' (Come in, come in,) Grandmother insisted that the man sit on the chair rather than the floor. She made the younger children run out to the kitchen to light the stove and make the stranger a hot, strong and sweet cup of Tanganda tea with boiled sweet potato.

After 30 minutes sitting in silence the stranger took his first sip of tea, he introduced himself as Mr Nkala who had been sent by his Chief in Tsholotsho. The younger children were sitting on the floor close enough to the fire to feel its heat but far enough to not cause Grandma to be angry. Children were not supposed to play or be seen by adults, especially when strangers came from far. The children had heard of Tsholotsho but nobody knew any member of their family in Tsholotsho. After an hour the stranger revealed to Grandmother MaNkomo that Mr Nkala, Anna's father, had died suddenly. Although Anna had never met her father she wailed loudly, tears gushing from her eyes onto her cheeks. Uncle Gabriel who had also never met Mr Nkala cried for his sister's loss and comforted her on his shoulders. Grandmother MaNkomo also cried for the man she had had a brief affair with in 1965 when she moved from working for Rev. Lewis in Essexvale. When the mood had lightened the stranger had told Anna that she looked like her father, which made her smile and wipe her tears. The stranger told Grandmother that it was important that Anna attend the funeral in Tsholotsho otherwise bad luck would follow her all her life and ancestral spirits (*amadlozi*) would not know to protect her from harm and evil.

When the rain stopped and the tea had gone cold, Grandmother asked the stranger to stay for the night but he could not as he had to deliver a message to another family. The stranger left at 9:3pm, long after the children had fallen asleep; even the loud sound of the front door being locked and bolted by Uncle Gabriel did not wake the children up. When the stranger closed the front door the old dog Rex made a long mournful howling noise that made Grandmother look at Uncle Gabriel, who looked at Anna who looked at Aunty Hetta. The sound of a howling dog in Ndebele customs was a bad omen: it meant that somebody was going to die.

'This dog is slow; he is barking but it has already happened, the death has already happened.' Uncle Gabriel broke the pained fear on all their faces. They could not believe that they had not realised that the old dog Rex was barking after the event. Uncle Gabriel and his little sister packed enough clothes to visit Tsholotsho for three days for Anna's father's funeral. Both Anna and Gabriel were born in Bulawayo, the second largest city in the country in houses that had electricity, running water, sofas and beds. Although they had relatives who lived in African huts with *Kraals* and slept on the hard floor they had never experienced it themselves. Although they both worried about this they decided to forget this and preoccupy themselves with packing a few clothes. Their mother had given an old brown and white dress, a red skirt and some blouses to the grieving relatives. Anna too had donated some clothes she had been sent by her eldest sister to any girls who might be her age. Uncle Gabriel gave two old jackets and a pair of trousers with a zipper that had broken two years ago. Baby clothes, balls of wool, old shoes, T-shirts, soap, cooking oil and anything they could find were gathered into two large suitcases for Anna and Uncle Gabriel to take to Tsholotsho.

In the morning Aunty Hetta helped her younger brother and sister with the heavy suitcases to go to the bus terminus. The buses went to the African homesteads that were occupied by the Ndebeles that had migrated from South Africa in the early nineteenth century. Those Ndebeles who had remained true to their ancestral beliefs and way of life did not move to the white man's suburbs to be their servants to take care of their children, who called men and women older than their mothers 'boy' or 'girl'. They carried on with pastoral activities in Nkayi, Kezi, Gwatemba and Gwanda and thrived even in areas that the British had renamed to their home country names.

Anna and Uncle Gabriel boarded the bus, which was packed full of people and their luggage, suitcases, sacks of maize, cooking oil, flour, sugar and tea. On the top of the bus were more passengers and makeshift chicken pens with frantic hens and cockerels tied to the roof rack with ropes and string. The bus was brimming full as it drove past Mzilikazi, which was named after the Great Ndebele King. It zoomed past Barbourfields with its great stadium and swimming pool on to the Old Falls Road. The bus choked its diesel fumes at a slow 40 km per hour as it meandered out of the outskirts of Bulawayo past the racecourse on to Richmond where King Lobengula had built his Royal household for the second time in 1871.

Bulawayo slowly disappeared until there were no houses, animals or people, just the freshly ploughed muddy fields that still seemed traumatised by the recent rain. Eventually houses with bigger yards than those in Bulawayo came into view. Bigger houses with sky blue swimming pools with garden boys picking out leaves from lawns. The bus driver slowed down and shifted his gear stick to turn left. The rains had fallen for a few more days in the north. The fields were greener and lusher on either side of the road, which had more trucks and cars than people. There were pickup trucks with garden boys in the back holding their hats from blowing in the wind. There were caravans towed in the back of European bosses going to and from the Great Victoria Falls and buses to Francistown in Botswana.

Anna and Uncle Gabriel both dozed off for what felt like a day when the bus driver shouted that they had reached Nyamayandlovu. Half the bus got off while others went to the toilet and others bought food sold by locals from under the tree near where the bus stopped. Anna and Uncle Gabriel were surprised to find fresh melons and *umxanxa,* a hot sweet broth made from a variety of cooked pumpkins and maize. There was a young boisterous boy selling freshly cooked beef with a helping of *isitshwala* with vegetables or *amasi* if you preferred. After the passengers were fed, more passengers joined the bus on their way to Kamativi mine homesteads or Detty or Victoria Falls. There were babies crying, sleeping or being fed from their mother's bare breasts. The passengers seemed to be united in conversations about the disenfranchised Ndebele freedom fighters, Joshua Nkomo's dissidents.

When Anna and Gabriel fell asleep in the midst of the heated debates, they almost missed their stop. Luckily for them the bus was going to stop for a little while minutes before it drove away towards the Gwaai river deep into the heavy Kalahari sands that the Ndebeles called *emaguswini*.

Lifting the suitcases from the ground, Uncle Gabriel thought about how profound it was that a moment that is late could have so much meaning. It reminded him of his niece and the time they had left her suitcases on the bus. He did not realise when she left for good that he was going to miss her as profoundly as he did.

Tsholotsho

Anna and Uncle Gabriel were led to Anna's father's village in the deepest part of Tsholotsho. Tsholotsho was named by King Mzilikazi and his army and meant 'elephant head'. The place was sandier and drier than Bulawayo. Dispersed amongst the tall Amarula trees were a handful of sand-coloured windowless round traditional huts with conical thatched roofs. Chickens, goats and dogs were sauntering around babies and old people who were sitting under the cool shade of the trees. Uncle Gabriel had never seen a mud hut except in a text book. The collection of huts belonged to Mr Nkala, Anna's father who had passed away two days ago. As soon as they arrived Anna's relatives welcomed them warmly. The Nkala family were gathered in the main hut where Anna's father's widow sat with a traditional Ndebele blanket and black clothes that showed that she was a widow. In her hands was a blue cloth that she sobbed into. Beside her were two women who sat on a grass mat with their legs folded modestly under their legs and their heads looking down. Next to the two women were three younger women between the ages of 15 and 22.

Three of the girls were sitting on old plastic bags of maize meal, which had been sown together to form a long communal mat. The oldest looking girl was rocking back and forth to calm her baby, which was tightly clamped to her back with a cream *Mbelekho* made from raw *calico*. Only the baby's round chubby cheeks and his sparse black head of baby hair were visible. The girl with the baby looked at Anna as if to say she would probably display a happier face if it was a happier time and continued to knit something using long, thin mismatched needles. The other girl on the other side concentrated on unrolling the wool from a giant ball of wool. Anna stared at the ball as it rolled from the green plastic bag inside another plastic bag from Haddon & Sly in Bulawayo. As the baby started to doze off to sleep, the girl that appeared to be the youngest moved the baby's head which had flopped onto its side. Anna and Gabriel shook hands with every elder and child in the compound, the younger boys bowing to them while the young girls curtsied. By late afternoon the guests were given a hearty meal with no meat. It was traditional to not eat meat so soon after the death of the head of the family.

As the sun set more guests had come from far and wide to come and grieve with Anna's stepmother and her sudden loss. Each arriving guest would bring a new chorus of grief, tears and condolences. Mr Nkala the dead man was now lying in the main hut. Mr Nkala's older brother's three sons guarded the hut in case witches came at night to take the body to cut out its body parts to make *umuthi* for their evil purposes.

Mr Nkala's brother told the mourners that a black goat would be killed for the dead man the next day. Uncle Gabriel remembered the last burial that he had visited where a black goat had been killed and a traditional healer (*iNyanga*) had mixed the first meat that was cut and mixed it with dried herbs, bits of dead insects, rats' heads and tails and then roasted it slowly. On the day after the burial, the iNyanga would call upon the ancestral spirits and everyone would bite a piece of that meat to strengthen the family and remove bad luck and more death coming into the family.

An old man and his wife had walked from Plumtree to Tsholotsho, sleeping on the roadside under trees and in fear of snakes but could not miss Mr Nkala's wake. The old man had grown up with Mr Nkala in a village near Plumtree. A fire was lit and more guests arrived to sit on every inch of the ground in front of the main hut, on wooden benches or on the edges of the steps that surrounded each hut. The crowd thanked the rain God of Njelele for bringing rain to Matebeland at last. A big drum of *amasese* beer made from sorghum and barley hops was brewing in the corner and the women started to sing songs.

'*Lumhlaba asikhaya lami, ikhaya lami lisezulwini …*' (This world is not my home, heaven is my home …) They sang as the weeping became louder.

As the communal jug of beer was passed around, the men became more passionate about the dissidents who were lurking in their area.

'*Kanti ngobani abantu laba? Ngobani?*' (Who are these people? Who are they?)

'*Akhula!*' (There is no way!) Another man wearing a grey coat and a brown hat wiped his mouth with the back of his hand. The others agreed with them and the general consensus was that the new Government that was not even a year old was deliberately oppressing the Ndebeles for spurious reasons.

Everybody went quiet to listen to what Mr Ncube, the oldest man in the group, would say. Mr Ncube was sitting close to the flames of the fire next to the bicycle which he had ridden from his own village to pay the family his last respects. Mr Ncube's only son Patrick had left the village late at night in 1977 to train how to use a Bazooka, how to throw grenades and outwit the Selous Scouts. His son Patrick had died during an ambush in the North East of Rhodesia. Patrick's limbless remains were brought back home three days before independence.

Mr Ncube was still grieving for his dead son when independence was declared in February 1980. On March 15th, 1980, however, a stranger had arrived in his village, on crutches hopping on one leg. His mother had recognised him straight away: it was Patrick the son they thought had died. He had been dropped off by the demobilising army truck that had driven all the way from Lusaka. Mr Ncube talked about how his son had been forced to walk for miles to a designated assembly point near Lupane to be demobilised. Trouble had started near St Paul's mission and his youngest son who had surprised them by being alive was killed by The Zimbabwean National Army. His body was riddled with six bullets: there was one on his left cheek which was still black and bloody. There was a bullet above his amputated knee, one between his right rib cage and his navel. The one that probably killed him was the one on his left temple that would have gone straight to his brain, shutting down his senses. Mr Ncube did not understand why a crippled, helpless man needed six bullets to kill him. When Mr Ncube stopped telling the story of his son everyone including Anna and Uncle Gabriel wiped a tear from their eye.

'*Bazasibulala vele,*' (They are killing us for sure,) said a man in his thirties who sat in the corner, his shirt unbuttoned showing a long, shiny diagonal knife scar on his torso. There was a pause that followed as all eyes looked up to the young man. He left everyone in no doubt that the man was a ZIPRA guerrilla who had returned home. Their bodies straightened up, their shoulders lifted their sagging heads, the women tightened their legs under their buttocks and shifted the hands that were pressed hard against the ground into a new attentive position. In one second the mood was clear, silent and respectful. The respect was directed at the young man with no name who had fought battles only he knew about. In the silence that followed, their minds wondered who he was and what he had done.

'*Liphendukhe nini?*' (When did you get back?) Mr Nkala's older brother who was almost 60 said respectfully to the younger man half his age.

'*Hayi, mina ngaphenduka ngasengisiya e Nyazura ...*' (I came back and then went to Inyazura …) The young man spoke with humility in spite of the palpable reverence by the mourners. The young man was one of the earliest freedom fighters to go to Boma Camp in Luso in Angola.

'*Ngathi ngifika e Nyazura bathi ngiye e Mozambique ngayala.*' (When I got to Nyazura they asked me to go to Mozambique and I refused.) The man told the crowd how the new Zimbabwe Army had tried to send him back to the bush in Mozambique to kill ex-members of the Rhodesian Army including Peter Wells and he had refused.

'*Ngayala, Ngayala!*' (I refused!) The man spoke with a maddened passion for refusing to be a mercenary after the Lancaster House agreement in December 1979. The man told the crowd how his brave comrade had been massacred with a machete. A bowl of hot water was passed to the 'war veteran' to wash his hands before eating.

The widow held on to her sister and started the wailing that reminded everyone that they were here to grieve for her dead husband. Everyone joined her chorus, mourning for their own dead brothers, uncles, sons and husbands, the 'boys' who had crossed the border and never returned.

Revenge of the Rozwi

The night was soft and warm. Anna shared a floor with three women who were her half-sisters and sister-in-law. Anna laid her head on a pile of clothes from her suitcase; the smell of old dried cow dung rose up her nostrils combining with the smell of a dying fire. A faint light from the moon came through the flimsy wooden door that separated the women from their dead father's corpse. Anna was so tired she dreamt of the father she had never met. In her dream Anna was sick and lying down in her hut and her father came down to give her a kiss before pulling her up to walk outside and show her his grave. The younger men had been digging it all day and night. Suddenly Anna's father jumped into the grave and pulled her in as she reluctantly peered down. When Anna's father saw the fear in her eyes he comforted her, his arms warm and gentle. She felt that he was comforting her, not just for pulling her into the grave but for not being there for her as a father. When Anna got used to his comforting arms he suddenly pulled her hair from her head. Anna felt scared again. He smiled back and pulled her to him again comforting her in his arms.

Suddenly, Anna's feet were cold and wet and she found that she was standing in a pool of stagnant water with dead fish everywhere, the weight of the dead fish on her feet overwhelmed Anna. When she realised he had gone, she woke up at the same time as she heard a scream and she was not sure if it was her own scream or someone else's.

'*Vukha! Vukha!*' (Wake up, Wake up!) She heard the sound of a man's voice shouting in the hut next door. She heard commotion, the baby started to cry and her half-sisters put on their dresses, rushed out to see what was going on outside. Only a few ashes were left on the fire. It must have been one o'clock in the morning; everyone was gathering outside to see what was going on. The huts were surrounded by a dozen soldiers wearing green and grey combat uniforms and red berets.

'*Mukhayi!*' one of the soldiers shouted in Shona as someone screamed and shouted in the next hut. Suddenly the rapid, deafening sound of a rifle being shot woke all the dogs, cats and goats. Everyone scuppered blindly in all directions. The mourners were dragged into the courtyard where they had been sitting telling stories. Anna was confused about what was happening as she pulled her hat over her face. She stood next to her brother Gabriel at the back of the crowd that had formed around the soldiers.

'What's going on Gabe, are these the dissidents?'

'I don't know,' he whispered back holding her hand. The soldiers separated the men and the women and asked the women to make a fire and sit down and not make eye contact with them.

'Don't look at me,' the main soldier with ammunition around his shoulder shouted in Shona to all the people who were all sitting down and looking at the ground. He walked around from the centre of the quadrangle stepping on spread-out hands and toes. The girl that was unrolling the wool ball made the mistake of looking at the soldier who was tall, muscular, dark and sweaty even though the evening was cool.

'What are you looking at?' he said to the girl who had not meant to look at him. Before she could look away or answer, he slapped her across the cheek causing her to fly on top of her father who begged the soldiers not to hurt his daughter.

'Shut up you Ndebele dog,' the soldier shouted at the old man who was old enough to be his father. The crowd of mourners looking down at the floor slowly moved away from the old man and his daughter and the sphere of trouble around them.

'*U-u- xolo, uxolo,*' (I am sorry, I am sorry,) the old man tried to apologise, his hands lifted up in the air to surrender.

The old man's stammer was suddenly truncated by the force that hit his head with the back of an AK47. His wife and daughters tried to keep quiet but when the third blow brought out a gush of fresh blood they screamed and protested. The other four soldiers that were wandering around at the edges came to the scene of the old man and his daughters, pulling the girls away.

'*Bulala!*' (Kill them!) said a tall, thin light-skinned soldier with small, shiny black eyes the colour of fresh tar. He had a high-pitched voice that was neither Shona nor Ndebele and he seemed to get pleasure from seeing the chief soldier beat the old man.

The three women, one with a baby on her back, were taken into a hut while the chief soldier beat their father. The first soldier pushed the oldest girl into the hut. The girl that was rolling the ball of wool seized the baby from her back. The force of being pulled back stopped her sister in her tracks. The soldier that wanted the girl with the baby was medium height, dark, stocky with a thick unruly beard over his thick lips. His eyebrows were equally thick and his eyes evil, dark and serious.

When the soldier realised the girl with the wool was pulling the baby he shoved the girl with the baby to the left, seized the girl pulling the baby and gave her two hard slaps. The girl with the wool fell backwards and the baby fell on top of her, cushioned by her bosom. This did not stop the baby from screaming, its tongue and epiglottis quivering rhythmically. The girl with the wool had the good sense to not utter another word which could have saved her life.

'*Thula, thula,*' (Hush, hush,) she held the baby tightly to her breast, her eyes defiantly locking with the stocky soldier's eyes. He spat at her while pushing her sister in the hut.

Outside the hut a soldier with a cigarette between his thick fingers asked the mourners in Shona, 'We hear that you people are holding some dissidents.'

Uncle Gabriel had heard that word on the radio and knew that a dissident was a former guerrilla fighter, *Abafana*, a comrade or *Bakhomana* who had gone bad. A dissident was a criminal that the Government wanted to silence, but he did not realise that they actually existed.

'If you don't show us your dissidents, all of you will die,' the stocky soldier continued.

When nobody answered the soldier, he picked up the old widow Mrs Nkala by her sleeves half-dragging her. Mrs Nkala stuck out like a sore thumb with her big Victorian black skirt, black *qhiye* and black blouse with puffed up sleeves. After an hour Mrs Nkala came out of the hut, sobbing. The soldier who had taken her into her hut was consoling her as if she was his mother. The mood was sombre; the crowd wondered if the soldiers had softened. When he got her to where she was sitting before, he pushed her down on the floor and she fell without saying a word.

The stocky soldier standing at the doorway of the hut where the dead man slept pushed the mother of the baby on top of a pile of clothes and blankets on the floor where Anna and her half-sisters had slept. Without warning he pulled down her skirt and shoved his hands under her jersey to feel her lactating breasts. His hands felt like thorns as they moved down between her legs. She suppressed a scream and tears could not flow from her eyes although her heart was burning.

The soldier forced himself into her with a force and a pain that reminded her of childbirth. It lasted for a second before he came down on her again this time feeling like a sharp knife searing her labia. He said something in Shona that she did not understand before he came down on her again, opening her wide. The pain of her elastic panties was pulling against her knees alternating with the fast pace with which he was pounding the top of her womb.

She realised that the more she kept quiet the harder he pounded her as if to want to see her in pain. She screamed loud and clear for him to hear and a smile came across his face. The older women in the courtyard held their cheeks in shame; the woman's father got up, no longer able to take it.

'*Gara pasi*!' (Sit down!) The chief soldier shouted at the old man, pushing him to the ground. Nobody dared speak a word. Another soldier who looked like he might be second in command was standing outside where the rape was taking place. He took three strides from the hut and picked up the old man's bicycle and threw it on top of him and then laughed. The other soldiers including the chief clapped and cheered as if they had just heard the funniest joke in their life.

'*Ndakakutawurira kuti Gara pasi,*' (I told you to sit down,) the chief screamed at the old man who was yelping in pain, his face poking under the shiny spokes of the wheels of the bicycle. Only the pedals were revolving making squeaky noises as they turned. In an act of defiance the old man stood and pushed the bicycle away from him. The chief soldier pushed him back down. The second in command picked up the bicycle chain and whipped the old man on his knees, his back and his mouth. His teeth were cracked and

299

smashed and blood gushed from his mouth. The mourners screamed.

The shortest of the soldiers came to the crowd. 'This is too sad, we need to sing. Do you know any songs here? Why are you so sad? You, why are you so sad? You need to sing, you Ndebele's like singing. *Pungwe! Pungwe! Pungwe!*'

The youngest soldier made the mourners stand up and salute him before making them do guerrilla marches on the spot for ten minutes. If their knees were flagging the soldier with the bicycle chain would swing the chain at their knees.

'*Pamberi ne* ZANU!'

'*Pamberi na* Mugabe!'

'*Pasi ne* ZAPU.'

'*Pasi ne* ZAPU.'

'*Pasi ne* ZAPU.'

The ex-guerrilla that had been telling the stories sat in front of the crowd on the three-legged stool. The crowd was now chanting louder and louder and could be heard from the road. Sweat poured from the chanting mourners as they were asked to denounce Joshua Nkomo, the man the Ndebeles had considered to be their leader.

'*Pamberi ne ZANU!*' (Forward with ZANU!) the crowd shouted, ululated and started to beat drums. The ex-guerrilla soldier was made to take all his clothes off, his hands tied behind his back and his legs tied together. His testicles were wired to an old car battery which the chief soldier pressed slowly until the man jumped and screamed. This was done eleven times while the crowd watched, their hands on their soundless mouths.

'*Pasi na Joshua Nkomo!*' (Down with Joshua Nkomo!) they shouted as the ex-guerrilla soldier that told the stories was tied to his chair, the plastic bag that had held the wool the night before was taken from the floor and tied around his head to stop him from screaming.

The day was starting to break and the sky had changed from black to a deep, dark quiet blue. Anna was next to be shoved into the hut after the girl with the baby had been raped by the soldier with the bicycle chain. The soldier was now carrying a bicycle pump from the old man's bicycle. He made Anna strip until she was naked. Then he called the young soldier who was one of the only two who had not been involved in raping any women. The crowd stopped momentarily while their boot camp officer walked into the hut to see Anna's naked body.

The young soldier and Anna stood looking at each other in shame: he could only have been a year or two older than she was. Anna was a virgin and had heard all of the screams and shouts from the other girls. He reached to touch her waist and the loud sound of a single shot was heard outside then followed by complete silence. The young soldier ran out leaving the door open. The old man that was being beaten up with the chain was lying on the ground with bright red blood seeping from his body onto the grey earth.

The soldier with the bicycle chain walked over to the chief who was smoking a cigarette and took a puff of the cigarette before giving it back. Three of the red bereted soldiers watched the mourners whose faces were dripping with sweat, their eyes overwhelmed with fear and desperation. The soldiers had a heated debate while the widow of the old man with the bicycle wept with her hands in her head, rolling her body from left to right. Nobody dared comfort her for fear of being next.

'Bury him, come on,' the chief soldier told the men to go and dig a grave for the old man with the bicycle. They moved towards the back of the huts where there were shovels, picks and hoes that had been used to dig Mr Nkala's grave the day before.

'All of you,' the licentious soldiers yelled at the rest of the mourners, some of whom were transfixed by the dead man with blood still pouring from his broken teeth and the gunshot wound that was somewhere between his chest and his stomach.

'Not you!' He pointed to the girl with the baby that had been raped first. 'Not you!' He pointed to another woman that had been raped by the second in chief. 'You. Kill that goat!' He pointed to Uncle Gabriel. Uncle Gabriel had to kill the black goat that was supposed to be the sacrifice to the ancestors.

The old man was buried in a makeshift shallow grave under a weeping mulberry bush. The women were told they had to cook food for the 5th Brigade soldiers who had come to a village in Tsholotsho in the dead of night.

Half-Filth

The bangles hurt Maya until someone came close to her and loosened them. The man she thought was a taxi driver was holding her bangles.

Handcuffs.

She was in a prison wearing handcuffs not bangles. The man who looked down on her was a black man. The man was ugly and repulsive with breath that stank so bad that it made her want to vomit.

'You white girl? he, he, he. You like black man? he, he, he.'

The man had a beard that stopped just below his jaw to reveal razor big bump spots some of which were red, some purple and some with thick pus. One minute she was in Datchett, ready to go to Rishikesh, the next minute she was in a taxi driven by a taxi driver and his apprentice. Now she was being molested by an African man holding her hostage.

'Why did you write this?' The man picked up an article that read 'Robert Mugabe is Dead.'

Splintered memories fused in her mind. She remembered the little girl in the train who had written a story about Zimbabwe. So why was Robert Mugabe dead and why was he asking her?

'Where am I?' Maya asked, her eyes looking at the window that was so high up it only let in a slither of light. The room was cold and grey and had a faint smell of cement and disinfectant. The bed she was sitting on was hard.

'Where are you? Who are you?' The man mocked her, looking at her erotically in an accent she vaguely recognised. 'You white girl?' The man asked her again, his fingers running over her lips and over the ridge of her nose. 'Beautiful nose white girl. Beeee—uuuuuu—tiful nose. Plastic nose? He, he, he, is it real air you breathe? You like black man?'

'Where am I?' Maya repeated frantically moving his hand away from her nose and looking at the man straight in the eyes. The man did not answer.

'The man is mightier than the sword. Or is it the pen is mightier than the sword he, he, he.' The man ignored her question and let her know that he knew something that she did not know about why she had got here.

'Can I go home?' she blurted, amazed by her own strength and forthrightness.

'Yes. Can youuuu?' he said enigmatically overemphasising the 'you' dragging it beyond what was necessary. 'That is the question, can you go home? Where is home? Will they recognise you there?'

'Who?'

'Your people?'

'My people? In Datchett?'

'Your people in Datchett? Ha, ha, ha.' The man laughed slapping his thighs leaving Maya confused.

'Robert Mugabe is dead? Why did you write such a thing? Did you want to kill him? He is alive and well you know. Did you kill her? Why did you kill that woman?'

'She took away my voice and separated me from my love?'

'Why did you want to kill Mugabe? Heeeh?'

'He took away my voice,' Maya said, her voice box moving without connecting to her mind. 'He took away my voice, our voice,' Maya repeated, finding strength to look at the soldier but not able to connect to the words that were coming out of his mouth.

'Do you know how much Mugabe himself suffered to set his people free?' the man hissed.

'I know he drove my people away and stood by as a generation lost their culture and their identity because he had to be right.' Maya spat out the words unable to

304

believe who was talking for her.

'He didn't drive your people away. You Ndebeles are cowards, you have been running since 1830, pillaging vaRozwi, taking their wives, making them speak your language. Now you are all running anywhere. To England. Any excuse. You Ndebeles, he, he, he.'

'I am not Ndebele,' Maya whispered in a dispassionate voice.

'Oh let me see, of course with that nose you must be English? Xle, xle, xle'!

'My father is Shona, if your father is Shona then you are Shona. My mother's family are Ndebele. When I was growing up they insulted me and called me *iSwina*.'

The policeman looked at Maya with her straight nose and peachy skin.

'You should know that *iSwina* is *iTswina* in Shona which means filth, so I am half-filth.'

Epilogue
Kieran and the Devil

'The greatest thirst that can never be quenched is the absence of love. It is an eternal void that mankind will try to fill. It is the toil of the soil that Adam had to endure. It is how the Devil enters the hearts of men. Where he steals, kills and destroys. He enters where there is an absence of love. Where the soul is in anguish and knows more clearly the abandonment. Being without divine love. At times it is better to be ignorant and not know it because knowing invites the Devil back.' Kieran's Grandfather read out loud from a manuscript in his hand. Kieran listened and was surprised when his Grandfather suddenly said, 'Kieran, how is it possible that the earth is a billion years old? If the world was created when the bible says it was then how is this possible?' the old man asked the boy with the humility of someone who knows nothing.

'I will tell you what happened, Grandpa,' said Kieran with a reversal of sagacity that surprised them both. 'The tree of knowledge is the pact with the Devil. Those born in darkness have dark skin and no knowledge; they live closest to the sun and in harmony with the trees and the animals and seek to not destroy because the Devil does not inhabit their souls. Those in partial light, their skin is brown and they see the sun and are humbled by what they don't know. They are aware of their limitations and seek harmony with the earth and the inevitable cycle of birth and death. There are those then who live in cold places who do not see hardly any light or sunshine. Their skins are pale and God has blessed them with knowledge that is closest to them. For God so loved Lucifer his favourite Angel and gave him the best of the best including knowledge.

Lucifer was full of pride and wanted more. He envied those in darkness and their dark skin for living in blissful worship, knowing that they did not know. He chose to change them by having them bite the apple again.'

Kieran continued. 'When you are arrogant you don't hear, not even God. Adam was not the first man on earth: God had already created people.' Adam and Eve were ignorant and arrogant, this at least Kieran and his Grandfather concluded.

'Ignorant and arrogant?'

'Ignorant and arrogant!'

'Ignorant and arrogant, yes, they could not possibly conceive other possibilities. This is the greatest sadness of this chapter of mankind.'

'Mankind only believes what it sees.'

'I suppose ignorance and arrogance lead to blindness of the soul,' Kieran said confidently.

'The biting of the apple is the truth about evolution: it will never end until man knows nothing at all and delights in his own blindness. This way all of mankind will move to that part of the world which is full of sunlight and abandon knowledge and greed for joy. They will not go there to steal, kill or destroy as they did in the past, they will ask those who live there what they know about joy.'

END

About the author:

Rachel Hawadi was born in Bulawayo Zimbabwe during the period of the Rhodesian Bush war. In 1985 she moved to Plymouth in the UK and completed her "O" and "A" Levels at Plymouth High School for girls. Following that she did an Honours degree in Medicinal, Agricultural and Environmental Chemistry at Brunel University. In 1994 she did a joint Masters degree at Aberdeen University and Seville University gaining a distinction. Her early career was with the burgeoning dot.com industry and was part of the teams that launched Amazon.co.uk and America Online in the UK. Recently Rachel has been working as freelance Project Manager whilst working on entrepreneurial and literary projects.

CPSIA information can be obtained at www.ICGtesting.com
Printed in the USA
BVOW082313140413

318169BV00003B/46/P

9 781909 593718